ALSO BY TREVOR TUCKER

Ned Kelly's Son

A saga of Australian heritage ... almost lost in history.

The Stolen Maps

Australia's greatest maritime secret?

Aussie Anecdotes

A collection of quintessential Australian short stories.

A Sense of Justice

A tale of retribution for two unlikely Australian heroes.

GOD ONLY KNOWS WHEN

TREVOR TUCKER

TREVOR TUCKER PUBLISHING

First published 2023 in Australia by Trevor Tucker Publishing
Copyright © Trevor Tucker 2023
All rights reserved
www.trevortuckerpublishing.com.au

God Only Knows When
EPUB: 978-1-922825-22-3
POD: 978-1-922825-21-6
Cover design by Leandra Wicks

In recognition of all those impacted by farm invasion and/or livestock theft which resulted in on-going chronic depression, bankruptcy, loss of family members murdered while trying to save their property, or while attempting to prevent theft of their precious stock ... and of those who believed they failed, and sadly succumbed to suicide.

1

Not every day does one's life start quite as shitty as this one did; thank God.

It didn't take much intuition after enduring the noise and power of last night's raging storm to realise I'd have more than a few things to repair or replace—just as a freezing cascade of dirty water and a sizeable chunk of ceiling plaster deposited itself on the back of my head ... rudely waking me from the nanosecond of sleep I'd had.

Shivering, I pulled all the bedding away from the overhead deluge then dragged on a T-shirt. I was in the process of hauling on my jeans when the next disaster struck, stopping me rigid as a most unexpected and excruciating pain wrought havoc upon my gentleman's region. Poor bugger me! In my haste, the zipper of my jeans had somehow heartlessly ensnared my manhood! And hey, that's *never* funny.

With great caution learnt from a previous identical encounter, I coaxed my member free, but not without bouts of noteworthy expletives while facing horrific pain which reduced me close to the point of blacking-out.

Breathless, yet congratulating myself on my gallant achievement,

I risked a quick look outside through probably the house's only unbroken window.

Undeniably I'd need a plan, for that glance confirmed an entire sidewall and two thirds of the roof sheeting had been removed from my new tractor and machinery shed ... plus half of the house's roof tiles based on the quantity now randomly scattered on the front lawn.

And you've probably guessed it, the outdoor long drop had disappeared! Oh shiiiit!! Typical; just when I desperately needed to pay it a visit ... and where my only supply of toilet paper had resided.

* * *

THAT RUN of hideous bad luck continued.

About six weeks later I was forced to take a redundancy package leaving me jobless and without any prospect of finding new employment; after all, our country was now in a recession.

I remember the night I got that advice from my boss; fretting all the way home about how I was going to break this latest news to my wife. But I shouldn't have worried, she had other more important things on her mind when I arrived home.

My wife wasn't a religious type, nevertheless I was greeted with some very energetic and rhythmic beseeching of our Good Lord for what she was receiving. She was also totally oblivious of my arrival and in complete synch with the well-intended physical exertions being not so gently shared with my next-door neighbour.

Oh yes, I was mortified and shocked, but through a fog of rage, opportunity knocked. Unnoticed, I backed away, located my .22 rifle then crept back into the bedroom.

Again unnoticed, I positioned the muzzle of my rifle between my wife's legs, then pulled the trigger.

The immediate reaction of both participants was unexpected: they first went rigid, then greedily consumed the intended reward for their betrayals ... as if that was the last thing they were ever going to do.

The wash-up of this was that my neighbour eventually woke from a serious concussion and spent two weeks recovering in hospital. My wife was last seen heading for Queensland, so I'm told.

Regrettably, the bloody police relieved me of my rifle and cancelled my shooter's licence. Of course, things could have been worse; I could have just as easily killed them both.

Mind you, I should have been a wake-up to this debauched eventuality; remember the night of the storm? It transpired that my wife chose to stay at my neighbour's house to comfort the lady of the house ... but who in hindsight I discovered had departed the previous week to live with her sister in Adelaide. Regardless, I must give my neighbour a big tick arising from this fiasco; he overlooked any need to press assault charges upon me.

The next few weeks went by in a blur of emotions, but unlike my usual interest in the weather which generally controls everything in a farmer's life, I ignored every forecast: until it was too late, when a raging bushfire demolished my house, shedding and fences and scattered my cattle, killing most. Of course, none of these precious items was insured.

Naturally I'm now destitute given that investors see no current value in my blackened few acres of dreams. Ah well, perhaps the record breaking floods which are slowly receding from my property will bring good luck for someone, some day.

2

———

It's amazing how quickly twelve months can slip by. Regrettably, during that time both my mum and dad passed away, no doubt due in part to the realisation that their only son was destined for failure.

But out of the blue emerged a glimmer of hope.

One Saturday morning while idly sorting through some of my dad's revered old hand-tools, my mobile phone rang. Nursing a sizable hangover from the previous night's drinking while enduring the thrashing of my beloved *South Sydney Rabbitohs* by the *Melbourne Storm,* I was hardly in the mood for a chat, but relented.

'Stevo speakin',' I mumbled.

'Mr Andrew Robert Stevens?'

'Who wants to know?'

'I do. My name's Beth, Beth Carmichael, your parents' solicitor. We met at your father's funeral.'

'Oh, yeah. More shitful news I suppose?'

'No need to be shirty, Mr. Stevens. Quite the contrary; what I must tell you just might improve your demeanour somewhat.'

'Well, go on, spit it out.'

'Not over the phone, Mr. Stevens. Can you spare an hour of your time to meet me at 10:00 am at my Randwick office: is this Wednesday OK for you? I'll give you the address.'

* * *

DRESSED in my best (and only) jeans, a clean though slightly stained T-shirt and Redback work boots, I dutifully arrived at the address I'd been given. Old money shouted at me, though externally it wasn't a real flash place. Nevertheless, the lawns were well-kept and bordered by an assortment of colourful flowers; roses mostly, I think.

No more than ten seconds elapsed, after I pressed the black button mounted within a highly polished brass plaque, before the door opened. A smiling woman in her mid-sixties warmly greeted me.

'Ah, Mr. Stevens I assume. We've been expecting you; thank you for being so punctual. I hope you had a pleasant trip to Sydney. Please come in and take a seat. Beth will be with you in just a few minutes.'

Beth! Bloody hell, I'd completely forgotten the solicitor's name.

Typical, as soon as I had succumbed to a Reader's Digest article on the benefits of abstaining from sex during an influenza pandemic, a very feminine voice interrupted my sex-starved cynicism.

'Good morning, Mr. Stevens, would you please come with me, I'm Beth, your father's solicitor.'

Any time: here, in the waiting room, or in your office would be just fine by me, I almost replied. Damn it, this woman was *hot*; in her early thirties, about five feet six tall and without doubt possessing an amazing figure beneath the elegant suit she was wearing. I must have been drunk or genuinely engrossed in my father's funeral not to have recalled running my eyes over this gorgeous woman.

She walked behind her desk, but before sitting, directed me to a seat immediately in front of and facing her desk. We reached across her desk and shook hands, then in unison, we sat.

'I see you have some outdoorsy work planned, so I'll not keep you too long, Mr. Stevens. 'I almost purchased a farm once, in Darwin.

Decided it was too humid for me, besides I have an aversion to creepy crawly things. So, what do you have on your farm, Mr. Stevens?'

Though a bit taken aback by her impression of my dress code, her genial introduction gave me time to get my mind from the gutter. 'Please, call me Andy. All my stock has gone; compliments of the recent fires and then the floods, so I'm trying to sell my property, as is, but haven't had any enquiries so far.'

'I see, that's a shame, Andy, but let's get down to it. By the time you leave my office, I suspect that your life is in for quite a change.

'Unbeknown at the time of dispersing the meagre assets from your father's Will, a further asset has subsequently and recently been discovered. In the briefest explanation that I can advise, the amount in question is considerable and given you are an only child and that the likelihood of any relatives being able to challenge this discovery is most unlikely ... you should be receiving an amount of approximately seven hundred and fifty thousand dollars, less my fees of course.'

'You're gotta be bloody joking!', I spluttered, then tried to stand but damn nearly feinted. 'How on earth could that be true? My old man always told anyone who wanted to listen that he never had two bob to rub together. And he seldom gave mum anything decent, like. C'mon, this has to be some sort of a put on. So how come, Beth. Out with it! And everything had better be legit.'

'Trust me, Andy, it's legit, my professional reputation would otherwise be at risk. So, take a deep breath and relax while I explain.

'It seems your father had a penchant for horses and had a close friendship and working relationship with a Sydney based bookmaker. That bookmaker, to your everlasting good fortune, met with me last week and upon my oath that I would honour his request for complete anonymity, explained the reason for his visit.

'It seems that your father, over a period of about twenty years, had been rather successful at tipping winners and had accumulated a "sizeable cash working account" with his bookmaker friend, a hidden sum which more than once rescued that bookie from bankruptcy. In other words that bloke was in debt to your father when he passed away, not only morally, but to the tune of seven hundred and fifty thousand dollars!

'Relax for God's sake, Andy; there's more. Honest bookies are generally as scarce as hen's teeth, but I'm now the current custodian of that windfall. I'm not empowered to give you further details, so I'd suggest that you accept this for what it is: an incredible stroke of good luck and reinstatement of faith in human nature. In fact, after I retire this story will definitely take pride of place in my professional memoirs.

'Now, Andy, I need your bank details so that I can transfer your money into *your* coffers. If you have them with you, I can do that for you now.

As luck would have it, I had my banking details with me and regardless of my $6.55 account balance, proudly read them out. It took Beth no more than two minutes to complete the necessary telephone funds transfer.

Now consumed by a series of unexpected emotions, blurred images, some regret, and a compelling need to cry, it only vaguely registered with me that Beth had walked over to her office door and locked it. However, it most certainly did not go unnoticed that she was now barefoot, her hair released in a flowing cascade and was in the process of removing her jacket.

In her next few strides, she sensually stepped from her suit trousers then made herself comfortable on my lap. 'Now, there's no need to cry, Andy, just relax and show me your gratitude,' she whispered while reaching for the buckle of my jeans. 'And congratulations, you've won the jackpot because this'll cost you nothing.'

Understandably, what followed was gratuitous, unrestrained, almost brutal sex; the hard desktop being only a minor distraction. No sooner had I experienced the most unbelievable physical pleasure than Beth applied one last breathtaking kiss then dismounted and proceeded to get dressed.

Still breathless, I soon followed her example and was about to offer up my heartfelt thanks, but she grabbed me by the elbow and almost frog-marched me to her office door. Before opening it, she muttered, 'I must admit, that was bloody good, but now be on your way. Look, here's fifty bucks. Get yourself down to the Randwick track just down the road and put that on the nose of number 6 in the fourth. You've got heaps of time to grab yourself a beer or two before they jump. All compliments of your dear father's good friend.'

Again, before I could say anything, Beth chimed in most professionally, 'A pleasure meeting you Mr. Stevens. Should you need further service, you've got my number. Cheers, and please drive safely.'

I stumbled back to my car, opened its door, fell in, started the engine (which fired first time, a most unusual occurrence), turned the car's air conditioner to full-bore, then mumbled most contentedly to myself, 'How the fuck did all that just happen?'

To this day I'm still not entirely sure how it did. And I still occasionally wonder if the finer achievements of our desktop liaison would really make it into her memoirs.

Anyway, I was now parched and full of a confidence I'd not experienced for years, so, I got out of my car, locked it, and then strolled down the street and made myself comfortable in the local pub. After downing two schooners of ice cold, cleansing Toohey's New, I took Beth's advice and wandered over the road to the Randwick racetrack.

Being the smart-arse I was on this glorious day, I placed a $40 bet on horse number six in the fourth at the odds of 25 to one, and, you've guessed it, the bloody thing won ... by at least three lengths! I wondered fleetingly if this remarkable good fortune was in fact my old man's genes at work.

As I strutted off to my car, unable to stuff any more cash into my wallet, I heard the bookmaker call out to me; 'Arsehole!'

'Yeah, maybe you're right mate,' I replied flippantly while waving at him with a fist full of $50 notes, 'but tough titty, sport, I'm much bloody luckier than you today, yah mug.'

3

Energized, the next morning I rose early, made a list of my debts, then methodically within minutes reduced them all to zero via phone banking.

At nine o'clock I rang my real estate agent, not so politely rejected their offer to settle into a joint listing, then dismissed them and refused to reimburse them due to their obvious lack of initiative.

By morning-tea I had engaged one of the State's most prestigious property investment companies, and to my delight was confidently advised I could look forward to a result within a fortnight.

True to their word, just ten days later they had secured a buyer for my small rural property. Apparently, that buyer was falling over himself to part with five hundred and fifty-three thousand dollars—thus elevating me to instant millionaire status—and further uplifting my previously flagging demeanour.

* * *

About six weeks later, after finishing a rather vigorous early morning workout at my local gym, I made a beeline to my favourite bakery to buy a vanilla snotbox and a choc-chip muffin to go with my takeaway honey-sweetened, double strength mid-morning coffee latte.

I was soon home, settled into my back-verandah deck chair and paused for a few minutes, to savour the view. The elevated location of my house afforded a magnificent 180° view over the bayside park which included the concourse, ancient pines, picnic lawns and of course, the Bondi beach proper that arched north and south to the bay's headlands. There was barely a cloud in the sky, and what there was of them were at high altitude and being swept in thin skeins to the offshore horizon. The ocean sparkled in the early morning sun, and was calm, barely a wave finding its way up the beach.

Though my mood matched the ocean, I did feel a bit sad for the half dozen surfers who sat forlornly beside their boards, no doubt hoping for the arrival of a rideable set of waves. 'No way boys, not this morning,' I muttered, 'maybe later this arvo.'

I glanced at the morning paper's sporting page headlines, took a bite from my muffin, and sipped my first coffee hit, when, wouldn't you know it, my bloody phone started chirping at me.

'Oh, piss off, call back later will yah,' I again muttered, getting agitated now, but after the sixth or seventh ring, I relented and answered.

'Andy here,' I said, not so politely, 'this had better be good calling a man at this hour.'

'Hello darling,' a sensual and almost familiar woman replied. 'It's me, Beth, Beth Carmichael. Have you got a moment? I've got some lovely news that I know you'll really appreciate.'

'Beth! Well, I'll be buggered. Ah, come on, don't tell me another bookie has come forward with another bloody donation.'

'I'm very well, Andy, thanks for asking. But no, nothing like that, *much* better I reckon.'

'Well come on, spit it out, there's no secrets between us.'

'Well, you're wrong, darling, there has been one I've been keeping to myself. I'm pregnant, how does that grab you!'

Silence reigned.

'Soooo, congratulations, but what's that got to do with me,' I whispered, never expecting Beth's words to have such a deadening impact upon my day which had otherwise got off to such a pleasant start.

'No, no, Andy, you misunderstand, darling; my sincerest congratulations to you are also in order.'

Another silence: my mind suddenly blank.

'But, but ...,' I eventually stammered.

'No if's or but's, Andy, I'm pregnant. I hadn't had sex for at least eighteen months before your visit to my office, I've missed my last two periods and my GP has confirmed my condition.

'Look, I was taken by your physique when we met at your father's funeral, despite your hangdog appearance, OK. And ever since I'd been fantasising about how much I wanted to get you back on the road, so to speak, so don't go blaming yourself for the indulgences I extracted from you. Perhaps I should have insisted that you wear a condom because I'd stopped taking the pill twelve or more months ago. And that too, is no fault of yours.

'That's all I want to say over the phone; please, can we meet somewhere, and soon? I reckon we need to iron out a few things because, Andy my darling, I am *not* going to have an abortion, no matter what.'

Strangely, Beth's insistence on calling me *darling*, was having a profound impact upon me; not pushy, relaxed, sincere, and natural ... as if we'd known each other for years. 'Yeah, OK, that'd be good,' I replied with what I thought sounded equally sincere and enthusiastic. 'I live alone, in Bondi. Can you come over today, at any time, or do you want me to come to you?'

'I've got your address; I'll be there in about an hour. I'll bring some lunch. And hey, I'm still infatuated by you, no matter what *you* might be thinking right now.'

* * *

THE INTERVENING hour before Beth arrived gave me time to think. At no time had I felt pressured during our telephone conversation. In fact, I felt rather good about this development, and besides she wasn't the only one who'd been doing the fantasising thing. Based on how my heart was now pumping and how suddenly my mouth had become as dry as a chip, it was time to admit it ... *I'm smitten,* there you go, I've said it, as foreign as it was coming from me, who, for a change, was not just thinking of myself.

On the other hand, an hour was more than enough time for me to pack a few things and head for the hills, but nah, that was the old Andy. Somehow my thoughts were totally focused on Beth and her little surprise. The truth was I liked her, and I felt that I really needed her ... besides I love kids.

* * *

WHEN I HEARD the side gate click open, I almost fell over myself as I pranced to the end of my verandah. Looking down the back steps in anticipation of Beth's arrival, I almost stopped breathing when she appeared from around the side of the house, where she then stepped onto the bottom step, stopped, and looked up at me.

Her beautiful beaming smile greeted me, a display of perfect white teeth between full, orange lips, a colour which matched her lightly tanned face, shoulders, arms, and legs. Sunglasses were planted on her head amongst a mess of blond hair which framed her face, a small straight nose in perfect unison with high cheek bones, and a squarish jaw line. And mind you, her white summer dress, which left little to my imagination, most definitely did not go unnoticed, nor did her orange sandals detract from her magnificent, sculpted legs.

But best of all, her light blue eyes sparkled as if she didn't have a worry in the world, and her expression oozed confidence and unadulterated happiness; in fact, she looked drop-dead gorgeous ... and even more beautiful than when we last met at her office in Randwick.

'Well, hello you, give a girl a hand with this shopping, and please, grab your jaw before it hits the floor.'

I raced down the stairs to unburden her of the large grocery bag and the six-pack of beer she was holding. But, before I took them from her, Beth daringly spread her arms as I swept mine around her waist, then gently pulled her into my chest and planted what was intended to be a courteous greeting peck—but which rapidly escalated into an unashamedly passionate kiss, the likes of which you only ever imagine could be possible.

Breathless, we parted. 'Well, that was nice,' Beth whispered, 'but please unhand me and quickly; take these, I need to use your toilet.'

I quickly grabbed her shopping, turned, and bolted back up the steps, not expecting to have my buttocks playfully squeezed when only halfway up; could this be foreplay?

'Andy, which way? ... quickly!'

Beth obviously made it in time, judging by the self-satisfied look on her face as she meandered back into the kitchen.

'Those sandwiches; how did you know ham-off-the-bone, Swiss cheese, lettuce, and love apples is my favourite? ... and on light rye!'

'Purely guess work darling. I had you figured for a love apple kind of bloke. And a coldie'd be good, eh?' Where'd you put the stubbies?'

'Freezer; top part of the fridge.'

'Good boy. I'll get 'em; you make a start on your sandwich. Out on the back verandah; yeah?'

We sat shoulder-to-shoulder, almost touching, eating steadily and slowly downing our ice-cold beers while casually scanning a very flat ocean. 'The surfers have snatched it; apparently, they've decided the surf's a no-go. What about you, Beth, can you ride a surfboard?'

'Yep, but I haven't had many opportunities over the past five or so years. My business and career have sort of got in the way. And you, my darling?'

'Yep, same. But my excuse is an unhealthy marriage. One day while I was at work, she threw my board onto a hard rubbish collection. Of course, I never saw it again. Said it was always getting in her way, and that I never used it anymore and even questioned why I got so annoyed. Thoughtless bitch, she never once wanted to come with me whenever I suggested a day at the beach ... and of course hated the ocean, and wasn't a bit interested in learning to ride.'

'So, why'd you marry her?'

'She knew a bit about farming, which I thought would be a great help to me, but she spent more time helping our next-door neighbour ... including which I eventually discovered, involved screwing him at every opportunity, including in our bed.'

'Oohh, what a nasty piece of work. And where is she now?'

'I've got no idea and couldn't care a tinker's toss. Thank God we didn't have kids; just in case the poor bugger's grew up to look like my neighbour.'

'Actually that's quite funny darling; just another of your endearing qualities ... that you've somehow managed to retain your sense of humour.

'But I must say, from a legal perspective of course, the timing of her departure was a blessing insomuch as you now have no obligation to part with any of your inheritances, even if she subsequently locates you. Legally, I've seen to all of that for you. And, if you're wondering, should our dalliance result in you believing that *I'm* out to relieve you of your fortune, then you've got it wrong, Andy, very wrong.'

'Thank God you've clarified that because I think I've fallen in love with you. And you?'

'Oh yes, right back at you Andy; I'm absolutely sure, too. My instincts are never wrong. But come on, let's go for a walk on the beach, I haven't done that for years. We can talk and walk, eh?'

We strolled barefoot, either holding hands or arm-in-arm, from one end of Bondi Beach to the other and back to where we started. I don't believe that I'd ever before felt so content and assured. And yes, we talked about many things that had shaped our lives and revealed most of our ambitions.

Suddenly Beth urged me into the sea, up to our knees. She then turned and faced me, smiling broadly while firmly grasping both of my hands in hers and said, 'Andy, please, will you marry me?'

'You've got a bloody cheek; that's supposed to be my job. But yes, absolutely yes, of course I'll marry you. And Beth, for the record, I'm rapt that you are coming with our special package. Nothing feels rushed, just so bloody natural and exciting. But hang on, why the Hell are you crying girl!?'

'Crazy, eh? I'm not sad or upset, Andy; really. These are tears of joy, from me and our first little-un.'

We hugged and kissed (and groped each other; just a bit) until a rogue wave tipped us both arse overhead.

4

____

Five years on, we still live in Bondi. Our wedding took place just three weeks after Beth's proposal, the one which preceded our near drowning. That conjugal celebration was a small, brief affair and the reception was a boozy meal with a few close friends, at the Randwick pub.

Our first born, Jack, has started primary school and he loves it. Our second child is impatient to enter the world: if it's a girl her name will be Kelly. If it's another boy, well, we both like Frank.

Beth is even more beautiful (if that's possible) and, irrefutably, she *is* my soul mate. Not all our individual likes and dislikes are shared but we nevertheless have many convergent interests which often result in delirious laughter and physical fun, most often ending in our bedroom.

We work-out together at least three times a week at the local gym and ride our bikes for typically forty kilometres on most weekends. However, Beth's condition will soon put an end to those activities for a while. Regardless, we still walk the beach most mornings. Oh yes, Beth is also a fantastic cook and has taught me many recipes; mostly those inherited from her mum.

There's a slightly sad note which intrudes occasionally: both of her parents were killed in car accidents. However, Beth's spirit soars above any depression she might be feeling in her moments of reflection. I wish I'd met her parents.

By coincidence, my parents passed in the same year as Beth's, and apparently, we are both the single product of both marriages, yet we never feel alone.

Beth works three days a week for the barrister whom she once employed, travelling to Randwick and home for no other reasons than she's bloody good at her chosen career, enjoys its legal challenges … and must support me, for I haven't worked for wages since we first met. I, however, have chased and invested in the stock market with considerable success, more than doubling our shared wealth and guaranteeing our now multi-millionaire status. Mind you, we don't make a fuss about our wealth, our greatest reward is the pleasure of just being with each other, and our kids.

It was during this time we took to the skies. Both of us obtained our pilot licenses' and soon after purchased an American made Beechcraft Duchess, a twin-engine monoplane which we stored in a hangar at the Mascot airport. Yes, perhaps an urbane lifestyle, some may argue.

However, about ten months later that lifestyle was about to change somewhat.

* * *

LATE ONE SUMMER AFTERNOON, while sitting on the Bondi beach sharing our favourite take-away meal of fish and chips, our kids, Jack, and Kelly, were finally showing signs of tiring after an hour or more of playing *tag* and racing away from waves as they clawed their way up the beach in pursuit of their toes.

'You had enough, darling? I need to pee, so I'll grab the kids and get them home; alright?'

'Of course, but I'll stay and finish our chips and my milkshake. I'll join you in about ten minutes.' Again, I don't know why I deserved it, but as usual, Beth's smile of acceptance almost took my breath away.

I was in the process of bundling up our rubbish when a bloke who had been sitting alone, about twenty yards away, wandered up to me. 'Nice day, eh? Your wife and kids have abandoned you I see.'

'Nah, not really. The kids need to have an early night; we're going on a drive to Warragamba tomorrow and I want to make an early start. Haven't seen you around before mate; you live local?'

'No, just passing through. By the way, me name's Beau, Beau Dickinson.'

'Nice to meet you, mate. I'm Andrew, Andrew Stevens; Andy will do.'

'That's good because I've been looking for you. But hang on Andy, relax. I just want to have a yarn with you about a few things that might be of interest ... you apparently come with the perfect credentials for what certain people would like you to consider.'

Yes, I did arc up a bit, but it's not every day that a stranger wanders up to you and wants to have an earnest discussion. But, as I studied this bloke, he gave no impression of being either an obnoxious lay-about or a God botherer, but rather more like a seasoned farmer: his rugged and suntanned face was a dead set giveaway, as were his green trousers, dusty RM Williams pull-up work boots and his beige, button down long-sleeved shirt ... and of course his nondescript leather hat complete with a very sweaty sweatband.

There was no threat in his demeanour as he dropped his spent cigarette into the roadside gutter and very deliberately crushed it lifeless with the twist of a boot. He then removed his hat, revealing an almost bald head and a few longish remaining whisps of white hair. And, not for the only time during the next half hour would I be amazed at how startlingly blue his eyes were. Mind you, it was a bit off putting that those eyes seemed to cause him continuous discomfort, judging by the tears which oozed from them before meandering down his cheeks.

'I'm intrigued mate; let's sit here. This table looks clean enough; there's a bit of shade and nobody's within earshot.

'So, let's get started; what really brings you to Bondi?'

'Just doing my job Andy. I'm employed by the Australian Federal

Police, but not in any role you've probably ever heard about ... or to fear for that matter. In fact, it's not a gazetted job; it's not something we want the public, particularly anyone with an inclination contrary to honest regional farming interests, to know about. Secrecy and our self-serving objectives will always be king.'

Beau then removed his wallet, from which he withdrew a single sheet of folded paper.

'Here, you'd better read this,' he said as he slid the note across the table. 'As you'll see, I'm empowered to "recruit certain parties" who, in my judgement, will become a valuable resource to help curtail farm invasions and livestock theft, primarily throughout Victoria.

'Mind you, my stated jurisdiction, and yours should you join me, will not prevent our activities from continuing should we find ourselves in any other state. In fact, all Australian states will be duty bound to provide us with policing support when, or if we need it.'

'*And you want to recruit me!?* You'd better start explaining how you know me and why I seem to fit your bill.'

'Not just you, Andy, but Beth as well. How about we three meet and I'll lay all my cards on the table ... fair and square, like?'

'And that includes our kids as part of your plans?'

'Yep, they're perfect cover and no harm will ever come to them, I'll commit to that promise with my life, if need be.'

'Very persuasive Beau. OK, let's all meet, tomorrow, at noon. Do you know where Warragamba is?'

'That sounds like a plan. Don't worry, I'll find the place ... and we'll both be there.'

'We?'

'Yes, I'd like you all to meet my mate, Aussie.

'OK. There's a nice shady park right next to the Town Hall; we'll keep an eye out for you both. Anyway, again, nice meeting you Beau, catch you tomorrow.'

With that said we stood, shook hands, then went our own ways.

5

———————

That night, after putting the kids to bed with the promise of an adventurous drive away from the coast and into the hinterland where we had never previously taken them, Beth grabbed my hand and almost dragged me into our loungeroom. 'OK darling, out with it; what took you so long to get home? I don't think I've ever seen you so pre-occupied.'

'Well, yes, that's because *I am* pre-occupied, and with good reason. You'd better sit down because what I'm about to tell you could be somewhat life changing ... for all of us. No, I'm not about to run away with another woman. But we might soon be on the move. What I'm about to explain could be an amazing opportunity, but nothing will transpire unless you're in total agreement. So, babe, don't feel pressured until you hear me out.'

'*Ooh darling*, well said; this does sound like a Biggy. Please proceed my handsome man of mystery.'

Excluding nothing, I didn't need to explain anything more than once about my meeting with Beau, and, as usual, Beth was very quick on the uptake.

Beaming her most thoughtful smile, Beth sat unmoving for a few seconds then said, simply, 'Let's do it. The only question I have is, who's funding this operation?'

'Dunno, you can bounce that off Beau tomorrow. C'mon let's get to bed, I'm bushed, and I want us to be on the road by no later than six o'clock. That OK with you?'

'Of course, but I need a cuddle.' In the few minutes that lapsed after Beth had had her way with me, and before sleep immersed me, I knew from her breathing that she was still wide awake, no doubt professionally weighing up our risks and options.

WE ARRIVED at Warragamba at eleven thirty the next morning. The park where we were to meet our friends was most inviting, and as luck would have it, devoid of other people. The grass was recently mown and neatly trimmed. Dappled light escaped beneath the branches of well-established native trees making perfect our selected shaded picnic location.

While the kids were off inspecting a small stream which flowed through the park, Beth and I went about setting up our small table and unfolded six camping chairs. As we started laying on our lunchtime spread, and as I had my undivided attention upon coaxing our portable stove into life to boil some water for an overdue cuppa, Beau's voice gently challenged us.

'Why six chairs' folks? My fault though, I forgot to tell you Aussie is my dog. Mind you, he's been looking froward to meeting you.'

'Bloody Hell Beau, you frightened the Bejesus out of me. Where were you two: the park was empty?'

'Something you'll need to practice Andy. And hey, you must be Beth; so nice to meet you.' Beau first shook hands with Beth, then me, then introduced Aussie to us who obediently walked up to Beth, sat, then raised his right paw while excitedly waving his tail. Beth returned the handshake. 'What a polite and handsome boy you are. I hope you enjoy roast lamb sandwiches; that's all I've got for you I'm afraid.'

'He'll be OK with that Beth, but I've got his tucker in me Landy if he gets peckish like.'

What followed was most unexpected. Aussie repeated the handshake routine with me, but as I took his paw, he let out a soft bark in greeting ... then walked to my side and happily leant his weight against my right leg.

'He likes you both; thought he would. But right now, I could do with that cuppa you promised, black, no sugar or milk thanks.'

'He's a bloody ripper, eh Beau, where'd you get him? Pull up a chair mate, while I pour the tea. Want some fruit cake to go with that? Beth's *the* greatest cook, so I suggest you get into some of it before I eat the lot.'

'Reckon I can handle both, but how about you call your nippers back Beth, so we can complete our intro's and so I can *tell all* about how Aussie came into my life.'

Aussie dutifully repeated the handshake routine, which put Jack and Kelly into fits of laughter, and it didn't take long before they enticed Beau and Aussie away to show them the small trout they'd earlier discovered in the nearby creek. I don't know what the three of them talked about, but it was a pleasurable experience watching them walk back to our table, each of our kids holding one of Beau's hands and with Aussie out-front, bouncing along and smiling; yes smiling, I swear!

During those fleeting moments, Beth gently grabbed and squeezed my hand then turned to face me and delivered a beautifully contented smile which I knew meant she was sharing the same feelings of pride, happiness, and love ... and not a single word from either of us was needed to magnify our feelings.

'Righto kids, just one more important thing you need to know, and I'll need your help too, Andy and Beth,' said Beau as he signalled Aussie to sit by his side.

'You see, Aussie's more than just a cattle dog, he's a fighter. Don't let his convivial nature fool you, though he'll never harm any of us. If he has a fault it's imbedded in his nature to protect me, mixed with some inbred trait that he's "King of the heap". He's such a strong boy all right, but he can't help it, there's something in his DNA which sets him apart. If he ever spots another dog, whether it's on a leash or not, he'll want to challenge it, regardless of its size, or age. So, if you see a dog at any time, let me know straight away; he'll obey me when I tell to mind his own business, but he'll probably ignore you folk. Mind you, he's still a gentleman when a bitch is involved; he gets all affection like, but that's nature, eh?

'Right now, you'll notice he's shivering, like it's cold, and staring over towards the creek. That's a sure sign he's already seen a dog, which we haven't, and he's waiting for me to give him the OK to send it packing.'

'Actually Beau, there's two dogs over there,' Beth quickly pointed out, 'they're both about the same size as Aussie.'

'Oh yes, and they're up to no good, I'd say. I'd like to give you a demo, but Aussie'd probably kill one, or both of 'em, and that's not something you'll want the kids to witness. Just keep an eye out for them and see what those two do. When Aussie stops shivering, he'll probably sort of cough, then walk around in a circle before relaxing.' As if on command, Aussie uttered a strange, quiet, strangling sounding woof, circled Beau's legs then flopped onto the grass; so *cool* that butter wouldn't melt in his mouth.

That performance complete, we sat around our picnic table and thoroughly enjoyed Beth's fabulous lamb and pickle sandwiches, potato salad, and of course the best fruit cake you'll ever taste. As I poured Beau's his third cup of black tea, he coughed quietly to get everyone's attention then gradually launched into how he met Aussie.

* * *

'IT WAS the '96 Australia Day long weekend, and one of our favourite "local" getaway opportunities was coming to an end. It had been a fun—sometimes hair-raising—few days, 4-wheel driving in the high country not too far from home. By "our", I mean me and my very special friend, Jill, an amazing woman who is not only a secondary school teacher but a successful farmer who, I should add, suffers fools badly. You'll get to meet her if you accept my recruitment offer.'

'Is she friends with Aussie too?' Jack asked innocently.

'Oh, yes, they're the best of mates,' Beau replied casually as he sipped his tea before continuing.

'Anyway, having packed up we set off for home. However, we reached the Winchester Crossing a bit earlier than usual so decided to boil the billy for morning tea before tackling the climb to the heli-port. Having crossed the river and set the billy boiling, we heard a dog barking nearby. 'Most likely some fishermen or shooters have left their dog tied up at their camp by the river,' I commented to Jill.

'However, there was a distressing tone in the dog's barking, so Jill walked down river intent upon testing my theory. She hadn't gone more than a hundred yards from our vehicle and by then apparently the barking was quite close yet muffled like.

'There are many abandoned and exposed gold mine shafts in these hills, and as soon as Jill recognised a tell-tale mullock heap she correctly guessed where the barking was coming from.

'She cautiously peered over the edge of the nearest shaft, and even in the gloom, about ten or so yards down, she could see a dog. It was looking up at her with what Jill described as a "desperate plea for help" on its face.

'Jill then ran back to me where I was making a brew and yelled excitedly, 'I knew it, a dog's fallen into a bloody mine; c'mon, we've to get it out or it'll starve to death!'

'Not sure if I could do that, I nevertheless grabbed a few ropes from the Landy and followed Jill back to the mine.

'He looks a good sort of a dog, a beautiful red kelpie I suggested while carefully peering into the gloom of the shaft, but quickly added, 'but there's absolutely no bloody way I'm going down there!

'Jill agreed, so we discussed a couple of strategies: for example, who was the lightest that could be easily lowered down and then pulled back up ... but that was ridiculous of course: Jill was having none of that either.

'Now, you must know, I'm rather handy when it comes to ropes, knots, and lassoes ... and just then, an idea struck me.

'I quickly fashioned a decent running noose from one of the ropes then lay on my chest and guts and edged myself forward so that some of my upper body was over the edge of the shaft. After issuing urgent instructions to Jill in terms which in no way could be misunderstood, she threw all her weight onto my legs, and with one hand, managed to grab a hold on a nearby sapling in the hope of making certain I didn't join the dog.

'I then lowered the noose, hoping it would slip easily over the dog's head, but I missed ... the damn dog was wriggling madly and trying to get up and out using its own best efforts. However, on my second attempt the noose dropped straight over the dog's head (not that I ever doubted it wouldn't), pulled the noose tight around its neck then hauled the squirming bugger to the rim of the mine shaft.

'It must be said, that in the excitement I nearly forgot the precarious position I was still in. But Jill, thank God, was gallantly hauling very hard on the belt of my trousers as I wriggled backwards as best that I could while trying to restrain the frantically twisting and squirming critter. But we did it; a great team effort.

'Anyway, on closer inspection he was looking a bit thin, and the pads of his feet were worn and almost raw. Nevertheless, we estimated him to be about ten to twelve months old, but already with an alarmingly large frame and muscle tone for a kelpie. Yet Jill agreed he was, indeed, "not a bad sort of a dog".

'Back at the morning tea camp, the dog drank half a bucket of water in one go and wolfed down at least a dozen or so dry biscuits, while Jill and I finally had our well-deserved cuppa and the few biscuits that remained.

'The dog, we decided, would be called "Lucky", and with no encouragement, he jumped into the back of my old Landy and settled among our camping gear.

'We headed up to the helipad to take in the view as we had originally intended the day before, and upon arrival checked on Lucky; he was "out like a light", still nestled on his back on top of our swags, snoring, legs up and leaving us in no doubt about his gender.'

'Gee whiz, Beau,' a fascinated Kelly chimed in, '*you* were really the *lucky* one; what if Jill hadn't been able to stop you from falling into that awful mine?'

'And hey, Beau,' Jack quickly interrupted, 'I'll betcha that was Aussie, and *not* Lucky, eh?'

'Well, you'd be right on both counts' kids, but let me finish my story. You OK with this Andy and Beth?'

'Mate, please go on; it's a great yarn,' I replied. 'Anyone for another cuppa?'

'No yarn, Andy, all of this is the Gospel truth. Yeah, I'll have a brew, and a bit more fruit cake if there's any left, please,'

'Right, where was I?' Beau continued. 'Oh yes, when we arrived back at Jill's farm, we set Lucky up with his own pen and kennel alongside Jill's other working dogs. However, it was only upon reflection the following day—as it had been Australia Day when we found Lucky—that we thought it would be far more fitting to call him, *Aussie.*

'To begin with, Aussie's work ethics and "cattle nous" left a fair bit to be desired. But with my instructions and the "tips" he acquired from Jill's more experienced dogs, Aussie has turned into much more than a "handy type". He's also a great and faithful friend to us both, as he'll soon become to all you folk.

'Anyway, a month or so later, my friend, Archie, called by to return something he'd borrowed. As we stood in the driveway chatting, Aussie trotted up to check out our visitor. Archie stared at Aussie and asked excitedly, 'Where the hell'd you get him?'

'Suddenly suspicious, I asked him, why pray tell?

'Well, my sister lost one of her dogs recently,' Archie explained, then quickly added, 'when she and her workers were mustering cattle down on the Winchester River.

'Apparently, they searched for days but finally decided her dog must have either drowned when they were crossing the river, or that it was bitten by a snake and carked it.'

'Archie went on to tell me he also has a full-litter brother of his sister's lost dog and that "Aussie is a dead ringer!"

'Of course, I told Archie our story, then he asked if he could use Jill's phone to tell his sister about Aussie. However, before he made the call, Jill chimed in and said to Archie in her most confrontational manner, 'Make sure you tell her that "possession's 9/10ths of the law" and that she's *not getting Aussie back*!'

'It turned out that Archie's sister was pleased Aussie had not died and had a good home. I think Aussie knew that well enough, eh?

'So, folks, that's how I met Aussie. But that's enough about you for the moment my boy. I've got a lot more to talk about with Beth and Andy.'

6

———————

Finally, Jack and Kelly succumbed to tiredness and retreated to the beds Beth had made up for them in the rear of our 4WD. In the deep shade cast by the nearby eucalypts, and caressed by a gentle breeze, all three members of our now extended family, Jack, Kelly and Aussie were all side-by-side and soon sound asleep. Which left me, Beth and Beau sitting comfortably, and in peace around our picnic table.

'Before we get into the nitty gritty,' Beth asked politely, 'who, pray tell is financing this recruitment drive you've spoken to Andy about?'

'And if I may ask Beau,' I interjected, 'how did my selection come about?'

'Both fair enough questions. But ladies first. The Victorian Police is the short answer. They successfully convinced the Victorian Premier and the Government's Treasury Department that crime in the bush can't be ignored and that something enforceable must be put in place to either interrupt or stop stock theft in Victoria. The Treasury agreed overwhelmingly, based on lost revenue and hence lost taxes. It was the Victorian Police's initiative—and their insistence —that an undercover branch be created and properly funded. Their plans obviously impressed both the Australian Tax Office and our

Governor General because within the following year's Federal Policing and Security budget, the *Regional Stock Protection Authority* surfaced as the prime law enforcement body. And I'm it, for the moment anyway.

'Mind you, the whole operation is emphatically rated *Secret*; its existence will be denied but will be overseen by Treasury *and* the Australian Tax Office, so Beth, I don't think we need to be too concerned about funding, eh?

'In fact, if you come on board with me, you will be provided with a three-hundred-acre property in Gippsland, near Sale. You'll each be given a vehicle, Jack and Kelly will be enrolled in a school, or boarding school of your choice, you'll be given funds to purchase all the furniture and household things you'll need ... and Andy'll receive a healthy salary when he officially becomes a Stock Theft Investigation Officer.

'Now, Andy, I'm not totally aware of how I got roped into this scheme. However, I've attended several meetings with the Victoria Police, Treasury and ATO officers, and even the Australian Defence Forces Special Operations Division. Between them, I can assure you that they mean business. They'll provide us with situation intelligence and give you firearms instruction, use of communications and self-defence tactics, some of which I'm already receiving and working on. The instructors are all good blokes, a bit intense at times, but bloody switched on in all aspects of staying alive.

'And here's the really good bit ... you, my fair lady, are seen as an important player in this job and therefore you'll get the exact same training as Andy, starting as soon as both of you sign on. Yes, *both* of you!

'Hang on, hang on Beth, let me answer Andy's other question. Then you can bounce all your questions off me, OK?

'To be honest, I don't know exactly *why* I was recruited for this job. I didn't volunteer. Anyway, I reckon we should just accept the wisdom, scheming, and judgements to our Federal Agencies. But I *can* tell you that an old schoolmate of mine who became a copper stationed in Stratford, was involved somehow. Apparently, it was his unbiased opinion that my understanding of how rural communities work, my farming expertise and general nouse and my ingrained notion of fair play had something to do with it.

'There was also a small matter involving my failure to lodge Tax Returns. Not intentional really, I just didn't reckon I ever earned enough to justify lodging 'em. However, the ATO investigated my excuses and suggested that if I would commit to becoming a secret stock theft investigator and enforcer, then the ATO were prepared to waiver all my pending tax penalties, in lieu, like. Fair enough, I reckoned, so I signed on the dotted line.

'There's also a dossier on you Andy. Something to do with previous questionable tax returns, and of your methods and bad luck while trying to turn a profit from your failed farming enterprises. I'm assuming the ATO knew of your strong held views that "someone" needed to crack down on those cattle duffing bastards who, unnoticed, can simply walk your cattle off your property and into a truck destined for the nearest knackery, or be shipped over the border to God only knows where.

'So, somehow the ATO put two and two together and here we are, not so long-ago complete strangers and now mates and potentially about to start working together ... all three of us, I hope.

'There are just two other things I need to clarify. First, you will be operating under my direction in accordance with intelligence I receive relating to other impacted regions other than in Gippsland, though I'm sure we'll get results soon enough operating as a team. And second, you may have to relocate to different parts of Victoria, depending on the need.

'So, what say you both?'

* * *

IT's NOW three months since that meeting with Beau. Beth and I are now officially Stock Theft Investigators and Enforcers; a secret only known to Beau and a handful of ATO special operations people in

Canberra, the Chief of Victorian Police operations, and the Victorian Premier, none of whom neither Beth nor I have met.

Life is as normal as Beau's strategies require. Our anonymity and "new chum persona" are operating very well, I believe. We are not exactly recluses, nor are we social butterflies. However, we do limit our socializing, targeting venues such as pubs, farming goods outlets and stock auctions, where our apparent farming ineptitude will be noticed, and, as we expect, will become a talking point and therefore likely to come to the attention of local felons who will in turn become hell bent on relieving us of our sheep. For example, our sheep are deliberately not ear tagged, and we have joked about the need to padlock our gates. In effect, Beth and I are bait.

Beau then discreetly follows up on our visits and usually has a laugh at our expense, while quietly, unbeknown to his audience, learns how effectively our trap is being set.

We discuss matters with Beau by phone, either on a *as need basis*, or every other day, bearing in mind that we are nevertheless on a 7/24/365 lookout, and must always be ready to move at very short notice. For that reason, Jack and Kelly are enrolled in a regional boarding school: on the surface, they seem to love this arrangement, and as a family we operate based on reciprocal visitations.

Similarly, Beau visits our kids as often as possible, and always with Aussie in tow.

7

———————

We also soon got to realise that any acquaintance of Beau was considered a friend. That was just the nature of the man.

However, it became apparent that for one bloke, Beau made an exception and over several cups of black tea, explained to us why.

That bloke's name was Zack, a rough nut by any standard. About my height, but slightly thicker set and dressed more like a tramp than a hardened stockman. I could only guess his facial characteristics for he sported a full-blown beard that rested on his chest, and long, filthy long hair tied in a ponytail that fell down his back, to below his shoulders. His eye colour, as best as I could discern, matched mine: his gaze was never still, an observant type.

Like Beau, he had apparently spent most of his life around cattle. But whereas Beau generally preferred a patient approach, Zack seemed hell bent on always trying to show how good he was by either cruelly using his whip—and often—or by callously urging his basically useless dogs to senselessly harass the frightened cattle that were supposedly in his care.

Worse though, Beau deplored the pleasure which Zack extracted from his maniacal overuse of his electric cattle-prod, something which really rubbed Beau the wrong way.

This other side to Beau was revealed to Beth and me when he suggested we accompany him to witness how cattle, sold at the preceding auction, were loaded onto the cattle trucks before being railed to Melbourne. Of course, our attendance was intended as another subterfuge, another opportunity to overhear potential criminal plans being hatched.

It started raining heavily when the loading yard supervisor deliberately teamed Beau with Zack in the hope everything would proceed quickly, yet in an orderly manner. From our vantage point under the kiosk's verandah, we watched horrified as Beau's "team-mate" screamed useless instructions to his dogs, and clearly enjoyed exercising some kind of personal vendetta, judging by the relentless attacks with his cattle-prod upon the confused, hapless cattle still held up in the loading races.

Beau, however, soon finished loading his assigned carriages then wandered over to the kiosk to get out of the rain, and to partake in a cuppa with some of his mates.

'Did you see that stupid bastard?' I heard him say, as he furiously shook the rain from his hat. 'You'd reckon he'd know something about handling cattle by now, eh? Mark my words he's gonna get his comeuppance.'

At this point, I recalled that Beau had recently purchased a new style of electric cattle-prod whose modern specifications really appealed to him ... just in case some bulls became uncooperative. However, there was only one bull in the yard, but it casually trotted up the loading ramp. Accordingly, Beau's cattle prod remained idle, and I quickly forgot about it.

Beau was on his third cuppa when Zack stormed into the kiosk, cursing and mouthing off about how unruly '*his*' cattle were ... and how '*he'd well and truly sorted the bastards out!*'

Because it had stopped raining and to avoid the man's company, Beau and his mates went outside to finish their drinks, but unfortunately Zack soon joined them.

Though wet underfoot, it wasn't cold, so Zack removed his Driza-Bone coat, then leant with his now naked shoulder against one of the steel posts which supported the kiosk's veranda. In that arrogant pose he continued ranting and big noting himself. Out of the corner of my eye I spied Beth slowly shaking her head, her disdain obvious.

Casually, Beau threw away the dregs from his cup and walked away, creating the impression he was going back inside the kiosk to return his cup. But as he strolled by Zack, apparently ignoring him, Beau deftly jabbed his brand-new, fully charged, high performance cattle-prod against Zack's leaning post.

There was an almighty 'crraaak!' as the cattle-prod discharged. Mid-sentence, Zack screamed and leapt into the air, hitting his head on the underside of the veranda. Raucous laughter erupted from the other stockmen, and I whole-heartedly joined them.

Beau was laughing too, not at his clever "execution of the cattle prod", but at the result: much better than he ever dreamt of, for it had suddenly started raining again, heavily … and Zack was now on his hands and knees, at the mercy of the weather, swearing most colourfully and getting soaked while searching for his false teeth in a puddle comprising fifty percent cow shit!

During the enthusiastic congratulations and prolonged laughter from the other stockmen, Beau casually put on his Akubra hat and jogged off through the rain to his 4WD. As he passed by, he briefly turned to Beth and me, nodded slightly, winked, and then chuckled, 'Well, that's him sorted, eh? Good luck him finding somewhere to wash his choppers.'

8

Thursday nights had become our "quiet night", and I was looking forward to making a start on a book I'd grabbed from the Sale library earlier that day. But damn it, I'd left it in my ute, and I didn't relish the idea of leaving the fireplace to go and fetch it.

It was now mid-September. Our first drop of lambs had arrived on time, and it was bitterly cold: gloves and beanie weather. It was near pitch black outside as I made a dash for my ute, the wind tugging at my jacket and the legs of my jeans.

Immersed in the possible consequences of how many lambs we could lose during such weather, suddenly a gap in the clouds allowed the moon to show its face ... and send a reflection of light from our forty-acre, roadside paddock where about two hundred of our ewes and their lambs were camped.

Totally forgetting the library book, I raced back inside. 'Beth!' I yelled impatiently. 'Grab your jacket and come outside ... quick!'

Seconds later, Beth was at my side and threw an arm around my waist. 'This had better be good, darling; what the hell's got you so damn excited?'

'Look where I'm pointing. There! Did you see those flashes?'

'Yes, absolutely, just before the clouds closed over. Reflections; yes?' We briefly looked at each other, then bolted back inside, knowing exactly what we had to do.

'OK, stay put, we're on our way. Be sure you're both armed.' Beau ordered and then hung up.

* * *

WE NEVER HEARD Beau's vehicle approaching; in fact, we were completely unaware he had arrived, until, about twenty minutes later he and Aussie walked quietly around the side of our house and stepped onto our back verandah. His greeting was hushed, and he wasted no time laying out his plan to apprehend whoever were presumably in the process of stealing our sheep.

'They could've simply driven through your unsecured friendly front gate, but they've cut the front-road wire fence a bit further along and driven what looks like a Kenworth prime mover and a twin deck trailer straight down to the holding yards. The cheeky bastards have already positioned their trailer up against the loading ramp ready to take on our sheep!'

'How do you know that?' I asked quietly, albeit just a bit aggressively.

'C'mon, let's get cracking. I'll explain later.'

About one hundred yards from our post and rail holding yards, Beau stopped and gestured that we squat beside him. I must confess that our army camouflage clothing was brilliant; the only features I could make out were our white, ghost like faces. As for Aussie, had he not been leaning against my leg, I'd have had no idea he was with us. Beau then indicated with unambiguous hand movements that it was time to blacken our faces. This we did, efficiently and noiselessly; the result being extremely effective for I could then only see Beth when she flashed an excited smile in my direction.

The wind had now dropped considerably, and the cloud cover was breaking up so that the moon was free to cast its light to create convenient shadows that would enable us to avoid detection.

Aussie was shivering; he'd obviously become aware other dogs were nearby. Better still, we were downwind of the truck and the holding yards where two well-trained kelpies were patiently urging the remnants of our flock into the yards.

The partially loaded trailer seemed to be eagerly awaiting those stragglers as two men walked slowly behind them, quietly giving their dogs some final commands.

It then struck me how quiet it was, just the occasional bleating of a confused lamb and a shuffling sound as some of the sheep attempted to create more room for themselves within the trailer. These stock thieves were no amateurs; they knew precisely how to muster sheep to keep them relaxed, cooperative and essentially, silent.

However, Beth, yes, my Beth, was to lead our assault upon these thieving bastards. Without hesitation she set off as Beau tapped her arm. We watched as she slid along the shaded side of the truck, then stop at the truck's cabin where, earlier, we'd seen a woman; now asleep we hoped. In the blink of an eye Beth was on the footplate and threw open the cabin door. The cabin light came on revealing her scrambling inside, her gun clearly visible and pointing at the occupant. No gun fire followed; thank Christ!

I was about to whisper something about how brave my beautiful wife was, but Beau silenced me in a hushed voice. 'Watch this Andy.' I didn't see the signal which sent Aussie off, full tilt towards the yards.

The largest working dog was clearly Aussie's initial target, but the poor beast, being so faithfully focused upon its job, never saw—nor expected—Aussie's brutal attack. A snarling, growling mass of tangled and struggling legs ensued. Though the working dog was a large, powerful looking animal, within just a few seconds Aussie secured a crushing grip on its throat, then thrashed his, and the hapless kelpies head, ruthlessly from side to side. Within thirty seconds the kelpie was undoubtedly dead, yet Aussie was standing over him, looking for the other dog ... for another challenge!

What followed, I'd never seen before. Aussie soon sighted the other dog, a smaller version of its deceased companion. It was just sitting quietly, its head cocked to one side. Aussie again set off at full charge, no doubt his fighting blood still at fever pitch. But when within a couple of yards of that second dog, he stopped dead and just sat, facing his adversary while mimicking its head movement and vigorously wagging his tail.

All this had been the perfect distraction for Beau and me to make our way quickly across the open paddock and up behind the two bewildered trespassers, all beautifully performed in concert with a slow-moving bank of clouds which, for just a minute or so, had eliminated any moonlight.

'Hold it you two! Get your hands up,' Beau suddenly yelled. 'You're both under arrest.'

Their reaction was immediate and somewhat comical. One, a small, lightly built bloke of Asian descent, fell to the ground, and lay on his back, arms up, whimpering and pleading. 'Please, please. No, no, you no shoot.'

At first glance, the other accomplice was vaguely familiar. He appeared most put out and growled, 'be *buggered* if we are'. He then very nearly made a bad mistake, reaching quickly for what I assumed was a firearm: hadn't the stupid bastard seen the gun that Beau was steadily pointing at the fool's chest?

Ignoring the Asian bloke on the ground, I stepped forward and jabbed my gun's barrel onto that idiot's temple. 'Yah luck's out, Smartarse. Don't do anything you'll regret; I can't miss from here,' I whispered, then added with certainty, 'and I'm not kidding matey. Now turn around and put your hands behind your back,' I said, '*now!*'

The bloke complied reluctantly, then with well-practiced execution I "cuffed" my first felon.

'Thought it was you Zack' Beau said with delight. 'Yah can't handle cattle and sure can't organise a sheep robbery. Now get a move on, your early retirement awaits you. You're going to have plenty of time to get a decent bloody haircut where you're goin'.

Beau and I escorted the two thieves back to their truck. 'So, what took you so long?' Beth quipped as she climbed down from the truck's cabin.

'The lady up there is frightened witless. Asian, hardly any English; from Vietnam I'm pretty sure, and she's got an infant with her and she's breast feeding, so she won't be going anywhere, besides, she's now cuffed as per regs. Mind you, she did have a gun in the glovebox. Here, you take it Beau.'

'Right, now Beth, would you please nick back to the house and phone the Sale cops. Tell 'em your husband has just apprehended a couple of sheep thieves on your property. Don't tell 'em more than where we're located. Insist they send a divvy wagon, now like, to collect this lot. Then get back here.'

By now a false dawn (or the Piccaninny daylight) was upon us, and to our ever-lasting embarrassment, Beau and I suddenly realised that we had both blundered... badly. 'So, where's that other snivelling sod got to?' I said, alarmed. 'I didn't cuff him, did you?'

'Bloody hell! The little shit's shot through. Yah can't trust anyone these days,' Beau replied angrily, 'Get after him Andy. Take Aussie with you and watch out! He might have a gun. I didn't frisk him, did you?' Ha, ha, so glad ... we were now even.

As I jogged down the paddock, I was looking for Aussie and wondering what Beau really meant by, *not being able to trust anyone*. I finally realised it was just his way of making light of our blunders; there was nothing personal targeting me; I had misinterpreted his underlying jest.

Aussie had gone out wide, and back and forth, searching for a single scent leading from the paddock, no doubt confused by the myriad of scents left by the thieves as they had worked the sheep up to the holding yards. And yes, I admit, I wasn't concentrating on where *I* was heading.

To my ever-lasting humiliation, I soon located the escapee, or rather, he found me when he abruptly stepped from behind the shed which housed our house-water supply pump. And yes, I got one hell of a shock because he was now pointing a handgun at my chest. No longer a snivelling wimp, but a desperate bloke, more than likely to pull the bloody trigger if I overreacted.

'Back to the holding yards, you bastard. Make any fancy moves and you're a dead man. Got it?' Interestingly, there now wasn't a hint of broken English in his speech.

Using his gun, which had settled into the small of my back, he pushed me hard. No point relying on Aussie, he was nowhere to be seen, nor Beau or Beth, who would no doubt be preoccupied, and the local police may, or may not, have arrived at our farm by now.

As we arrived at the yards, I was quickly put in a surprisingly strong headlock for such a small bloke and dragged up to Beau and Beth who were standing, both looking confused, but hopefully both worried for my safety. Beth had obviously wasted no time in returning to the yards after calling the police but, bugger it ... no sign of them.

'OK, release my mate right now, or this 'ere mug (yes, me!) gets one in the head. I mean it, so get on with it!' I believed him.

Daylight was now with us. It was bloody cold, exacerbated by a not too friendly breeze. Beau never moved, but strangely, ever so strangely, Beth did.

Like a demented ballerina she danced to one side, slowly and sensually removing her fleecy jacket, then her jumper, then her singlet ... and yep, then her bra! I knew just how beautiful her boobs were, but what the *hell* was she doing flashing them about for all the world to see.

The penny dropped. She'd been executing *the* most unexpected diversion. Momentarily the gunman's arm relaxed then, stupidly, dropped from around my neck. Overtaken by lust he'd forgotten all about me to ogle at my wife's "brace and bits". I don't blame him for that, but it wasn't his last mistake of the day. All I needed now was two more seconds.

I took a quick step to one side, and now unimpeded, swung the best right cross I've ever delivered. *Whack!*

The little fool slumped to the ground, blood oozing from his nose. Groggily, he worked his way up onto all fours, then spat out at least two teeth. 'Why you do dat? No need be so bloody rough,' he muttered. Yeah, right.

His second mistake soon followed. Though obviously still dazed, he tried to get to his feet. But, alas, his intention was short lived as Aussie launched himself, fiercely latching onto the bloke's left wrist, just above the hand still holding the gun! Before too much damage could be done, Beau called Aussie off as soon as the idiot dropped his weapon, which I quickly added to our collection.

Thereafter, the only consideration he received from us was that he didn't get the shit kicked out of him before the police arrived. Nevertheless, in the interim, the two of them seemed content lying face down on the wet grass, albeit separated by ten or so feet.

'I suppose it's useless asking if either of you two have a Bill of Sale, or a receipt for these sheep,' Beth asked casually, yet full of sarcasm, 'No? So, I suppose the next time we meet will be in court where I'll be assisting the prosecution.' There was no response from either thief, but if their looks could have killed ...!

When the Sale police arrived, we unburdened our prize upon them, and so started the official paperwork. Regardless, it was of little surprise to learn that the Asian man and woman were apparently married. Regrettably, it seemed, their innocent child was now destined to cope without law abiding parents. But that's not our problem.

As soon as the police and the trespassers had left our property, we released the ewes and their lambs back into a fresh, fully fenced paddock. The prime mover and its trailer were to stay where they were until the police returned to officially seize them to collect further evidence.

Only then could we repair the damage to our roadside fence. Those stupid *tea leaves* could simply have opened the road gate—invitingly left without any padlock and chain—and driven straight into the yard's paddock and saved us hours of hard work ... the inconsiderate bastards!

We learnt a few weeks later that these same thieves had been on a "watch list" for the past two years and were to be subsequently charged with another six, historically successful stock thefts.

A rewarding result, from our perspective, was that an illegal Dandenong abattoir, albeit abandoned, was "discovered" by the police. I don't recall that we advised the police about that abattoir, and, regrettably, no people were arrested. Mind you, several unregistered firearms and boxes of ammunition were found.

Oh yes, not a word was printed in any regional or city newspapers about these events; our names therefore, according to plan, would remain concealed. We were, after all, just normal farmers going about our business: yes?

As for Aussie—always the gentleman—he and the red kelpie bitch have become inseparable.

And now, if I ever feel like a laugh to perk me up, I sneakily look at Beth and suggest, with a couple of meaningful flicks of my eyebrows, 'hey, gorgeous, you got time for a private strip tease?' This wasn't always a successful ploy, but when it was, I will never forget the look on her face; pure seduction without equal ... followed by a subtle side-flick of her head indicating "oh, alright, if you must".

9

———————

Our first successful operation was now done and dusted, but three months later, Beau received further intelligence from our employers, which he promptly shared with Beth and me.

Apparently, the solitary police officer who manned the Stratford Police Station had been receiving a few theft reports: a stolen brand-new tractor (yes, brand spanking new, with less than five hundred kilometres on its odometer), machinery parts (predominantly chain saw chains), a plethora of hand tools, fencing wire and fuel (usually diesel). That officer had a gut feeling all those reports were linked and that he knew the culprit, or culprits, but had neither the time nor resources to uncover evidence, let alone catch the offender, or offenders. His appeal for help was about to become our business.

Initially, we unanimously rejected the command to assist with such an operation; after all, no stock losses were involved. Beau argued our point of view and to our surprise, our friends in high places agreed and cancelled their request.

However, we weren't particularly busy, there being few demands upon our farming prowess. So, to satisfy her curiosity, Beth made several phone calls then completed some sums which clearly

43

revealed the huge impact these sorts of thefts were having upon innocent farmers, some of whom were our near neighbours.

Beth discovered, through her former legal colleagues, that a huge social issue was emerging throughout regional Victoria; a phenomenon not well known to the city centric populations of Australia's capital cities. Many "theft demoralised" graziers, grain growers and dairy farmers were finding themselves penniless and were either walking off their properties, or being driven to committing suicide, not only because of their inability to repay bank loans, but from the shame they felt for somehow being put in that situation by good-for-nothing thieves.

Livestock and farming equipment theft was becoming big business; stolen machinery and spare parts were always available "at the right price".

Yet, illegal meat markets were still flourishing in all States of Australia.

To our surprise, Beth also learnt that a *lot* of money (also that from which of course no tax revenue could ever be obtained) was being racketeered, not only via interstate overland cattle and sheep droving, but by the shipping of stolen stock to convenient, secret locations around Australia's coastline ... and, to Vietnam.

But shipping? Droving theft was almost a traditional custom but known to be in decline. Undetected road transportation? Yes, that was old hat, yet manageable despite its unpredictability. But ocean shipping was a very new twist on things about which very little was known. Most farmers, including us, believed our laws governing the illegal movement of stolen livestock by ship either into, or from Australia, was unlikely given the strict oversight and policing of biodiversity risks. These laws were slanted towards the movement of thoroughbred horses, *not* sheep and cattle.

Unless some immediate interventions occurred, that appalling, systematic trail of theft (which conservatively exceeded two million dollars annually) was set to continue.

Beth also discovered that such thefts tended to coincide with certain local events such as farmers either being absent from their farm to attend a funeral, or when pine plantation staff were rostered off early to get a good start to upcoming long weekends. Indeed, the hasty departure of workers from their remote workplaces was the perfect opportunity for felons "in the know" to secretly remove anything valuable that was left unprotected ... even if it was (securely?) locked!

An intervention action appealed to Beth's legal instincts and human rights, and when she pointed out that "our doing for the powers that be, a timely favour would most likely *not be forgotten* by them", our sense of fair play overrode our previous selfishness.

So, the next morning, Beau, a little humiliated I suppose, formally acknowledged to our long-suffering employers that a "genuine need *did* exist", and respectfully accepted their initial request on our collective behalf.

* * *

A PLAN WAS NEEDED; a simple no-brainer, and I reckon I had it in one. 'Greed, not necessity,' I confidently blurted, being the occasional know-all that I am. 'All we need to learn is where the plantation workers will be operating when the next public holiday is due. Their vehicles, chainsaws and fuel will become our bait.'

'Labor Day falls on the thirteenth of March,' Beth said, and quickly added, 'that's just a fortnight away.'

'You won't believe this,' Beau chimed in, 'I was talking with Fossy, the farm equipment supplier in Maffra a few days ago, and he reckons he's just got an order for two front-end loaders and a mid-size bulldozer to be delivered to a pine plantation out our way. In fact, one of those front-end loaders is scheduled for delivery next week, just a few days before that long weekend.'

'They can't be operating too far from our property,' Beth said excitedly, 'we can hear their noisy bloody chainsaws at all hours during the night.'

'Right, I know a couple of blokes working with that crew,' Beau said, 'so how about we all go and pay their camp a visit, on the pretext they're making so much noise that you two can't get any sleep.'

'*Pretext be damned,*' Beth and I growled in unison.

The following day, we easily found the plantation workers site huts and the operation's supervisor. He listened sympathetically and agreed to cease overnight operations after 10:00pm and alter the morning shift start time to 6:00am; not a bad outcome, even though "normal shift times" would have to resume in two weeks' time. That suited us just fine; by then, our operation would be over, and the direction of tree harvesting would have changed to proceed *away* from our house.

Better still, we also learnt that the current site hut's location would remain the operations hub for at least another month, which meant that all plant and equipment, including the arrival of two brand-new front-end loaders and a bulldozer would be stationed there, completely devoid of a caretaker or any other security ... not even a resident guard dog.

Labor Day arrived soon enough, and our plan swung into action on Friday night. As darkness fell, we arrived on foot, and as expected, the entire site had been abandoned. Nevertheless, we took up separate watching locations about sixty yards apart, just within the tree line. Oh yes, Aussie was with us, in close company with Beau.

But, despite the best laid plans, the site remained silent right throughout the night. An hour after dawn we retreated.

The following night we repeated our stake-out, still perhaps a little jaded from lack of proper sleep but determined to see this action through.

Around midnight, Beth was first to hear an approaching vehicle. As planned, she immediately flashed her torch twice, our agreed "be alert" signal.

A few minutes later a white Toyota 4WD ute rolled into the hub site. The car's headlights remained on, and when it stopped, two men emerged, both apparently without a care in the world and carelessly slammed shut their respective doors.

So far so good; no dog, or dogs. However, both men carried

torches and wasted no time in plying powerful beams of light probing first on and around the huts, and then, more patiently around the surrounding, nearby tree line.

We had anticipated such a routine and chosen our concealment positions carefully, and as was now *our routine*, our paper-white faces were now covered in black and green military camouflage paint.

As planned, we watched as these blokes brazenly sought out specific chainsaws, grease guns, two large drums of diesel, chains and links, the urn from the mess hut, and, from the supervisor's hut, the keys to the brand-new front-end loader. It was clearly an informed, determined collection process, not a ransacking, which would otherwise have been the case had they not been "in the know" where to locate those items.

We gave them about half an hour as they confidently went about loading their stolen contraband into the 4WD's cargo tray. Then, just as they completed that task, the tallest bloke casually unlocked the loader's cabin and climbed aboard. Seconds later he turned on the loader's running lights and started its motor. As planned, the three of us immediately broke cover and stormed the hub. So far, so good ... only our guns were in play.

'Arms in the air you two,' I yelled on top note, 'you're *both* under arrest!'

Of course, the bloke in the loader couldn't do that, but Beau had already ordered Aussie to get up to the cabin. Our canine champion was soon into the cabin and snarling menacingly at the would-be driver, and in just another unchallenged second, Aussies jaws were very firmly clamped around the hapless man's wrist.

Aussie struggled backwards out of the cabin dragging the now screaming bloke with him. The more that bloke tried to be rid of Aussie's embrace, the harder Aussie growled, as, no doubt his fangs sought and then sunk further into soft flesh.

Abruptly, man and dog fell with a thump onto the ground beside the loader. In a flash, Beau called Aussie off, then rolled the stunned bloke over onto his chest. Now with one of Beau's knees firmly pushing into the felon's lower back, his captive obviously saw the wisdom of not resisting. That submission enabled Beau to easily drag the bloke's arms together behind his back, and, in the blink of an eye, expertly snap his handcuffs shut around the thief's wrists.

To my surprise, (no that's not correct, for I should have known better), Beth had single-handedly hauled the other, older bloke from the ute, cuffed him and was reading him his rights.

Without further ado, Beau and Beth started escorting these blokes back to our hidden car. I drove carefully behind them in the evidence-loaded ute, providing them with a well-lit pathway.

* * *

THESE BLOKES, father, and son as it turned out, were not only our nearby neighbours but trusted employees of the plantation owner's company. Their properties were searched, and a veritable treasure trove of goods and fuel were found, most of which was subsequently identified then returned to their rightful owners.

But it was *where* their hoards were found that was quite remarkable. Hidden deep within the pine plantation which bordered their properties, cleverly concealed storage tunnels were located, their contents being the accumulation of more than a decade of unchallenged larceny. Had these fools hidden their (well worn) tracks to their tunnels with the same attentiveness they had paid to the construction and concealment of the entrances to those tunnels, their prison sentences would no doubt have been considerably less.

10

———————

Beth's performance at both trials, as "Barrister Assisting", was nothing short of brilliant; concise, cutting quickly to factual evidence, demanded nothing but the truth and successfully implored the Judge to impose maximum prison terms.

Those findings were important and had the desired outcome; reports of large-scale thefts in our region dropped to nil overnight and stayed that way for at least the next three years.

However, early during this time, we had heard whispers of a bounty on our heads, probably funded by an overseas consortium. This *most unwelcome* news drove Beth and I to (sort of) retire from our secret occupation. We relocated to Western Australia and maintained a low profile; nevertheless, we were on *"standby"*, (at full pay mind you) if Beau ever needed us, whereupon we'd fly back to join forces with him, or to take over his duties to give him a decent break.

Our lives continued in the same previous vein of acting on intelligence: mostly operations in Victoria, yes, though some of our successes would not have occurred without the efforts of dedicated cohorts within the New South Wales and South Australian special police forces.

These exploits remained out of the public eye, but not the results:

many would-be cattle duffers and sheep thieves were soon either in "enforced retirement" or thinking twice (even thrice) about making a quick quid at the expense of honest, defenceless farmers. Though all the reported thefts we investigated during this time were relatively minor in nature, of late, worrying reports of brazen, well-orchestrated thefts of more than a just few hundred sheep have again started to surface despite our previous best efforts. It would be fair to say Beth and I were getting just a wee bit anxious, and wondering when, and how, this blight on our nation was going to end. 'God only knows,' Beth would say. I agreed unashamedly.

* * *

'WELL, G'DAY AUSSIE,' I said with pleasure as he raced unannounced onto our back verandah, smiling as usual, followed much more slowly and sedately by his very pregnant soulmate, who we'd decided to call, RB (short for, red bitch).

'And hi, RB, you're looking absolutely elegant and beautiful for one so advanced.'

Beth was sitting beside me; she too was smiling as Aussie raised his paw and shook hands with her. After she had patted him on the head, Aussie joined me and repeated his greeting, just as Beau walked onto our verandah with the morning paper tucked under an armpit and carrying a bottle of milk and a loaf of bread.

'G'day, Beau, welcome back' Beth and I chorused, both of us delighted to have our stalwart mentor back in our company.

'You look really fit, mate. Rearin' to get started?' I quickly added.

'G'day you two,' Beau replied, 'Never felt better; in fact, if I was any fitter, I'd buck me brand off. But first, you've gotta see this.' Beau clicked his fingers. RB wandered over, sat in front of Beth, and raised her right paw, which Beth took gently. They shook hands, and, so help me, RB had now learnt how to smile like a loon, just like Aussie did when he was happy to see us.

'You didn't have to bring those things with you Beau,' Beth said cheerfully, 'but thanks anyway. Fancy a cuppa? We were just about to toast some raisin bread; like some?'

'Thought you'd never ask,' Beau replied. 'By the way, where're the kids?'

'They stayed over-night with their friends, in Maffra,' I said, 'they're all going to basketball practice this morning; should be home just after lunch.'

'Might be just as well. I've got some news which we need to think about. Here, Andy, read this little gem,' said Beau as he handed the newspaper to me and tapped an article which appeared on the top left-hand corner of the front page: not a huge piece, but one which would no doubt also intrigue Beth.

The County Court has delivered their verdict upon an appeal by an Asian couple imprisoned for five years (for multiple stock thefts throughout Gippsland) to be overturned, citing their child's serious ill-health, and a preparedness to accept immediate deportation. The Judge agreed with the defendant's submissions and ruled in favour that they be released immediately.

Beth returned to the verandah carrying a tray with a mountain of buttered toast, plates, a small jug of milk, a large pot of tea and our favourite mugs. 'Here, let me take that Beth,' said Beau as he sprung to his feet. 'Now, sit girl and relax, we've got something to show you. Andy, go on, hand her the paper.'

As Beau passed around the plates and mugs, I watched as the expression on Beth's beautiful face changed from curiosity to alarm, then rage.

'BULLSHIT!' she hissed heatedly. 'The stupid bastards can't do that; they'll re-offend in just five minutes and our months of work will have bloody well been for nought!'

Not quite the reaction I was expecting, for Beth seldom swore. But understandably, she was entitled to be pissed off given the time and effort she'd sacrificed to bring about meaningful punishment for the thieves' misdemeanours. An even better measure of her annoyance was the way she hotly shrugged my intended calming hand from her forearm.

Obviously, Beau heard and saw Beth's reaction but continued to make our mugs of tea, and to share around the toast. He then sat facing Beth and me and raised his hands, appealing to our undivided attention. 'Right; at first glance I agree this development is, indeed, out-and-out offensive bullshit.

'But ... I've been contacted by our friends in Canberra who were at pains to explain why they've engineered this situation and to detail how they would like to have us continue with their plans.'

'Mate, this has better be bloody good,' I replied. 'When did they contact you? Before or after this news item?'

'I was completely in the dark until about five o'clock this morning. Of course, they were very apologetic, especially to you Beth.'

'OK, I'm all ears,' she replied, now considerably more relaxed, and no doubt professionally intrigued as she reached for and gripped my hand. 'Best get on with it, Beau; there's no point pre-judging anything until you tell us everything.'

'Of course, but there's another issue that we need to come to terms with,' said Beau as he turned his attention upon me. 'Andy, are you aware that you have a twin brother?'

Beth and I immediately looked at each other in astonishment, and all I could do was shrug my shoulders and then settle my gaze upon Beau. 'That's utter bullshit too, mate. I'm an only child, for God's sake! Who's making up this crap ... and for why?'

As the enormity of this revelation settled in my consciousness, I suddenly felt lightheaded and struggled to breathe: there had never been an inkling of this little detail at any stage in my life to date. Oh yes, I was agitated all right, but I had to do something before I totally lost my temper. So, I stood up quickly and started pacing about, sucking in deep breaths ... which proved to be not such a good idea; I soon became even more dizzy, compelling me to grab the back of Beth's chair before I blacked out.

'Look, Andy, I'm only relaying what our friends told me; it's a bit of a shock for all of us, eh? Just hold your horses and let me explain. However, for Christ's sake man, sit down and relax before you take a turn.'

Ehhm; good advice of course. Now was not the time for me to step off, I've got kids to raise and a wife to protect. And Beau is doing his best to soften the news, not belittling it, but also not wanting to lose me to the fast-landing reality that I may one day need to arrest my own brother ... or, worse.

Most unexpectedly but gratefully received, Aussie and RB were now nuzzling my hands expressing their concern, I suspect ... so I sat.

'Let's all take it easy for a few minutes because there's more you two have gotta hear. Come on, let's have our tea and toast before it goes stone cold.'

By the time we had finished our breakfast, a calmness reigned, but it was evident Beau was keen to continue as he leant back in his chair. 'Andy, I'm sure you still remember that bloke I so professionally electrocuted at the Sale stockyards?'

'That smart-arse, Zack, you mean. Of course, how could I *not* forget that dopey bastard?' I chuckled and leant forward to return my empty, favourite mug to the table.

'Well, it so happens he's your long-lost brother,' Beau announced with little formality, and by the pained look in his face, was no doubt hoping for a more mature response from me this time.

My mug never made it back to the tabletop; instead, ending its life as it effortlessly slipped from my hand and smashed into a hundred pieces onto the verandah floor.

'C'mon Beau, how could they possibly know that? That's gotta be a bloody joke, surely?' I responded, flabbergasted ... yet there was still no sign of mirth on Beau's face.

'You know what darling?' Beth, ever the calm realist chipped in. 'Now that I think about it, that chap is your size and has your build to a T. Take away his mangy beard, and if he were to have a decent hair-cut, you'd be two peas from the same pod ... *and* by the way, you've both got the same eye colour.'

Beau was nodding sagely, putting the three of us in agreement, I suppose; for I unreservedly had to accept Beth's flawless observations and intuition.

11

———————

Beth and I spent the next twenty minutes taking in every word as Beau continued unburdening himself with parts of the conversation he'd had before dawn this morning with our Canberra supervisors.

Beau, never an orator, but intent on brevity and clarity of talk, suddenly changed tack. 'None of us are obliged to accept the project we've been offered but I've been requested to pass on our friend's genuine congratulations. In their words, "we are all getting results no one expected of us. And apparently, we are to throw a prime cut of fillet steak onto our next barbecue; just for Aussie". Not bad, eh?'

Thoughtful bunch of folks, eh, but as much as I love Aussie and his amazing prowess, I'm still not sure that we three are deserving of such praise. But what now worries me is that Beau has gone quiet, the usual precursor signalling there's more enlightenment to follow.

'OK, so if our next job is apparently not to take place in Victoria,' Beth interrupted my exact thoughts, 'then where, pray tell?'

'For us, mostly New South Wales,' Beau replies firmly. 'For your brother, Levy, possibly in Vietnam though that was vague. Anyway, as at today, we need to keep an eye out for him because our friends in

Canberra have received a coded message which indicates he's nearby, in Bega as a matter of fact.'

Silence reigned for a few seconds, but suddenly unable to control or contain myself, I yelled angrily. 'Not only do I now have a twin brother, but it seems his name's no longer Zack, but Levy! *And* Christ almighty, you want us to accept him as part of our team?

'Jesus wept, Beau, are you winding us up, or what? You'd better come clean mate; I for one have had this secrecy stuff up to pussies bow!

'What's more, I can't stand Zack, or Levy, or whatever his bloody name is, and I certainly don't trust the thieving bastard.' And ... his little Asian mate has already put a gun to my head, remember?'

I could have ranted on, but Beth's calming grip on my nearest forearm had an immediate impact ... I shut my mouth, took a deep breath though my nose and flopped back into my chair.

'Look, Andy, I can understand why you'd feel that way,' Beau replied, 'and our friends will not be offended if you were to withdraw your services, but they earnestly appealed to me to pass on their need for your help. Same goes for you too, Beth. That both of you are registered pilots and own your own plane makes you doubly important to them.

'Apparently, they have access to ways and means of unearthing all sorts of non-public, archived information. In Zack's case, they assured me he *is* your blood brother, and they have a dossier on him even thicker than those they have on the three of us.

'He's been working for our friends for nearly three years, including in Vietnam; that's about two years longer than we've been active. He's been extensively and professionally trained in working with cattle in Queensland, armed combat, disguise, infiltration, and survival techniques ... *and acting.* However, he does recall all of us, of course, but only as livestock theft investigators. Regardless, Zack has no idea that he's related to you Andy, and Beth, of course. He just knows me as a skinny old bastard, who knows a bit more than him about how to handle cattle humanely ... and when to use a cattle prod.

'Anyway, he's been advised he'll soon be teaming up with another three likeminded officers, *us*, so no doubt it'll come as one hell of a surprise for him to learn he'll be working with family.

'Look, we'll have to give him a fair go, after all he has a lot to tell us about the background to this new operation and we must respect his judgement and advice.'

'It still irks me that I'll have to apologise to him for treating him so roughly and belittling him,' I quickly added, 'but he really did give me the shits.'

'Understood darling, but we'll have to accept his involvement to date has all been an act,' Beth added astutely while intently gazing into my eyes. 'However, you'll have to ask him up front how close his little Asian friend came to *actually* blowing your brains out! Mind you, had he done so, I'd have personally seen to it that they'd both now be permanently missing persons.' Typical Beth, the velvet hammer of justice.

'For your information,' Beau continued, smiling slightly, but with his usual pragmatism. 'Our learned friends in Canberra have been right about everything so far, so I suggest that if you want to continue with our unfinished business, we'd best all accept their strategic intelligence as also being correct on this occasion.

'There's another matter you need to know. Zack has already put his life on the line to gather intelligence and may need to do so again. He has already infiltrated a well-organised gang in Vietnam which apparently controls most major livestock thefts in Australia. Apparently, much of the livestock which goes missing from Victorian farms ends up illegally overseas. Too many people within that trade already know him as, Zack, so his real name, Levy, *must* remain top secret.'

'This news is most intriguing and has many legal ramifications,' Beth quietly interjected, 'so I hope our immunity privileges as livestock investigators and law enforcers will prevail if we undertake this assignment ... but what's triggered it.'

'Fair enough Beth, Beau replied. 'I can assure you both that we have nothing to worry about, all the previous safeguards and interstate cooperation protocols remain in place and have been expanded to ensure the safety of Jack and Kelly because we will most likely all be interstate for extended periods. And fear not, you will both be rostered-off, so to speak, to enable you to fly home to catch up with your kids.

'The trigger? Well, about three weeks ago, eighteen hundred sheep were brazenly stolen from a stud farm in Central Victoria. You might have heard about it on the radio, before our friends in Canberra slapped a broadcasting ban on it quick smart like. All part of their grand plan to make the bad guys reckon they've got away with it; letting them think that there was no news worth reporting because our authorities are useless. The theft was briefly reported by a couple of local newspapers, but they were also hit with the same ban. No witnesses have since surfaced, and based upon surveillance of known illegal, and legal abattoirs, no such numbers have been processed during recent times: all those sheep have just vanished!

'It'll be our job to work out how that happened ... and put a stop to this bloody racket.'

I'd been itching to ask a question that had been puzzling me, so I just blurted out, 'what about Zack's sidekick, the Asian bloke we arrested along with Zack; the one who got released on a plea deal?'

'Good point, Andy,' Beau replied seriously. 'That arrest we made at your property was all part of a larger plan to get Zack ingratiated with the big nobs in the gang running the show in Vietnam.

'That Asian bloke, known sometimes as, Ho Hua, is a known felon in Australia and quite a dangerous piece of work. Coincidentally, it seems he has a senior position within that gang and is apparently quite buddy-buddy with Zack. That's why they were all released, or rather deported, simultaneously ... and with a total news blackout, particularly about Zack.

'So, Zack, we hope, is now a trusted and entrenched member of that gang—though his loyalty is firmly in step with us.'

Silence reined; a new respect for the bloke I knew as a despicable *smart arse* has surfaced. Surely, he's one of a kind. Well, no, that's not quite right, but he's a damn sight smarter and gutsier than me.

'Anyway,' Beau continued, not quite finished with his briefing, 'based on some very sketchy info recently supplied by Zack, the stolen sheep are being shipped via "special ports" somewhere in southern New South Wales, then transported into Vietnam and possibly into the Philippines.

'Are we all in on this one, or not? I've gotta report back to our friends in Canberra, first thing tomorrow.'

Beth and I nodded. Aussie smiled.

12

Those adventurous souls who first sailed down the southeast coast of The Great South Land, must have been in awe of its daunting, rugged beauty: yet many still perished for not heeding the power and danger of the massive waves which exploded against a seemingly endless shoreline of perpendicular cliffs.

So too, I was to learn, that despite the obvious unrelenting navigational perils of this coastline, nature still threw up hope for some of the petrified, but very blessed, ancient mariners. Through the ever-present cloud of sea spray at the base of those cliffs, an occasional small bay would appear offering both an anchorage safe from the worst that the ocean and wind could muster ... *and* in some cases, unexpected access to the inland, and fresh water.

Flying at four hundred feet above that coastline, such bays were relatively easy to spot, as were the huge sharks which occasionally inhabited them. Of course, modern technology ensures that all shipping is kept well eastward from this coastline.

But our search on this day was not for sharks, but rather to locate every small bay two hundred and fifty miles north of the Victorian and New South Wales border. We found seven which met our general criteria of interest. However, only four provided relatively easy access to the inland; all of which were remote and surrounded by dense bushland. Beth, with her eagle-eyes, glimpsed almost obscured vehicle tracks leading into each of those bays, which she duly high-lighted on the paper map resting on her knees.

Our observations correlated perfectly with Zack's intelligence about the existence of such land and ocean features: surely, we were now onto something exciting and well worthy of much closer scrutiny!

This flight was memorable for another reason: we discovered that Aussie loved flying. At the airport, without invitation, he muscled past me and jumped on board as soon as I opened the plane's side door. Much to our surprise he commandeered the co-pilot seat, but Beth, being Beth, simply buckled the seat belt firmly around Aussie's body then crawled past him and into the back seat.

Aussie sat proudly upfront for the entire journey, looking straight ahead, or occasionally either smiling at me or licking the side of my face, or barking softly when something held his interest far below, often a container ship, albeit way to seaward.

When we returned to Bega Airport that afternoon, Beau was waiting for us as planned. But understandably, he was a bit shitty that we had failed to leave a message to let him know we had taken Aussie with us. 'I was beginning to think some bastard had souvenired him, or that he'd been bowled over by one of the vehicles scuttling every-where on the tarmac.'

'Apologies mate,' I said as Beth sidled up to me to provide her moral support, 'but you'd better hear what we have to tell yah.'

'Yeah, yeah, alright,' Beau replied with no real venom. 'It's not your fault I missed the plane. I ran into an old mate, and we got chat-tin'. He's a nice old bastard. Gave me my first job musterin' cattle and then drove'n 'em from Benambra to Bairnsdale. He's in his early nineties and still smokes like a bloody chimney; rolls his own, hates filter tip cigarettes ... and reckons he knows the names of all twenty-seven of his grand kids. Bloody amazing, eh?'

Anyway, after we'd finished describing our aerial recce, Beau pushed his weather-beaten hat to the back of his head, wiped his rheumy eyes, and then, with hands on hips, said to Aussie in his usual considered manner, 'I suppose you'll want to fly the bloody thing for them next time?'

We all had a good laugh at this, but I don't think Aussie was offended.

On the way back to our motel, Beau though seeming preoccupied, gently broke into our conversation and said in a quiet, almost bewildered manner, 'I'm buggered if I know what Aussie was expecting. I don't reckon he's ever seen a plane up close before, let alone just take one over. Anyhow, you three ... well done today.'

A few minutes of silence followed, but then Beau reverted to his serious tone of voice. 'Most of the players in this caper are predictable, eh? For most of 'em, Australia's vastness is their greatest ally, and as we know, over time they generally get caught, receive a token fine and a slap on the wrist, then, at the very next opportunity, they reoffend.

'Clearly, they still reckon the risk of disposing of stolen stock through remote stockyard sales is low ... and they're right, we just don't have the manpower to respond and stop 'em. They're cunning bastards, and seem to know all the bent auctioneers who, for a few quid, will turn a blind eye to anything missing an ear tag, or with a freeze brand, or over-brand. But, my dear friends, that's all changing. From tomorrow I reckon we're leading the charge into a new world of policing stock theft.'

He didn't need to elaborate; it was clear we all had to keep our wits about us. I must admit that at this juncture I was seriously considering quitting this upcoming escalation of activity and returning to WA, but Beau wasn't quite finished and continued in a reflective tone.

'Back in the early 1800's, once all those original seafarers from England disembarked in Oz, which as you know included convicts, soldiers, and sailors—they were followed down the gangplanks by 4 cows, 32 pigs, 44 sheep, 19 goats, 6 horses, 5 rabbits and 87 chickens. I got those figures from a library book a few weeks ago. Convicts' *way* outnumbered those soldiers and sailors.

'Of course, once our luscious grazing land was surveyed, arrangements were made for thousands of such animals to be sent to Australia. And it wasn't long before cattle and sheep numbers significantly outnumbered people. Mind you, criminals seriously outnumbered free citizens for a long time and the ongoing impact of those *crims* grew unchallenged, their thievin' habits were impossible to stop.

'In fact, so bad and constant were their activities that the livelihoods of free settlers and their dreams were ruined, which led to many of those poor bloody farmers committing suicide. The actual number was probably grossly under-recorded ... as is still the case today. Not a lot seems to have changed over the past couple of hundred years, eh? It's almost as if stock theft in Australia has *always* been seen as a birthright. But it ain't! Therefore, we must do our utmost to reverse that culture ... but God only knows when that might happen.'

I knew some farmers who suicided: good men who'd give you the shirt off their backs.

Beth, who'd not said a word to this stage, squeezed my hand and said, emphatically, 'We're in, when do we start?'

13

Ho Hua was born in Vietnam during the Vietnam war. He died, forty-five years later, in Australia, having not only been recognised in some circles as the most condescending and ruthless stock thief, but as one of the most cold-blooded murderers to ever walk our land.

By design, his infamy may never officially reach the public domain, nor should it ever do so, after all, his highly imaginative (and successful) tactics would no doubt inspire some impressionable idiots, copycats no less, thinking their risk of making a quick fortune would somehow be worth it.

* * *

As you would expect, over time, Beth and I became privy to most of the ins-and-outs of Ho's colourful profile.

He was born in a small village not long after the Vietnam war commenced. Barely two weeks later, the American air force bombed that village killing his parents and three sisters. By some miracle, Ho survived.

The following day, baby Ho was found by Australian infantry soldiers and taken to a nearby village where, fortuitously, he was off-loaded into the care of relatives.

For the next few years, Ho essentially lived underground in tunnels provided by the Vietcong. He was a smart, likeable boy and quickly learnt how to ingratiate himself with both the Vietcong and with American and Australian troops. Outwardly, butter wouldn't melt in his mouth, yet he was one of a young brigade who, on more than one occasion, rolled Chinese made hand-grenades into peaceful gatherings of unsuspecting Western allied troops.

At age thirteen, the Vietcong shoved a gun into Ho's hands and taught him not only how to shoot and set deadly booby traps, but also the art of pilfering, and how to bargain. Yet Ho also attended an Allied run school where he became very proficient in both English, and "Aussie speak".

At seventeen, Ho killed for the first time; a medium ranking Vietcong officer found himself looking down the barrel of an American Army issue handgun, for repeatedly questioning Ho's indifference to Vietcong discipline.

The killer and the murder weapon were long gone before that officer's body was found. There were no witnesses, but because these two were clearly antagonists, Ho's involvement was rumoured, but never proven.

Just four days later, an African American soldier made the mistake of questioning Ho too closely about his stolen handgun: his body was found a few days later beneath a small river-jetty. It's hardly likely this was suicide for the hole in that soldier's forehead suggested another execution. Again, there were no witnesses and the judicial system at that time had far more important issues to worry about than investigating a couple of well-planned murders, and so, Ho's conscience remained unaffected.

It's unclear how Ho made his way to Australia. The official line is, that during the mad scramble to evacuate "worthy" Vietnamese citizens from Saigon, Ho somehow obtained a South Vietnamese soldier's uniform and his identification papers, then assumed that soldier's name.

In that role, given Ho's near perfect Aussie speak, he not only assisted the Australian Airforce personnel with supervising the loading of refugees onto rescue helicopters, but by so doing, made himself indispensable when it came time to reload those chosen few onto the huge Australian C-130 Hercules troop transport planes *en route* to Australia. One of many such flights no doubt included Ho.

Once Ho had arrived in Australia, and before he was processed by the authorities, he disappeared.

Three years lapsed before the Australian Federal Police got wind of a significant escalation in livestock theft in regional Australia—in particular, in Victoria—and to their credit, they immediately called for input from the various Chiefs of Police in every state, on how to mitigate this practise.

The Police Chiefs dutifully lodged some brilliant suggestions; none more intuitive and likely to succeed than those submitted by the Victorian Police. This report recommended the ATO oversee and adequately finance and resource a nation-wide secret operation employing trusted, pragmatic, and dedicated individuals with rural backgrounds.

Each state was to operate with its own well-trained team of no more than four operatives, each sworn by oath to make this task a success. All these individuals were to be given authority to carry firearms—and to use them "as required"—plus have access to any property at any time, and to make arrests on an "as needed" basis. However, regardless, neither their role nor names were ever to be revealed under any circumstance.

Co-operation between the states was a given, as was unregulated operational presence (I think they meant autonomy) throughout Australia. This was a stroke of genius because each state's policing budget was assured by the ATO and therefore did not reduce day-to-day policing manpower requirements. However, where, and whenever any livestock investigation team required backup, local police support was mandatory and given the highest possible response priority.

And so, without any fanfare, this idea was adopted. Shortly after, Beau received an unexpected visit from the ATO: the rest you know about.

I must say, at this time, I had some genuine sympathy for Ho; his early life must have been shitfull without ever having parental love or guidance, expecting any day to be blown to bits or maimed by an Allied forces bomb, forever wondering where his next meal would come from and being poor, dirt poor.

But things were about to alter my attitude towards Ho.

Beau had previously versed us on the five or six recently perpetrated "successful livestock thefts" in Central Victoria and in the Monaro district in New South Wales. In each case the stolen stock had disappeared without trace. But what he hadn't told Beth and me until today, was that one of those NSW farmers had been found dead at his property … a single bullet hole in his forehead indicating this was not suicide.

Beth was first to voice her instincts. 'This, surely, has to be the handiwork of our acquaintance, Ho Hua!'

'My immediate gut feelings too,' replied Beau, 'and that my friends, is why we're here … to either catch, or kill him.'

* * *

THE FOLLOWING MORNING, Beau received more information from our friends in Canberra. 'Remember the police raid conducted on that illegal abattoir in Dandenong?' he said as we sat enjoying our breakfast outside a bakery in Bega. 'Well, I for one did not tell the police about that abattoir. I didn't know it existed.'

'Likewise,' I added, as Beth shook her head and shrugged her shoulders in affirmation. 'So, go on, spit it out Beau, what gives?'

'Subsequently, four arrest warrants were issued in relation to that illegal meat business, but all four were found dead before the warrants were served: all were executed by a single bullet to the head.'

Beth and Beau were now looking at me, no doubt thinking, like me, just how bloody lucky I'd been—*before* we arrested him—that this demented idiot hadn't headshot me when we last met.

14

The balance of that day was spent going over our plans to apprehend this fiend. Based on Zack's sketchy tipoff, our aerial survey had given us reason to explore on foot those bays most likely to be utilised for any livestock smuggling operation.

Over the next four days, Beau drove us in his old Landy to each location. Our routine was to park at least two kilometres from each destination, hide the Landy, then, carrying fishing rods and tackle boxes, make our way to the coast. If challenged, our response would be that we were simply looking for a spot to fish from the rocks, our favourite sport. If further threatened with trespass we would depart without argument, but not before asking for directions to "any other accessible fishing spots". A nice twist of subterfuge, but luckily it wasn't put to the test.

Only one bay was "obviously workable" though all four were checked out. The approach track was well defined by deep tread impressions and recently broken overhanging trackside foliage. Within hearing distance of the ocean, the air became charged with ozone, the trees were either banksia or hakea and the track's soft sand was imbedded with leaf litter, twigs, and the occasional larger dead branch... which presented no significant test for any driver experienced in hauling transport trucks over loose surfaces.

Suddenly, a wire fence emerged. A closed gate fitted with a hefty chain and two padlocks displayed a not so welcoming sign which read: ALL TRESSPASERS WILL BE SHOT ON SITE. The spelling may not have been perfect, but its message was crystal clear.

Vehicle tracks passing through the gates opening were deteriorating; made maybe two weeks ago.

'We're definitely onto something,' said Beau as he climbed through the fence about five yards away from the gate. 'Keep off the track as much as you can from now on, we don't want to advertise our visit.' Aussie led the way, no doubt delighting in a smorgasbord of unfamiliar scents: only once did Beau have to call him into line.

We soon emerged from the coastal scrub and stopped to admire the splendid, unobstructed sight of advancing, unhurried waves. As each wave entered the bay, it gave the impression they were being welcomed by two huge, tree-lined arms. By the time the waves reached their destination, the water held captive there appeared to lack energy and was probably quite deep. I was not surprised when I soon spotted two dorsal fins cruising nearby, indicating this place could carry some decent fish. Should've brought the fishing tackle Andy.

My gaze then followed the sandy track down to the waterline. Well, well, what do we have here? I quickly turned to Beau and Beth intending to suggest we extend our explorations, but to my amazement they were both already marching down beside the track.

I caught them up just as we arrived at water level. To our surprise, it became very clear we'd found a pivotal place; perfect to enable a loaded semi-trailer to manoeuvre and position its release doors up against a crude but sturdy "L" shaped jetty which extended about six yards from the shore. The real giveaway for its purpose was the built-up sides on the jetty, perfect for guiding livestock to the end of the jetty.

'Quite an operation someone's got going here, eh,' said Beau while giving Aussie permission to inspect the jetty. 'I wonder who built it? I don't reckon this would 'ave been a one-man job. Anyway, we'll give it the once-over ourselves, but first Beth, would you get as many photos as you can. Include everything; that hut over there, this cleared area where the trucks get to turn around, and of course the jetty.'

'I'm on it,' Beth said in a most business-like voice, then added. 'That's a bloody lot of scrub they've cleared. I'll bet we won't find any documentation permitting it.'

'Or a permit for building the jetty,' Beau replied. 'Anyway, Andy, would you please pace out the size of this clearing.'

'Yeah, no problem,' I replied, 'Strange though, there's no sign of a fire to burn that scrub, so what the hell did they do with it?' My guess was that it was dumped into the ocean at the entrance of the bay where the currents could have carted it anywhere. We never did learn the answer.

The hut could only, at best, be called rustic; any decent onshore breeze would most likely blow it over. However, it was shelter from the sun I suppose. Inside was a military style, wood and canvas stretcher, a waterproof navy-style haversack which contained two blankets and a badly stained pillow. A circle of rocks filled with charcoal, ash and a few unburnt logs indicated this place had been occupied, and not so long ago.

While inspecting the end of the jetty, Beau measured the water's depth using some string to which he had tied a lump of rock. Using arm-over-arm retrieval of the weighted string, he estimated the water's depth at fifteen feet; more than enough to allow a fully laden merchant vessel to safely navigate its way too, and from, the jetty.

The purpose of the weird and crude wooden arrangement we'd found leaning against the outside wall of the hut also became obvious: with its fold out sides, it had to be the means of transferring *whatever* from the jetty onto a vessel moored alongside. A loading ramp no less. And yes, Beth had taken photos of it.

Before we commenced our walk back to the Landy, Beau presented Beth and me with leafy branches he'd cut from nearby hakea trees. 'Never leave yah tracks, me hearties,' he chortled, 'just watch me, and learn.'

'Hang on a second,' Beth demanded, 'where's Aussie?'

'I think he's still under the jetty trying to haul that dead sheep out of the water,' replied Beau. 'I'd better give him a call; I don't want him rolling in it.'

'You'd better be bloody quick,' I pleaded, somewhat alarmed, 'I hope to Christ he's seen that dorsal fin heading his way.'

HAVING RETURNED to where we'd hidden Beau's Landy, we brewed a cuppa and gave Aussie a drink of fresh water. Our return drive to Eden was basically uneventful though Aussie disgraced himself a few times, farting loudly and then looking around as if wanting to blame one of us for the horrific smell.

15

———

Three days later, Beau broke the news we'd all been expecting. Apparently, a farmer, north of Boort in Central Victoria, reported at least two hundred and fifty of his prized Border Leicester sheep had disappeared.

Our best guesstimate was that, by now, if the thieves drove non-stop, they would arrive at their intended destination, just north of Bega, by mid-morning tomorrow. Providing of course our assumption was correct, we had ample time to prepare and insert ourselves into hiding places around the jetty site before they arrived.

But first, as planned, we had to contact the Australian Navy, in the hope they could dispatch a patrol boat to the head of our "bay of thieves". This was probably a long shot at such short notice, however, using the secret phone number provided by Canberra, Beau identified himself with a pre-arranged code and made his request. 'No problem, we'll be there as required,' was our Navy's immediate response. 'We're underway; out.'

Of course, timing was to be everything; the patrol boat was to arrive (if possible) at the bay, *after* the livestock vessel entered the bay; then intercept it red-handed as they exited. I remembered thinking, 'confidence is an amazing thing, but what if our light-fingered friends have chosen another rendezvous to offload those sheep; then we're all going to look a bunch of mugs.' I kept that thought to myself for the time being.

* * *

WE ARRIVED at the vacant jetty site as the sun speared its first rays of the day into the coastal scrub behind us. A slight zephyr brushed our camouflaged faces, but the water's surface was essentially a millpond, apart from a small, lazy swell. There was no sign of any other trespassers since our recent visit.

'Look, I know the waiting can be bloody boring,' Beau sympathised with us, 'but we need to maximise our advantage of surprise. This camo gear really is fantastic, nobody's going to see us once we get a yard or two back into the scrub. Regardless, when you hear that truck coming, you must keep any movement to an absolute minimum: so, if you need to pee, now's the time!

'Right; now check the safety on your firearm and then put one up the spout. Remember, we let our friends get started on the unloading. Beth, if you can get some photos during that time, do so, but don't risk blowing your cover. We'll let them finish their loading drill then move in and arrest those turkeys, before their boat can leave. OK? Any questions?'

'Yeah, just one,' Beth said evenly, keeping a straight face. 'What if the boat doesn't show up?'

* * *

I HAD time to pee twice more before finally the unmistakable sound of a labouring diesel motor graced our ears. Maybe another ten minutes passed before a dull red Bedford prime mover towing a twin-deck trailer rolled into the clearing.

The unmistakable frame of Ho Hua jumped to the ground before the truck started a manoeuvring routine. Under Ho's watchful eye, the driver, utilising all of the cleared land adjacent to the jetty, competently positioned the rear end of the trailer snug up against the jetty: he'd obviously done this before.

The driver, a bearded bloke about thirty-five years old dressed in a navy-blue singlet, matching shorts and RM William's work boots that had seen better days soon joined Ho. Together they manhandled the "make do" loading ramp to the end of the jetty and secured it with ropes, albeit not so that it extended out from the jetty; presumably that would happen once the ship was moored to it.

The two dogs which had appeared from the cabin of the truck, raced to the nearest patch of scrub and both expertly cocked a rear leg to relieve themselves. Having completed that somewhat lengthy task they dutifully and most energetically performed the customary ground-scratching routine expected of all good dogs, before racing away to explore. My thoughts were with Beau; I was positive Aussie would have seen them by now, and somewhat impatient to greet them. But I detected no movement whatsoever from the location where Beau and Aussie were hiding. Good boy, Aussie.

From my hiding position, that closest to the jetty, it was clear Ho was pissed off about something for he launched into a most unexpected rant of some note for such a little bloke. His dogs didn't immediately respond, but obviously thought better about things and reluctantly sauntered back to Ho; tails now slung below their belly's. It then dawned on me why Ho was so hot under the collar; there was a whiff of decomposition in the air, an exotic invitation no dog could resist.

As soon as the dogs got within about three feet of Ho, he savagely kicked one, then the other, while screaming something at them which I interpreted to mean *if you dare get back in the truck smelling like that, he'd kill both of them*. The dogs yelped, more for effect than actual hurt; after all, most of their early training and subsequent success as reliable working dogs depended on safely evading flying hooves. To my amazement both dogs withdrew and commenced vigorously pushing their heads and torsos through the long grass which surrounded the clearing. Believing they had suitably addressed Ho's threat, both dogs disappeared beneath the old Bedford.

Suddenly the driver yelled, 'It's here Ho, spot on time, eh?'

Ho harrumphed, shrugged his shoulders then replied sarcastically, 'about time I'd say, you stupid skippy.' It wasn't difficult to sense that the hapless driver and Ho shared a mutual disdain for each other: just another one of those mysteries surrounding the events that were unfolding.

The approaching vessel, a hybrid craft about sixty feet long and comprising the features of a barge and a patrol boat, was slowing, and manoeuvring expertly toward the jetty; bow to seaward. The mooring process was completed within two minutes and the engine was left idling. This was fascinating to watch in its efficiency given that only three crew members were on board. Even more strange, no handshakes were exchanged. Clearly this too was a well-rehearsed routine requiring no thanks or orders to be issued.

Ho impatiently laid the boarding ramp into position then vigorously gestured for loading to start. Not more than fifteen minutes later, two hundred and forty-eight sheep were safely on the vessel's deck and apparently content with the real estate they individually occupied. The crew then set about lowering rows of canvas blinds, which I correctly guessed, would make it impossible for anyone onshore to see their live cargo.

Money now changed hands. How much I had no idea, but it was quickly split among the three smiling crew members. With no further ado, the securing-lines were released and the vessel's engine, now open full throttle, seemed hell bent on clearing the bay. However, as if from out of nowhere, the two working dogs appeared. They raced flat out along the jetty and with practiced ease launched themselves onto the deck of the departing boat. This too, we later learnt, was *the normal routine* for their main job, which would start once the boat reached its destination.

The bodies of two sheep which had probably succumbed to some unnecessarily rough handlings were unceremoniously heaved overboard when the departing boat was about two thirds of the way from greeting the open ocean.

But not all was scheduled to go well for our "pirates" ... for, at that moment an Australian Navy Patrol boat swept into the bay. *Well done boys* I wanted to yell. But our congratulations could wait, we'd be meeting them soon enough back at Bega's port facilities.

In retrospect, Ho must have spotted the patrol boat first because he was now ruthlessly shoving the truck driver back toward the truck, having no doubt instantly realising that he needed to clear out. But things now deteriorated quickly. Far too quickly.

Whatever was said by Ho must have finally pissed off the truck driver. Not only had he stopped and turned to face Ho, but he had started to push back. But as if by magic, a handgun was resting upon the now petrified driver's forehead.

Before we could intervene, a single shot rang out. The driver slumped to the ground; his earlier look of defiance now replaced by bewilderment. Unbeknown to him of course, a small, almost blood-less hole located centrally in his forehead was a significant blemish by any measure... and potentially our best witness to most of Ho's other homicides was lost to us.

Reality returned somewhat as Beau, Beth and I, guns all unmis-takably aimed squarely at Ho, advanced in lockstep. 'Drop that bloody gun, or so help me God you'll join that bloke in five seconds. One, two, three, four...

Recognising his hopeless position, Ho released his grip on the gun, allowing it to rotate on his finger within the trigger guard. The gun soon dropped at his feet. 'Right, now kick it away, and if you have any thoughts of escaping, you'd better think twice because if I instruct my friend behind you, he'll gladly rip your throat out.' Ho spun around, obviously not doubting Beau's threat, but nevertheless anxious to see what he was up against. The look on his face was priceless when it dawned on him, he'd previously seen Aussie in action.

'On the ground Ho, face down and put your hands behind your back,' Beau ordered. Begrudgingly Ho cooperated, not unexpectedly because Aussie had been sitting obediently at Ho's shoulder, growling threateningly every time Ho moved.

'Well, well, we meet again Mr. Ho,' said Beth while she clamped her handcuffs firmly over Ho's wrists. 'This time we've not only got you for several violent property thefts, but for multiple cold-blooded murders. What we all witnessed here just now was callous, first-degree murder Ho, and I'll be doing my absolute best to have you put away for at least fifteen years for that crime alone.'

As soon as Beth finished reciting Ho's legal rights, I couldn't resist adding, 'that's right, arsehole; you're now officially under arrest. By the Jeezus you're a slow learner.' That said, I felt a bit better I must say. Nevertheless, it troubled me how on earth I ever experienced some empathy for this nasty piece of work.

But Ho wasn't finished; he slowly turned his head in my direction, ignoring Aussie's warning, and whispered, pleading. 'You let me go and I'll give you twenty-five grand each, in cash ... today! We talkin' big money; what you think? You wanna be rich, yeah? Just tell me how much yah want.'

Ignoring his pleas, I stood and said to Beth and Beau, 'did you hear any of that? Seems we can now add attempted bribery to his charge sheet.'

'No deals, you mug,' said Beau as he heaved Ho to his feet. 'Right, now walk back up the truck. But first, I'll relieve you of its keys; I hope you don't mind, but it's our property now.'

Ho showed very little dignity or appreciation when we manhandled him into the bottom deck of the trailer as company for Aussie.

Beau drove the truck together with Beth and me in the cabin, back to the gate. Once through, we stopped, closed it, reset the padlocks then strung blue and white police crime scene tape all over and around the gate.

Neither Ho nor Aussie had moved. However, Aussie smiled at me and wagged his tail a few times. Ho looked daggers at me, then spat in my direction. Aussie stood, took a step forward, snarled and menacingly bared his fangs to remind Ho of his predicament.

We stopped on the track where we'd hidden Beau's Landy. I retrieved it and drove back to the truck where we agreed I'd follow Beau and Beth and our "cargo" to the docks in Bega.

16

Having arrived in Bega, we immediately saw that Ho's livestock transport vessel had docked: in front of it was the Navy patrol boat. Three men were being loaded into a police divvy wagon and, presumably, a local vet was leading two working dogs away, presumably to the local pound.

Being the positive man he is, Beau immediately started manoeuvring the Bedford and its trailer into a position as close as possible to Ho's moored vessel, ready to *again* receive the by now totally bewildered sheep. Considering the limited space on the dock, Beau's first effort was commendable.

As we exited our vehicles we were greeted by curious uniformed police. 'And what can we do for you folk? I hope you all have authorised business here.'

'Thank you, officers, indeed we do,' replied Beau. 'We're all Victorian Livestock Investigators. Pray tell, who's in charge here?'

'Our super over there, sir,' the nearest officer replied while pointing to a small gathering about fifty yards up the dock. 'Name's Donnie. Oops, I mean Superintendent Mr. Donald Watt.'

'Thanks officer. Would you be kind enough to keep an eye on our payload. The bloke in the trailer is under arrest; he's a nasty little bastard. But my dog, well, he's a good guy and would let you eat from his tucker bowl. Nah, I'd never put that to the test. Anyway, we'll be back shortly to keep this show on the road. Won't be long.'

We were in luck; the group of men were just the blokes we needed right now. They greeted us warmly and it was exhilarating to meet three of our kind, all recruited from the region around Bega.

'G'day. Superintendent Donald Watt, I presume?' Beau asked in his matter-of-fact voice. 'I'm Beau Dickinson; Gippsland Regional Livestock Theft Investigation squad leader.'

'Terrific to meet you Beau,' Donald replied as the two men shook hands, both smiling broadly, and obviously comfortable in each other's company. 'Word has it your team is kicking goals, but I'm not supposed to know that; the privilege of rank, eh.'

You could not have chosen two more different men to be in charge; both oozed an innate confidence. Beau, six foot three inches tall, broad shouldered but skinny as a stick and slightly stooped; age, well, mid-sixties I recall. His battered leather hat was pushed to the back of his head revealing a few wisps of white hair and a rollie cigarette tucked behind his left ear, awaiting its turn to become another smouldering death donor.

And Donald, fortyish, about five foot four inches tall (just), a round energetic face to match his rotund girth and a shock of black hair, a strand or two of which hung across his forehead. But his eyes sparkled with intelligence, and I suspect, an eagerness to co-operate. By some fluke of nature, his eyes were the same intense blue as Beau's, albeit not weeping uncontrollably as that which tormented Beau's eyes.

'I must ask you Donald, can you arrange for the captain of that Navy patrol boat to return to where they've just come from and collect the body of a bloke that's just been murdered? He was the previous driver of that truck I parked down the dock a few minutes ago. No offence intended, but I reckon they can get there and back a lot quicker than your boys, besides your blokes won't be able to easily access the murder scene. There's a padlocked gate in the way which they'd have to remove. I've taped it off by the way; you can't miss it... *if* you'd rather retrieve the body.

'For the record, I think we lost our best witness in that deceased bloke. But we've got photos of him alive, and shortly after, very dead.'

'Any singing bird is worth two dead ones, anytime, eh?', Donald replied with genuine understanding. 'I'll get into the skipper's ear straight away. Anyway, well done you lot.'

'Hang on Donald, you also need to know we have the murder weapon, the murdered bloke's wallet which contains about eleven hundred dollars, his driver's license, and the keys to the Bedford. Apart from those keys, I've separately bagged the other items for later as evidence. Beth has also taken a hundred or more photos of the jetty and its surroundings, all which should be quite handy at the murder trial. But we need another couple of favours please.'

'OK, I'll note that information in my report; again, well done. How else can I help?'

'Well, the Asian bloke locked in the trailer is one Mr. Ho Hua. He's killed several innocent farmers in Victoria and made life a misery for more than a dozen honest farming families. He's a very slippery type if you know what I mean?'

'"*Alleged* slippery murderer", but I get the drift. He'll be properly protected in my cells, and I can assure you he won't be going anywhere until you can arrange to take him out of my hands. And ... anything else?'

'Yeah, as a matter of fact, there is mate. When you talk to the patrol boat skipper, you could suggest his crew might appreciate some target practice ...'

'Meaning, what?'

'That they blow the bejeesus out of an illegal jetty; can't have any more smartarses thinking they could use it, can we?'

'Agreed; too good an opportunity to waste, but I'll suggest it would be prudent I accompany them; could be fun, eh?'

'Thanks heaps Donald, I'd like to stay and talk but I'd better get back to the truck; we've still got work to do.'

As I slid open the tailgate of the trailer, Aussie wasted no time engaging the nearest bollard. The look on his face, staring ahead with eyes half closed, was so intense I too suddenly got the urge to find the nearest toilet. On the other hand, Ho, now in a *most surly mood*, had to be unceremoniously hauled from the trailer and then marched by his ear to another divvy wagon. He spat forcefully in my direction as the van door was being closed and locked behind him; thankfully he missed.

Initially, I didn't know who arranged the events which followed, but a team of five men were now in the process of hefting bales of hay and bags of stock feed pallets onto Ho's boat.

Another young police officer and a teenage girl were in the process of placing a walkway from the rear of the trailer to the side of the boat.

'No use trying to load 'em just yet,' the girl called to Beau. 'They need to eat and have a drink first. Why don't you men go and have some lunch at me mum's pub; it's just up the road ... the Commercial. This lot should be OK to travel in an hour or so.'

'Now that sounds like a plan. You're not just here for your good look's young lady; thanks heaps. My name's Beth by the way'.

'Yeah, well some of us have to be switched on,' the girl replied. 'I'm Abbi; nice to meet you. We'll check your oil and water, and let you know if you need diesel when you get back.'

Hearing that brief conversation, my faith in human nature and our future generations skyrocketed.

THE COUNTER LUNCH at the pub was superb and the company of The Bega Livestock Investigation team most convivial. Their respect for *our* team grew enthusiastically as the abbreviated version of our story unfolded. Aussie's reputation no doubt went up a notch or two, given the many friendly pats of congratulation he received.

We were about to pay for our meals and bid farewell to the publican and his kitchen staff when the young, uniformed police officer approached us and asked politely, 'which one of you is Beau?'

'That's me,' replied Beau. 'Is there a problem son?'

'No sir, I just wanted you to know the sheep have been fed and watered and are being loaded as we speak.'

'Fantastic, we'll head back to the truck straight away. If the stock transfer paperwork is complete, I'll sign 'em off and hit the road. I should be in Boort late tonight if there are no roadworks to slow me down. I reckon that farmer will get one hell of a surprise, eh?'

'I beg to differ Beau, I mean, sir, the farmer who owns those sheep arrived here about an hour ago! Our Super contacted him as soon as those sheep arrived here. Apparently, it was Abbi who ID'd 'em ... from the few ear tags that remained in place. Anyway sir, the Super has given permission for the farmer to drive his sheep back to his property ... and Abbi has already seen to it that the Bedford's tanks are full.'

'Well, I'll be buggered; that's what I call service. She's a bloody good kid that one. I wouldn't mind having her work with us. In private, young fella, let her know I said that, would you? Your Super will know how to contact me should she be interested.'

'No problem, sir, I'll be having dinner with her tonight; Abbi's my sister.'

'Well, how about that! By the way, what's your name officer?'

'Reginald, Reggie Park.'

* * *

IN HIS LANDY, Beau and Aussie followed Beth and me to the Bega airport. We slung our kit bags into our Duchess, then Beth said as she flipped a twenty-cent piece into the air, 'Heads I get to fly us home darling, tails you lose.' It landed *tails*.

As we climbed on board, I turned and yelled to Beau, 'See yah tomorrow arvo at our place; a small celebration, yes?' A quick thumbs up followed in reply. Beth flicked on the cabin power, and we ran well-practiced eyes over the fuel gauges and the various other dials. All good.

We waved to Beau and Aussie from the cockpit as Beth fired the

Duchesses' twin engines, one after the other. She next carefully increased and synchronised the engine revs, released the brakes, and confidently taxied toward the designated take-off position.

But I noticed something was wrong as we waited for permission to depart. For, back at the hangar, there sat Aussie looking abandoned, ears down and, I suspect, glaring doggie-daggers at us for not taking him with us. 'Next time mate,' I promised.

Beth acknowledged the all-clear to depart, then caressed both sets of controls to their full-power, forward position. We soon reached our permitted maximum altitude then Beth finished setting the navigation coordinates for the West Sale airport. I gently squeezed her left knee and thought, *bloody hell, you'd have to be the most beautiful pilot in the world.*

* * *

THE STEADY THROBBING OF THE DUCHESSES' powerful engines lulled me into a deep sleep. I'd never done that before when flying with Beth; I must have been *really* tired. The bizarre thing was the dream I was enjoying was somehow morphing into a nightmare. Why the hell was Beth screaming at me!?

17

————

Being snatched from sleep for any reason is infuriating but surfacing to see your wife on the verge of panic, struggling to retain control of a rapidly descending plane, is something else entirely.

'What gives?'

'No fuel; none whatsoever!'

'C'mon babe, you know the drill; first, take a few deep breaths, right now, we must stop the props from windmilling; too much drag and we'll sink even more quickly without any power.'

'OK, I'm about to feather both engines and then stop them; right?'

'Yep, you've got it. As soon as they stop, feel your pedals, you've got to find the best glide angle and focus on gently lowering her without losing too much forward speed.'

'Would you like me to cut your hair while I'm doing that sir?'

I smiled, not so much from her gallant attempt to inject some mirth into our situation, more so in relief that Beth now had herself and our plane under control. 'Where the hell am I going to put her down?' There's nothing but pine plantations wherever I look.'

Our glide speed was around one hundred and twenty knots and rapidly plummeting as I stared at the ground ahead, and then to port.

'Look,' I yelled, while pointing maniacally. 'Thank Christ; there's a plantation maintenance track ... at about twenty degrees to port.'

'Got it!' Beth replied, back in charge and self-confident.

'Let's hope to God we'll have sufficient wing tip clearance. Got your seat belt buckled up tightly, darling? Good; OK, here goes.'

With the last of our forward glide fading rapidly and with huge pine trees now flashing by on both sides, Beth expertly juggled our Duchess to align with the centre of the track. A quick glance at the air speed indicator showed we were doing eighty knots and I estimated we'd probably touch down at around forty knots.

The track was racing to meet us; its surface littered with crushed bluestone rock and overgrown in summer weed, and scotch thistles.

Beth brilliantly executed a light touch down, but nevertheless the Duchesses' wheels thumped harshly, and the undercarriage groaned. We bounced about twenty yards before landing—fundamentally undamaged—whereafter Beth gamely wrestled the control wheel while dancing her feet across the brake and aileron pedals to keep our Duchess running straight and from fishtailing.

However, the track was starting a downwards slope into a creek bed which Beth had no way of averting. The far side of the creek loomed rapidly. We braced. A bone jarring thump followed almost immediately. This flight was well and truly over: we'd survived our first and only ever crash, albeit having miraculously avoided being downside up!

Beth was looking at me, in a way which I thought was to be her enquiry into my health, but instead she said, most earnestly, 'just as well you didn't invite Aussie, he'd probably be most put out.'

We dragged ourselves outside our once beautiful Duchess and staggered about ten yards away from the extremity of her starboard wing. Hugging tightly, Beth and I collapsed into the grass. Then, for some primeval reason, I guess, we started laughing like demented loons, refusing to stop laughing until our sides damn nearly burst. Our shared near-death anxieties and fears eventually evaporated, but they were never forgotten.

Eventually, Beth, now draped over me whispered a fair enough question into my ear. 'Darling, did you forget to have the tanks refilled?'

'No bloody way,' I replied, just a bit too firmly. 'Remember, you confirmed with me during our preflight visuals that they were one hundred percent full. My first thought was sabotage, but who and how?'

'Me too, I can think of someone who'd like to see us both dead; none other than that unpleasant Mr. Hua.'

'Nah, the timing's all wrong. He had no idea we were in Bega or how we got there. And he was running his own agenda from the time we got that report of the Boort theft.

'The "how" we got into this situation is more intriguing, I reckon. Do you remember during our training sessions with Russell at the flying school ... how he harped on about always personally checking that the tank refill cap is always properly seated before taking off?

'Well, come on girl, get up; let's check out my theory. If I'm right, we won't be able to make an insurance claim, bugger it.'

'So, you're a lawyer now my darling? But you're right, it would prove quite costly to defend.'

'Nah, you're the best there is Beth; you'd get a result in our favour for sure ... and for nix, eh?'

'Sorry darling, but have you heard of *conflict of interest*?'

* * *

It only took a few minutes to discover what had almost cost us our lives.

The fuel cap, if fitted correctly, should have been seated flush with the plane's outer skin. Ours wasn't. The lugs on the fuel cap had not engaged correctly, leaving a part of the fuel cap's circumference ever so slightly elevated, thus exposing the fuel to atmospheric pressure.

At some point in our flight, a pressure differential developed such that our remaining fuel syphoned from the tank ... probably within just a few minutes.

We had both missed this near fatal detail. I vowed that from this day, I'd personally supervise *our every* future refuelling routine.

* * *

THANKS TO AN OBSERVANT, concerned farmer who had recognised our potential plight, we were soon, very gratefully, being driven to his nearby farmhouse. His wife immediately put the kettle on and while waiting for it to boil, phoned the Sale police to report what had happened, and where.

Next, I rang Beau and briefed him on our accident. Amazingly, he knew exactly where we were and said he'd be on his way to pick us up in about an hour's time. 'Say g'day to John and Mary for me,' he said, and then rang off.

As Mary poured us our cuppa's, I rang the Gippsland Flight Training Centre.

Thanks to their switched-on staff, they immediately offered to retrieve our Duchess and deliver her to the West Sale Airport where an assessor was on hand to "give her a thorough going over".

18

Our next task was to phone our kids Kelly, and Jack, to placate them about our accident and put their minds to rest about our physical condition. However, they still made three demands; their first was *that they wanted to return home straight away, even though it was mid-term at their boarding school.* We rather neatly deferred that by promising them a lengthy home stay-over during the next Term holidays. That sort of worked God love 'em.

Their second demand—*that we both immediately resign from our jobs—w*as going to be far more difficult to dodge. In their eyes, we were getting too old to continue risking our lives ... but we both had unfinished business.

We had to make our kids understand Beth still had a legal ambition to fulfil, and we were both witnesses to one of Mr. Ho's cold-blooded murders. Effectively we were *on call* regarding his upcoming trials. This time we were going to do everything possible, whenever needed, to see that he was going to jail for a very long time, besides, we had no intention of missing a second of the judge's sentencing speech.

Kelly was OK with this, *but Jack wanted more certainty about when he and his sister's wishes would take priority over our jobs.* Ouch, that hurt, but I got the message.

Beth gently relieved me of the phone, whereafter I heard her announce with a hint of excitement, 'By the ways kids, while we were away, we met some really nice folk in Bega. We've been thinking of inviting two of them to come and stay with us during your Term holidays. Your father and I reckon you'll like them. They're just a bit older than both of you; so, would you like to meet them, or not?

'Oooh; that's great,' Beth cleverly shut down that conversation. 'I'll start organising things with them straight away.'

I heaved a sigh of relief and thought to myself, *'Well done again, Beth. Curiosity always gets the cat, eh?'*

I didn't need to have their fourth demand explained to me; Beth nipped that one in the bud immediately too. *'No, you can't have one of the pups come and stay with you*; not yet anyway ... they're too young and they may soon need to be neutered. But I tell you what. Remember that story Beau told us about how he rescued Aussie and how that farmer lady initially reckoned Beau and Jill stole him from her? Well, how about we give one of the boy pups to her? You two can explain that while she may have lost Aussie; she *will* be regaining his very best genes.'

For the time being, Beth and I had won at least two weeks of R & R entirely on our own, to do not much of anything, well, almost nothing. But just as things were returning to something resembling a pragmatic farming enterprise, we received an ominous sounding phone call from Beau: apparently, we needed to be updated.

* * *

No sooner had Beau's Landy clattered to a stop in our driveway, a pack of red dogs led by none-other than Aussie and RB, charged on mass around the back of our house but then stopped dead when they saw Beth and me. Of course, Aussie knew it was us; he was smiling, barking excitedly, prancing up and down like a lunatic, furiously wagging his tail: in other words, he was just showing off. And why not?

By the time Beau had climbed from his Landy, five magnificent pups, about eight weeks old I guessed, had gathered around RB (for security?), all fidgeting to attack (perhaps?) but otherwise inquisitive and eager to check us out.

In response to a subtle hand gesture from Beau, Aussie sauntered over to him and lay at his feet: a huffed, mid-tone yelp sent in RB's direction followed immediately. In a few strides RB was alongside Aussie, nuzzling and licking his face. Just moments later, the pups were all over their parents, growling, biting, and tugging at their ears and anything else they could grab.

Beth slowly lowered herself onto her knees and gently clapped her hands. All the pups stopped what they were doing, turning in unison to gaze at Beth, then at RB, and back again to Beth. By this stage, Beau had beckoned for me to join Beth.

I never saw RB's movement which must have somehow empowered the pups to investigate us. But gradually, ever so cautiously, they advanced upon us until one came within reach of Beth's outstretched hand. A nose touched her fingertips, then that brave beast rolled onto its back, legs moving as if running in the air and body wriggling madly. Beth looked at RB who instantly pricked her ears ... and good God, would you believe it, those two girls were now smiling at each other: honest!

Any reservations those pups may have had, dissolved in a flash as we were mobbed ... just as they had earlier thrown themselves upon Aussie and RB. I must say I was almost overwhelmed with joy, and perhaps a tear or two *may* have welled in my eyes.

* * *

ONCE WE'D SETTLED on our back verandah, enjoying a piping hot cuppa and yes, an ample wedge of Beth's special chocolate-iced, cream filled sponge cake, Beau quietly asked, 'Are you both absolutely positive you haven't been injured in any way?'

'My left wrist is giving me a bit of grief,' Beth replied, 'just a slight sprain is all, probably from the jarring I got through the control wheel when we first hit the deck. Otherwise, I'm all good.'

'Yeah, I'm good; stop worrying mate,' I added as I casually folded the local paper which Beau had brought with him and tossed it onto the table.

'Before you bring us up to date Beau, I'd like to say something,' I said, not only to change the subject but to get everyone's attention. 'It's quite a personal thing actually.'

'We're all ears ... go for it Andy; what's on yah mind?'

'Well, given all of those reported murders, which can surely only be attributed to Ho, plus his brutal execution of that poor bloody driver—which we all witnessed—it seems strange that he didn't do the same to me; he had the chance *and the time* when he and Zack tried to steal *our* bloody sheep, remember?'

'Agreed darling, that *is* a bit of a conundrum,' Beth interrupted gently, then added sagely, 'but, for all intents and purposes that attempted robbery at our place was just a trial that went wrong. Remember too, darling, that in his defence *he was otherwise distracted* from popping one into your handsome forehead.'

'Nevertheless, it feels goddamn weird that I'm still on the right side of the grass. Just more of the Stevens' innate good luck ... *anyway, I bloody well hope so.*'

A reflective pause in our conversation followed. Beth reached out, took my hand and squeezed. Beau returned his empty cup to the table, leant back in his chair, and stared at me with those incredibly blue eyes. After a few seconds, he said earnestly, 'Do you want to give it away Andy?'

'Mate, I really do want to be around to see our kids reach adulthood, but I'll let you know what I think after you've told us why you're paying us a visit this morning. I've got a gut feeling this isn't just a social visit.'

'Well, you'd be right. I've just been advised that Ho escaped from the Bega lockup yesterday!'

19

———————

'*Whhaaat!?*' Beth and I yelled: both of us gob smacked. By the equally startled look on Aussie's face, he wasn't impressed either. Perhaps I misinterpreted that look; perhaps he was just reacting to the fact that when I suddenly jumped up to vent my anger, I'd sent my chair sprawling backwards onto the back lawn, just missing his head.

'Beau, c'mon, you've gotta be joking!' Beth demanded. 'How?' And I take it he hasn't been caught yet?'

'It's no joking matter, please believe me,' Beau responded firmly, raising his arms to indicate we both should sit, and just listen. Beth and I sat; our fists clenched with rage, and both of us seething with incredulity.

'Even though Ho was searched at multiple times before his transfer to Pentridge Prison, in Melbourne, he overwhelmed one of the police officers with a blade from a safety razor. Apparently, the cunning little bastard had kept it hidden between the layers of leather in the sole of one of his sandals. And no, he's still on the loose; God only knows where.

'Apparently, the guard was alone in the police station and was in the process of handing Ho's meal tray to him, and probably juggling the ring of cell keys ... meaning both of his hands were occupied, like. Ho obviously saw his opportunity, produced the razor blade, and slashed the guard's throat.

'It's only conjecture, but in that initial moment of shock and distress, the guard would have dropped the meal tray and the cell keys. It seems Ho then somehow relieved the guard of the cell keys; possibly under the pretext that if the guard opened his cell, Ho would save the officer's life in return. But once let out, he disarmed the copper and shot him in the forehead; the calling tag of that bloody maniac.'

By this stage I was not only feeling sick, but extremely angry. 'Did we meet that officer?'

'No,' Beau replied, 'he was on leave when we were in Bega. But he was well known in the community and respected; he'll be sadly missed by all accounts.

'But I think we got a small break,' Beau continued. 'That officer never carried his handgun loaded, so presumably, Ho must have wasted some time getting that fatal bullet into the gun's chamber before executing him and then taking off. I know it's no consolation prize, but that may have limited his lead a bit. And thank God, we found the officer's gun, so perhaps he panicked and just threw it back into the cell ... but that doesn't make him any less dangerous.

'Our friends in Canberra and the Victorian Police Commissioner have put a reporting blackout on this. Homicide Squads from every State have been notified and provided with Ho's description, and every available police officer is now involved in trying to locate and capture the prick. Canberra has also involved the Federal Police to monitor every airport and shipping terminal from Adelaide to Darwin, and up to Cairns.

'The Fed's will also be keeping a close eye on Jack and Kelly; twenty-four hour surveillances, I've been told.'

'Do they really think that scum bag will try and harm our kids?' Beth asked.

'As at right now, he's the most wanted criminal in Australia,' Beau answered, but added, 'Who knows what he might do if he's desperate; let's hope he gets picked up quick smart, eh?'

Silence circled, then came to rest on me. 'Do you think Ho got any help?'

'Our friends in Canberra won't say,' Beau answered matter-of-factly. 'What makes you say that?'

'Where pray tell is Zack?' I replied. 'And when was *he* last sighted?'

'I'll check with Canberra and get back to you asap,' Beau replied quickly.

* * *

OUR JOURNEY in life as Livestock Theft Investigations (LTI's) had been interesting but had morphed into something more akin to a vendetta with death an ever-present guarantee if we cocked up. Beth was of the same view but felt compelled to see this assignment to its conclusion. Regardless, this was definitely going to be our final commitment. We may have become quite good at what we were doing, but things had rather abruptly changed and become much more than we originally bargained for. On the other hand, it was rewarding, acceptably challenging work. But it was also now loaded and potentially very bloody dangerous: we'd wait until after we knew of Zach's whereabouts to tell Beau of our decision.

* * *

AT 7:30 am the following morning Beau arrived at our farm armed with the newspaper, milk, and crumpets ... and Aussie's eager to please family of possessed, tireless ratbags. But it was great to have their company. RB was happy to sit beside Beth who she knew would deflect some of the attention the pups constantly demanded.

'Well, what gives mate? I dare say you're itching with some enlightening news.'

'You could say that, but uhm, you'd both better listen carefully. First, we're now all officially authorised to shoot to kill one mister Ho Hua on sight, no less! And second, that authorisation applies to any of his cohorts whether in Ho's company, or not! In other words, from this moment on, *no* questions are necessary to save either your own life, or that of any of us, or of course, that of any farmer.'

Beth gasped audibly. I threw my arms in the air and shouted, 'Bugger me and hi-ho Silver, here we come Ho! Best watch yah back now boyo.'

'Hang on, hang on,' Beau pleaded, 'there's more.'

'Our friends in Canberra went to great lengths to apologise for not coming clean about Ho. It wasn't that they wanted to feed us bull-shit, but they were waiting for information from Zack before enlightening us, as you so elegantly put it, Andy.'

'This should be good to hear,' Beth chimed in. 'I suspect what you're about to say is going to trump the news that we are now authorised bounty hunters; right, Beau?'

'Yes, I'd say it will. Andy, your intuition was spot on. Ho did get help ... from Zack!'

'Whhaat?' I bellowed, 'I knew it, that bastard is only out for himself: goddamn it, I knew he was on the double cross!'

'Sorry to disillusion you Andy, but you've got it wrong. Please, just listen mate.'

'No! Bugger it, I'm going for a walk. Besides, I think I'm about to throw up; this can't be happening.'

* * *

I DIDN'T THROW UP. But I did seethe before accepting I had no way of changing history, and realising Beau had a lot more to say which could shape my life and the lives of my family. Thirty minutes later and feeling a bit sheepish about my unwarranted outburst, I rejoined Beth and Beau, and apologised.

Beth repositioned her chair so that we were touching shoulders, her nearness as usual putting me at ease.

'I was advised last night that Ho had a visitor three days before he escaped. The name entered in the station's diary was Bruce Van der Linden, a bullshit name, and of course of no fixed address.

'But it was Zack—sent by our Canberra friends to somehow thrash out an escape plan for Ho. Zack's contribution was to provide transport and to drive him to any place of sanctuary that Ho might nominate. Zack didn't provide the murder weapon, that razor blade, or provide him with a firearm, though Ho was gifted five hundred bucks as a gesture of gang solidarity.

'As you can no doubt realise, Zack is held in very high regard and trust on both sides of a sting which eventually, we hope, will not only bring Ho undone but lead to interruption and cessation of farm theft on an international scale. We've been assured Zack has not jumped ship and is now being relied upon to keep us informed of Ho's plans, and if possible, let us know how and when he intends to make good his exit from Australia.

'Yes, yes, I know it seems absurd to go to these lengths given his murderous ways, but the larger picture is what matters.

'Mind you, Zack will be in constant danger while in Ho's company, and particularly so if he's with Ho when he's finally apprehended. So, Andy, there's the answer to your questions: your brother is a bloody brave fella.

'There's just one more thing of note you both need to know about; Zack got a coded message to Canberra yesterday that Ho mentioned "friends in Vietnam are no longer expecting him."'

'Which means that little shit has decided to continue trusting his luck to make his fortune in Australia.' Beth assumed correctly as upcoming events were to show.

* * *

AFTER WALKING with Beau and the dogs back to his Landi, we watched the last of a brilliant sunset together.

'Well mate, we've thought long enough about the next stage of this job. Beth and I have decided that *we're in*, but only while Ho's operating in Australia.'

'Thought as much ... so we'd better nail him quick smart, eh?', Beau replied, all matter of fact, like.

20

Three weeks lapsed before our lives would be transformed yet again.

No major regional thefts were brought to our attention during this relaxed period, but that didn't mean local stock theft was under control. However, we did receive some great news; Abbi Watt and her brother Reggie from Bega were coming to stay with us during the upcoming End of Term holidays.

A lovely time was had by all: however, little could we know where this friendship was headed.

* * *

Early one morning not long after Abbi and Reggie had returned home, and when we least expected it, Beau arrived unannounced with some amazing news: Zack had contacted our friends in Canberra; not just a few words but this time a message which ran into several very valuable sentences.

Beau quickly read the message to us: -

'Confirming H2 intends to remain in Oz. Unfinished business??

Boasting about well-advanced plans. His ideas inventive, which must be exchanged verbally asap. Mtg nearest Wagga2.'

Beth was first to respond. 'We can be in Wagga Wagga inside two hours with the right plane. Beau, you've got to get the exact meeting place, his desired date, and time to meet us; *like, asap*! And while you're at it, agree upon an *"aborted"* code word, just in case. Andy and I'll hire a plane from The Gippsland Flight Training Centre immediately and have it fuelled and ready for take-off on twenty-four stand-by. It's not going to take us long to get organised and drive to the West Sale Airport. Surely, we can be airborne in thirty minutes, tops … weather permitting of course.'

'Now that sounds like a plan my gorgeous bride,' I quickly chimed in, 'but will we have Aussie's permission to fly without him?'

'Ha, bloody ha,' replied Beau. 'Won't be necessary, he's coming with us, just make sure there's room in the back seat for me and one of the pups.'

* * *

Barely fifteen hours later, at 3:15*am* we were airborne with our full team; me, flying, Beth co-piloting and Beau, Aussie and a pup we'd named "Betta" (as in you'd *better* be good, or else) were in the back seats. I'd made a deal with Aussie that he could sit up-front on our return flight.

Yes, Beth and I had both checked that the fuel cap was correctly seated and locked. The plane, a twin-engine Beechcraft which Beth and I had previously flown while training for our pilot licenses, was still responsive and a joy to fly.

At 5:45-ish am, we sighted the handful of lights which lit the small airstrip we needed about five kilometres west of Wagga Wagga, a country town in New South Wales. The airport was owned by the Wagga Wagga Aviation Training Centre, and I was elated that a kind-hearted volunteer operator had not only turned the landing strip lights on for us but was on hand to welcome our arrival.

'Don't take all day Mr. Stevens,' the operator quipped, 'breakfast is almost ready; does mango juice, scrambled eggs, snags, toasted raisin bread and coffee sound OK? Over.'

'Nah, me dogs won't go for that. Over.'

'No problem, I'll see what I can muster up. See you in ten. Out.'

Gerry, our welcoming committee, greeted us as we approached the only office building on the airfield. The seven hangars nearby were obviously quite new and closed, and probably locked.

'Great to meet you all, my name's Gerry Traynor,' he said cheerfully, first shaking Beth's hand, then Beau's and finally mine.

'Nice dogs you've got there; no prize for guessing who's your father young fella,' said Gerry as he playfully patted the pup's back and ruffled its ears. 'You can all go through to the kitchen; just help yourselves and I'll join in a few minutes; landing protocols must be observed, eh.'

As Gerry was walking from the office to give our hire plane the once over, he turned and said, genuinely concerned, 'The boys at the Sale Airport reckon you two are bloody lucky to be alive. I hope that Duchess of yours fares just as well.'

* * *

THE BREAKFAST we'd all eagerly been anticipating was first class, and Gerry's company was most hospitable, yet it was just as well we'd rehearsed our reply to his next question.

'So, what brings you folk to Wagga?' Gerry asked naturally and politely enough, as most country people do.

Beau was quick out of the blocks. 'These two here want to keep up their flying hours and I'm on the lookout for a smallish property where I can grow cherries. Well, either cherries or almonds; depends on the available soil types and a regular water supply; irrigation water I'm guessing.' Gerry hummed and nodded his head in approbation.

'So, where are you heading? I'm assuming into town, so, can I give you lift? Otherwise, I can call a taxi to come and collect you if you'd prefer.'

'A lift into town would be lovely; thank you Gerry,' Beth decided as quick as a flash, also part of our planned response if such hospitality was offered to us.

However, our breakfast had to come to an end. Again, Beth took the lead by gathering up our plates and mugs and conveying them to the sink.

'Beth! Please, leave that lot, I'll take care of them when I return this arvo.

'So, what time will you be flying out? I'll need some time to refuel your Beechcraft and I've got two inbounds at about 4:00pm to look after.'

Beau replied with conviction. 'We'll be back here by not later than 3:00pm; is that OK with you mate?'

'Perfect. But come on then, all aboard ... the blue Nissan parked out front of hangar 4.'

21

On the northern side of Wagga is the football ground; abandoned at this time of the morning. I drove our hire car through the un-gated perimeter fence opening and headed for the grandstand which was proudly adorned by a large Wagga Kangaroos Rugby League Club signboard.

I parked the car then clambered out, leaving the engine running. 'Stay here,' I said firmly, 'but Beau, you take the driver's seat and be ready to clear out if I'm not back in thirty seconds.'

It didn't take me long to climb the twenty or so steps up to the viewing area: no sign of Zack! Disappointing.

I then leant over the guard railing and whistled, twice, our agreed "all safe" call.

The others joined me soon enough; Beau lugging a large supermarket paper bag containing sandwiches and cake, and three thermos flasks of black tea… compliments of our very obliging friend at the airport. Thoughtful bloke, that man, Gerry.

From our elevated perch in the seated viewing area at the very top of the grandstand, we had a nearly 270°view. However, Beau commanded Aussie and Betta to *stay* at the top of the stairs; their role being to let us know if anyone approached from the rear of the grandstand. Honest to God, I'd swear that Aussie smiled and nodded as if he knew exactly what was required of him.

About twenty minutes later, Aussie growled, not ferociously, more of a gargling whining sound coming from deep within his chest.

Beau clicked his fingers and Aussie went quiet, instantly. Betta was doing his best to emulate his father, succeeding in remaining quiet, but failing to contain his excitement and fidgeting. Again, I swear, Aussie was now looking directly at Betta; a look on his face which said, "if you don't sit still, I'll bite one of your bloody ears off!"

Betta slumped to the floor, chin resting on his front paws, now motionless, his full attention settling adoringly upon Aussie.

No more than a minute lapsed before a face appeared at the top of the grandstand stairs. It was bearded, unsmiling and cautiously sweeping the grandstand seating arrangements ... Zack for sure.

We all stood while Zack finished ascending the steps. Suddenly he froze; Aussie had also stood to greet him, their faces no more than two feet apart. 'It's OK mate,' Beau says, 'c'mon up, he's been fed. But watch out for his sidekick, his disposition is untested.'

Beautifully put I thought; just a subtle reminder for Zack not to try anything problematic, for he had experienced Aussie's effectiveness firsthand. Zack shifted his gaze downward to see Betta, now sitting beside Aussie, fidgeting, and ever so slightly raising his immature hackles and showing his collection of brand-new fangs. No doubt Zack called upon a reserve of guts and caution as he slowly walked past his initial greeting party.

Anyway, as soon as he reached us, Beau stepped forward and offered his hand, which Zack grasped with obvious relief. 'Good to see you safe and sound, Zack. I doubt if I'd ever take on what you're doing.'

'Hang on boys,' Beth chimed in, 'how about a cuppa and some Anzac's before we get started?'

'Tea black, thanks Beth.

'I say, Beth, the last time we met you were champing at the bit to put me away.'

'Yeah, well, that's all water under the bridge: we're definitely all on the same page now.'

As Beth started opening the thermos flasks and arranging mugs, I walked up to Zack, offered my hand, and looked him square in the eyes. 'Well brother, I hope you're being clean with us because if ever any harm comes to either Beth, Beau or our kids, you're a dead man.'

Zack's handshake was firm, his eyes searching mine, but also pleading. 'The safety of all of you has been paramount since day one; please believe me. We're all working for the same outfit and for the same outcome. We've got a lot to catch up on Andy, I know, but that'll have to wait; I've only got a few hours before I need to get back. Shall we get started now?'

22

———————

'I was only vaguely aware Ho had any interest in horses,' Zack started unexpectedly, 'until a few weeks ago anyway. I'm only saying this up front because it seems there's no limit to what he'll pull to make money, and although what we're trying to do is arrest him for multiple murders and sheep thefts, he's now added blackmail to his repertoire.

'Look, I'm pretty sure his main focus is still with hijacking sheep, judging by what he's hatched and what he's spending heaps of money on. But I'll describe all that in a few minutes.

'Recently I had to help him relieve two stallions from a horse breeder's property in Singleton. It was easy enough doin' the deed and hiding the horses, but he demanded over a million dollars ransom from the owner. For whatever reason the owner doesn't want the police involved and has agreed to pay the asking price. The exchange is scheduled for next week at this stage, but he hasn't told me which day just yet. Anyway, I'm supposed to accompany Ho to ensure everything goes down smoothly, no problems like.

'Which means I can't advise when we can go into action against him.'

'I can just imagine the threats he's made to the owner,' I pressed.

'Oh yes, he's a ruthless little bastard alright,' Zack replied. 'Threatened to kill one of the horses if he doesn't get the money on time; and he'll do it, I know what he's like.

'I can almost guarantee you he'll hit the bottle to celebrate his success and then suffer for days afterwards like a bear with a sore head. I make a point of keeping out of his way; he always carries a gun and he'll use it if something gets under his skin.'

'On the other hand,' said Beth thoughtfully, 'it might be just the right time to pay him a visit; his guard might be down while he's feeling so hungover.'

'You could perhaps have a drink or three with him to ensure he gets well and truly shit-faced,' I suggested enthusiastically.

'That's not a bad idea actually,' replied Zack, 'but by the bejeezus he can drink. I've seen him knock back two thirds of a bottle of whisky without taking a breather, then carry on as if he's as sober as a judge!'

'Let me add my two bobs' worth, you sneaky buggers,' Beau quietly added.

'Did I ever tell you about the woman who owned the pub at Omeo, many years ago now, like? Nice enough lady, even after she'd drank most of her best paying customers under the table. Confided in me that she had a trick up her sleeve: always swallowed two raw eggs about half an hour before she had her first drink. Claimed she never threw up and was never hungover the following day.'

'And it *really* worked?' Zack asked tentatively, not quite sure if he could believe Beau's anecdote.

'Yeah, apparently,' said Beau, 'but I also reckon she had an advantage. She was a *huge* girl, at least sixteen or seventeen stone, I'd say ... and that's roughly twice your weight, mate.

'Anyway, we'll have to play this by ear, Zack, until you know Ho's plans. Same arrangements as this time. Let me know when you believe he's most vulnerable and we'll be back here asap. All agreed?

'OK, now, please enlighten us about Ho's most inventive plans regarding sheep theft.'

'Ho has two properties, one in Narrandera and another in Cootamundra, both in his wife's name. Well, she's not legally Ho's wife, but they've lived together for years. So, the name on both titles is Hguyen, not Hua.

'That'll be the lady we met when you and Ho tried to steal our sheep,' said Beth.

'Correct. Her name's Lily. A nice enough woman and a good mother from what I've witnessed, but I'm buggered if I know what she sees in Ho. I sometimes get the feeling she holds the purse strings. And, oh yeah, she has a degree in mechanical engineering which brings me to what Ho's been working on.'

Interestingly, Aussie and Betta were now lying almost at Zack's feet, a social gesture I dare say, rather than one of distrust.

'Both of Ho's properties are about forty, maybe fifty, acres. Both have got large sheds and are well hidden from any roads. Another of his words of wisdom comes to mind; *"it never pays to have all your eggs in one basket"*. So, he reckons, even if he gets taken down on one property, he can get back to business at the other without too much delay.'

'He's got that wrong, the silly bugger,' Beth added. 'He seems to be forgetting he's murdered a dozen people, and that after we've nailed him, he'll *never* see either of those places again because he'll never, *ever*, either escape or be released.'

'That's what I mean about Ho,' Zack replied, 'his thinking's skewed by his ego, or he's a total nut job ... or both, I suspect. Regardless, he seems to like my company and confides in me about heaps of stuff which perhaps he shouldn't. And he can be quite *"normal"*—and happy—when his daughter comes to visit.'

'Which means,' said Beau, 'he currently doesn't know we know the whereabouts of both properties, thanks to you. Which by the way, are both properties permanently inhabited? And if so, by how many people, what vehicle types and how many guard dogs' etcetera?'

'I'll be getting to that, but what it really means Beau, is that you are going to need two teams of reliable and sufficient LTA's for when we swoop. Do you have the resources for that?'

'No, not yet, but I reckon I know where to recruit them. Mind you, I'll have to shake a leg to get 'em on board and fully briefed. Timing's going to be everything, so we'd better crack on. Tell us what you've learned about Ho's sheep theiven' plans and what he's working on.'

'Well, it's quite clever really,' Zack jumps straight in, 'he's in the process of converting two furniture removal vans—those that have high sides—into two basic compartments. The one closest to the prime mover is essentially a thermally insulated cold room with rows of head-high tracks for supporting the sheep's carcasses. Everything is stainless steel, even the leg hooks.

'Now, cop this; the rear compartment of the van houses a purpose-built, transportable animal slaughter vehicle—basically a small Bedford truck with its original cabin, engine, and chassis—which can be driven down another ramp, essentially the van's rear door, and then be positioned on flat ground, wherever it suits ... obviously out of site from any homestead. In no time at all they then offload from the van a flatpack of aluminum fencing sections and a gate which all slot together to form a pen which can hold about three dozen sheep.'

At this point Zack takes a few sips of tea, smacks his lips in appreciation then stands up and stretches his arms above his head. He then casually sits, scratches the back of his neck, and presses on.

'Oh yeah, there's only six blokes involved, Ho of course and five lackeys, all brawny unsavoury looking types.

'The slaughter vehicle has hydraulic holding arms, a stun gun and leg lifts that make it easy for his slaughtermen to bleed out the sheep and gut them. There's even a powered chain designed to pull the skin from the animal's carcass, made so easy while the body's still warm.

'There's also an arrangement of steel panels hydraulically operated which direct all the guts into a holding tank for later disposal at a disposal point somewhere on his properties; or anywhere else he so pleases. Anyway, another panel shoves the skins into a separate holding bin. Apparently, he's met a bloke who'll take as many skins as Ho can supply.

'Having loaded all the carcasses, the van's cold room door is closed and locked. The temporary holding pen is dismantled and stacked along the inside walls of the van, thus allowing the slaughter vehicle to be reversed back up the ramp and secured.

'However, before the van's rear door is closed, they start a generator—which also powers the cold room refrigeration system—to operate a sluice pump to wash everything down. This also lightens the load for the return trip; pretty smart, eh? The water's held in a forty-four-gallon tank that's been bolted into place behind the prime mover's cabin. It certainly doesn't attract any attention to the untrained eye.

'The van is then driven back to one of Ho's properties with little probability that anyone, particularly the police, would question the bona fides of a furniture removal van. It's then garaged in the large shed, completely out of sight of course.

'They usually repeat this procedure twice before packing up, which means each van returns to one of Ho's two storage facilities with about seventy head of dressed sheep ready for sale. In other words, if both his modified vans go out on the same day, he's probably netted at least one hundred and forty head, which just disappear ... and are all unidentifiable, even if they are found.

'It's only once the van is garaged in the front half of the shed that you realise why the van also has a standard sized door on both sides. You see, the rear half of each shed is also a huge state-of-the-art insulated and refrigerated storage room. The van's two side doors therefore reduce the effort and time it takes to transfer its load into the much larger, permanent cold storage room. And when the onloading is completed, the van is driven to the very front of the shed—behind the closed front door—in readiness for when Ho identifies his next target.

'When you think about it, Ho *is* on to something big. He has unlimited countryside to prey upon, and the unpredictability of *when*, not *if*, is always to his advantage. So, his entire operations must be stopped!

'By the way, just about everything is made from stainless steel so that nothing will rust. Must be costing him a bloody fortune.'

Zack pauses for a swig of his tea, and I grab my opportunity.

'Bloody amazing enterprise if you ask me. But tell us more; you were saying two of those slaughter vehicles are to be built. Who on earth has he engaged to build them and to modify the furniture vans?'

'And how the hell does he dispose of all the bones, the heads and the entrails and organs for God's sake,' Beau interjected, 'he can't be just dumping that lot willy-nilly all over the countryside.'

'Good questions,' replied Zack as he handed his empty mug back to Beth for a refill. 'One van and one slaughter vehicle are complete. I was with Ho and Lily as they tested everything; I even helped to adjust the lifting apparatus and tuned the Bedford's motor. Mind you, Lily's fingerprints are all over everything: that lady's quite an accomplished mechanic.

'The second build is very close to completion; it's my guess they'll start testing it next week.

'As for who's doing all the fit out, Lily has a family in Shepperton who specialise in stainless steel fabrication and motor vehicle repairs and rebuilds. How convenient, eh? They are all bloody good workers, but I'm sure Ho put the fear of Christ into them not to ask too many questions and otherwise keep their mouths shut. Mind you, given the money that's been involved it wouldn't surprise me if Lily was also the paymaster. If it had been Ho, they'd probably have got bugger all.

'As I said earlier, in Ho's usual indifferent, uncaring manner, he has no qualms about dumping the sheep heads, bones and their entrails wherever he chooses; that's not his problem, he reckons, particularly where long hauls are involved. On the other hand, Lily must have scruples because she's had several large holes dug at both properties; not for dams I'll bet, but for offal disposal.

'Anyway, before I make tracks, here's the company name and address, and some of the names of those workers. Beau, you'd better include in your manpower planning, a separate team to raid that workshop address, simultaneously with the main operation to capture Ho. And you'll need these; my mud maps of where you'll discover Ho's properties.

'That's about all I can pass on for now; any questions?'

'Yes, I have,' Beth replied. 'How will they go about getting customers and deliver everything without getting caught?'

'I'm not entirely sure,' said Zack, frowning and scratching his head, 'but I suspect word of mouth must play a part. Some will drive to the storage sheds to pick up, Lily has told me that much. Come to think of it, I've recently seen the Wagga butcher and the owner of one of the pubs talking with Ho and Lily.

'Deliveries, well, I'm sure those two have got something in mind, otherwise how can they make a profit? Ehm, I wonder, perhaps they're waiting for the military training camp that's been rumoured for Wagga; they'll need plenty of meat.

'In the meantime, it makes sense to me that Ho'll need a couple of quickish refrigerated panel vans for home deliveries. I'll let you know asap if I hear or see anything.

'Regardless, the butcher and the pub owner should be arrested for complicity, so Beau, don't forget to include them in your plans for when we make our bust.

'Just one more thing,' Zack continued. 'Have you been notified of any sheep thefts local to Wagga in the past couple of weeks?'

'No, nothing,' Beau answered. 'Why do you ask?'

'Well, I can assure you that at least one robbery of about fifty head *has* taken place during that time, about twenty kilometres northwest of Nerrandera. I even watched them unload.'

* * *

FAREWELLING Zack was something akin to how it must feel to run onto the MCG to play in a VFL Grand Final. Everything had to go right from that moment on to hold up the trophy.

Nevertheless, we parted with genuine handshakes of trust and even a hug for Zack from Beth. And believe it or not, Aussie allowed Zack to pat him on the head and ruffle his ears. Betta, however, not to be out done, sidled up to Zack and raised his right paw. Zack, not wishing to ignore the pup, squatted and took the offered paw.

23

During a lull in our conversation as we drove the hire car back to the Wagga Airport, I had a strange thought.

'Do you know what? This plan we're about to execute is a bit like ferreting for rabbits. After laying all your nets over every nearby burrow entrance, including any secret bolt hole of course, then you send a ferret down a selected burrow ... and next, wait. Zack of course is the ferret, we, and the raiding teams Beau is about to organise, are the nets. Ho and his merry offsiders are rabbits destined for the pot.'

'Very good darling,' Beth replied happily, 'that's a wonderful analogy. And it's my guess that the more confused and anxious the rabbits are, the faster they'll make a bolt for freedom ... not ever expecting to be nabbed by the nets of course.'

At the airport we were met by Gerry, the ever-helpful airport operations manager. 'I trust your business was successful. Everything's done here; your Beechy's been refuelled and she's ready as soon as you are. She's over in hangar two.'

Gerry tapped a green button on his console and hangar door two kicked slightly, then rose steadily.

'There's coffee on the go and some assorted sandwiches in the fridge; help yourselves. And for these two boys there's a fresh bag of dog biscuits in the cupboard above the sink; beef and prawn flavour no less.

'Don't worry about returning the hire car, I'll take it home tonight and drop it off at the Avis depot first thing tomorrow morning.'

'Thanks mate, everything's paid for I believe, but if there's any shortfall, I'll square things away with you when we return in about a week's time,' Beau assured our friend.

'No problems. But if you want to be back in Sale before it gets dark, you'd better shake a leg.'

The return flight was smooth and without incident. Aussie and Betta were my co-pilots sharing the same safety belt, while Beth and Beau were both sound asleep within half an hour of takeoff. And yes, if you are wondering, Beth and I both carefully checked the cap on the fuel tank's fill pipe.

24

———

The next morning, Beth and I sat in our lounge room eating breakfast and listening to the rain pelting on the house's galvanised iron roof. The fire was in good shape and wafting warm air over us, filling the room. I'd been contemplating the flames, dreaming of nothing specific, and glad that bugger all was going to get done outside this day, when out of the blue a thought struck me.

'Hey Beth, my gorgeous bride, has it occurred to you that it must have cost Ho and Lily an absolute fortune to set everything up to this stage of their shonky plans? Where, and how on earth, could they have accumulated that sort of dough?'

'Seed money darling, seed money.'

'Yeah, maybe, but who in their right mind would want to be Ho's goddamn sponsor?'

'I'm more worried about *the why*.'

'Ho's trying to impress someone; he's after power I reckon, more than accumulating wealth, though I suppose both do go hand in hand.'

'I agree darling. Based on what Zach's just told us, I think what we're seeing is just the infancy of a potentially very prosperous industry, one very capable of growing much faster than our existing law enforcement manpower has any chance of dealing with.'

'So, we absolutely must nip things in the bud before it gains any real traction. And to get that outcome, our planning must be spot on and well-executed. Which means we must give Beau as much support as we possibly can; he's sure got his work cut out.'

'I'd say *strangled*, not nipped in the bud, my darling. But we also have a chance to impress Canberra that simultaneous destruction of an entire supply chain is not only feasible, but well-worth financing properly ... not just the same old, same old random raid mentality.'

'Well said, you two,' Beau's voice from behind us shattered our contemplations, sending us both into defensive and impressive lounge chair dismounts.

'Ahhh, bloody Hell Beau! Yah frightened the shit out of us. How'd you get inside?'

'Easy as; just walked straight in the back door. I'd say it's high time you got yourselves a guard dog; I could've been anyone, perhaps even someone worse than Mr. Hua. But fear not, look who's come to say g'day.'

As if on cue, Betta poked his head around the lounge room door with a look on his youthful face which for all intents and purposes said, 'well, can I come in too, or not?'

I barely saw Beau's hand movement which sent Betta racing towards me, all four legs scrambling and his toenails clattering on the polished timber floor, desperate it seemed for him to get a purchase that would propel him onwards. But the floor won. Betta tripped, fell, and then slid into my waiting arms. I was immediately engulfed in a squirming, almost frantic display, the highlight being the smothering of my face with fast, warm wet licks which I chose not to deflect.

This was a beautiful surprise; I never suspected I was admired quite so much; that's if you exclude Beth, of course.

'What do yah reckon Beth,' Beau asked somewhat smugly, sure he already knew her answer, 'can he move in, or what?'

'Andy, just point casually to the floor and he'll get down: try it when he settles down a bit.'

While Beth prepared breakfast for Beau they chatted happily enough, however, it was evident Beau was keen to get on with the reason for his early visit.

As Beth started to clear the table, I recognised the glance she sent in my direction. Aha, here was my chance to test Beau's advice. No sooner had I pointed to the floor, than Betta slid off my lap. Just seconds later the tea towel that Beth had lobbed in my direction landed on my shoulder. How was that for teamwork, or was it a demonstration of who was the better trained?

WITH ALL OF us now gathered around the kitchen table, Beau launched into his news. 'I had quite a lengthy talk with our friends in Canberra last night ... discussing the intelligence Zack provided. Not only were they putting their total trust in Zach's information, but they agreed we should proceed with the plan I put to them regarding Ho's arrest and in shutting down his operation. How about that?

'Canberra has graciously agreed to finance everything and has already created for us, an "as required, no limit working account" with the Commonwealth Bank, in Wagga. The three of us are signatories to that account by the way.

'Not only that, but I've been accepted as Team Leader and Coordinator for our raids on Ho's enterprises. Our friends reiterated their earlier advice that nothing has changed with respect to how to deal with Ho should he not cooperate peacefully.

'They've also elevated the importance of arresting Lily; clearly, she's a collaborator and probably in possession of a sizeable stash of illegal money which is of interest to the ATO who are keen to learn its origins.

'And cop this, Canberra will provide Federal Police Officers currently stationed in the ACT ... and has authorised the secondment of as many police officers and LTI personnel which I deem necessary.

'All I need to do now is advise Canberra of how many officers I'll need at each rendezvous location, and by *when* they all need to be in place.

'There'll be a total news blackout on this project, so we must make sure all our operatives remain tight lipped, and do *not* turn up wearing their uniforms; but rather, I expect them to be dressed as if they are either on holiday or just average farmer Joes. However, they must all be armed.

'Regardless, we don't move until we get Zack's feedback regarding Ho's arrangements. Therefore, timing will be king, and in our case, I suggest that in the meantime, we should brush up on our handgun skills. Any questions so far?'

'Yep,' I replied, 'I take it everyone involved needs to be in position ready to pounce and catch each target red handed, but how will we know when they'll be where we want them?'

'Good point, but remember, time and surprise are our primary advantages.

'Let's start with the good local citizens; the butcher and the pub owner identified by Zack. They know Ho of course, but not Zack. On the day we strike, two out-of-uniform police officers will arrive in an unmarked vehicle at each address, at an appointed time; I think around twelve thirty. Those offenders will be arrested, hand cuffed and driven straight to the Wagga Police Station where they'll be charged with receiving stolen goods, and they'll remain there until the main event is concluded before they're released. They won't get a chance to tip off Ho.

'Those charges will change significantly should anyone be wounded or killed during our main actions, which means these unsuspecting clowns could also be up for aiding and abetting in a homicide.'

'Those four officers will then be available as back up, where, and if needed later in the day.'

'Ehhm, that sounds pretty good to me Beau,' I said, 'but how do you intend to pull everything else together on the day?'

'Well, as it so happens, Canberra have two Federal Police Officers earmarked to stay with the Wagga Airport duty manager, to supervise the setting up of our operational headquarters adjacent to the airport. A few students who are about to graduate from Duntroon will be flown in to install military tenting, probably a marquee and a handful of tents. These lads will also be on hand to assist the airport manager with catering as required, but they'll report to the Feds.

'Bloody Hell Beau,' Beth interrupted as she handed him a cuppa, 'you should have owned a logistics company.'

'It's in me blood I reckon; me dad was a logistics manager in the Australian Army during the First World War. But look, we'd better press on, there's heaps you need to know. Interrupt whenever, OK.

'As soon as we hear from Zack, all our standby operatives must get underway from their respective depots and time their journeys to arrive at the Wagga Airport, at least five hours before we strike. Once everyone's arrived, I'll be conducting a full briefing, with emphasis on timing and the element of surprise. That'll be followed by a question time and then an early buffet lunch.

'I may get overruled in my request that all those involved in the on-farm arrests must be armed and have one ready up the spout, but I hope not. Anyway, given we'll all be dealing with Australia's most wanted murderer, I'm convinced Ho *will* be armed and won't hesitate to shoot, as will any of his offsiders if they're armed.

'So, what I've got in mind, is this.

'You see, Canberra has also authorised two RAAF helicopters to be on standby for when we get Zack's advice that Ho's on the move. The pilots will arrive at the Wagga Airport in plenty of time to receive whatever information they need.

'Apparently, they'll have military aerial surveillance maps with them which'll greatly assist getting both arrest teams into place, at approximately the same time, and into locations chosen for their ease of chopper access despite the surrounding vegetation. Anyway, each chopper should be able to off-load our teams not more than five or six hundred yards from each shed.

'As soon as the choppers take off to return here, each team will then leg it to within one hundred yards of their target, then spread out to surround it. They'll all be wearing army camouflage ponchos but must still take advantage of whatever cover the scrub provides them to get into position undetected.'

'I think we should assume there will be some guard dogs at each location,' I suggested. 'And there will no doubt be at least two working dogs. What do you suggest?'

'I'm pretty certain the working dogs won't be any trouble,' Beau replied thoughtfully. 'They might bark a bit, but they won't be trained to attack, so just ignore them.

'On the other hand, the guard dogs will attack once they get a whiff of intruders, but not if they can't see the threat. That's why our boys must stay out of site, *absolutely do not smoke* and if they want to pee, they must retreat slowly and quietly at least fifty yards from their position.'

'No farting aloud either, I presume?' I suggested wearing my best poker face.

'Right, moving along,' Beau replied with a chuckle as Beth rolled her eyes and grinned in amusement, I think. 'Regardless, patience will be needed by all to maintain position out of sight, until the vans return.

'It must also be understood by everyone that should the guard dogs be off leash and attack, then everyone is at liberty not to mess about, but to just shoot them; *no one is to risk* being mauled, in fact, nothing should impede our assaults on the sheds.'

'So, *when do we leave our positions?*' Beth asked.

'Good question Beth', Beau responded with his usual logic and calmness. 'Ideally, we wait until the van has been in the shed for at least twenty minutes. That should give Ho and his men sufficient time to be well and truly focused upon transferring and hanging the dressed sheep carcasses into the refrigerated storage room; so, that's when we burst into the shed through the front door and both side doors, guns blazing if necessary, and arrest the bastard's red handed.

'Well, that's it in a nutshell, what do you reckon?'

'With all the resources at your disposal,' I chimed in, 'and given the inherent simplicity of your plans Beau, we stand a bloody good chance of pulling this off without too much collateral damage.'

'Logic says things may not go as we ideally hope, but that's why those chosen for this project are known for their initiative. So, once we launch this attack, the outcome rests in their hands; Ho's elimination being paramount, regardless of whether he's dead, or taken alive.'

'Just two more questions,' Beth asked thoughtfully, 'have you invited Aussie to join us? And where will Zack be during this little event?'

'Oh yes. Aussie would be most put out if I didn't include him in our plans.

'As for Zack, well, his job will essentially end once he delivers the info I'm waiting on. Canberra has given him instructions to make himself scarce until the law decides whether he'll be needed as a witness.'

25

———

Four days on, Beau's Landy skidded to a halt beside our back verandah. Betta was barking on top note, no doubt annoyed at being unceremoniously woken. I switched on the bedside light, not meaning to wake Beth: bloody hell, it was ten to six and still dark outside!

'No doubt the bearer of absorbing and meaningful news awaits our immediate and undivided attention my darling,' Beth said blearily. 'So, get your hand off my arse and get out of bed, or else. I knew exactly what she really meant, but I *did* hesitate, but only for a second or two while I contemplated the potential ecstasy inherent in her ambiguous threat.

Betta suddenly stopped barking, heavy footfalls purposefully traversed the verandah, the flywire door opened with its usual *screeeech*, the main kitchen door then quickly clattered open, and the kitchen light was switched on.

'Come on you two, rise and shine,' Beau's voice boomed. 'We've got a job to do. Some people would have done a day's work by now.' Cheeky bugger, I muttered.

When Beth and I surfaced into the kitchen a few minutes later, Beau already had the kettle on and had placed two thermos flasks on the sink waiting to be filled. 'No time for breakfast, we're on the move. I've phoned the West Sale Airport to let them know we'll be there in about fifty minutes; they reckon your Beechcraft has been refuelled and will be ready for immediate take-off.

'I've also spoken with our good friend Gerry at the Wagga Airport to let him know our ETA. He said all's clear weather wise, and bless his cotton socks, he'll have breakfast waiting for us, including something for Aussie.'

We had previously packed *everything* we might need in advance of such an eventuality, so it only took Beth and me five minutes to transfer our belongings into Beau's Landy.

Upon returning to the kitchen Beau had just finished filling both thermos flasks. I grabbed a fistful of tea bags, a packet of sweet biscuits, a box of sugar cubes, quickly filled a small jar with milk, sealed the lid tightly and then after placing these essentials into a fabric carry-all bag, headed for the Landy. Beau immediately followed me outside carrying the flasks and Beth quickly followed him after closing and locking the back door. No prize for correctly guessing who was already camped on the front passenger seat, seatbelt pulled up firmly around his chest and (yes) *smiling* in anticipation of another flying adventure.

* * *

No sooner had we finished our breakfast, than members of our strike force started arriving. The two ACT based Federal Police Officers were first, shortly followed by a convoy of three unmarked, military style trucks, no doubt conveying our tents and headquarters marquee and the lads from the Duntroon Military Academy.

'What the Hell's going on?' Gerry suddenly asked, his arms flapping in concern at this invasion. 'I've got a bloody airport to run!'

'It's OK Gerry, believe me,' Beau answered quickly. 'Please, sit down with us and I'll explain what's about to happen.'

Fifteen minutes later Gerry leant back in his chair and said, 'Well I'll be buggered. I'm at your disposal of course, but my priority must be attending to any air traffic movements. Mind you, there's nothing on my flight schedule until this arvo.'

'Not so Gerry,' I chimed in, 'if I'm not mistaken there are two RAAF choppers due here within the next few minutes.'

'Oh, right, then I'd better get ready to usher them in.'

As soon as the choppers landed, Gerry joined us when we filed outside to make our presence known and to introduce ourselves. 'Good luck', Gerry said as he turned and headed back to the control room. 'If you need anything, just ask; you know where to find me.'

A sort of managed chaos followed. However, order soon reigned, just in time for morning tea and for Beau's scheduled briefing of all parties. So far, so good.

26

By eleven o'clock the job was on. Most men who emerged from the Operation Centre marquee had an air of determination and self-confidence. Those not wearing their camouflage outfits retreated to their assigned tents and having changed and secured their firearms, jogged back to the marquee.

Chopper engines simultaneously coughed loudly, then settled into an even throb with their accelerating, rotating blades slicing the air which produced an unmistakable *whup, whup, whup* sound.

Within a minute both strike teams were on board their assigned chopper which then, in what seemed to be a well-practiced dance, both rose slowly, side by side, then advanced forward in a nose down attitude, before rapidly lifting and accelerating up, and away from the airport.

I had my arm around Aussie at this stage just in case he panicked, but instead, he simply leant into me and occasionally licked my chin. Even so, there was a slight trembling coming from his body; not from fear I'm sure, but exactly how Beau described it when he sensed action. Before long, Aussie left my side and planted himself at Beth's feet. One of the Duntroon lads, Will, I think, was with us, up front and calm.

Ten minutes lapsed before the choppers separated onto their respective flight paths. Another twenty minutes lapsed before our pilot looked back over his shoulder and gave us a thumbs down to indicate the target was in sight and our landing approach would now commence.

We flew in low over treetops towards a predetermined clearing, where, as if by magic, the chopper seemed to stop in midair, before descending gracefully. As we touched down, I slid open the chopper's side door and exited; with too much haste as it turned out. I took one step, tripped arse overhead and landed flat on my back.

Beth followed elegantly, suppressing a chuckle, but Beau was remorseless, 'Ya clumsy dolt, ya could have broken something, or shat yourself in the excitement. C'mon, on ya feet, and follow me.'

Embarrassingly, I did need help to stand; young Will got behind me and effortlessly hauled me up. I don't think Aussie cared a tinker's toss, for he was standing about two yards away, leg cocked and peeing forcibly up against a tree while sporting a look of total contentment on his face. And I'm sure I also got a glimpse of the pilot's face contorted with laughter as he eased his chopper into the air before sliding it away, back over the surrounding trees.

After putting on our camouflage ponchos, our next task was to get as close to Ho's shed without being either seen or heard. The surrounding undergrowth provided just the right amount of cover; for instance, if either Beau or Beth moved more than twenty steps away, they could not be seen. It still took us about twenty minutes to navigate our way through this scrub.

Young Will was the first to see the shed, quickly grabbing Beau's arm to alert him, and pointing. We all knew the drill, fanning out to be about fifty yards apart and to approach to be within no more than fifty yards from the shed.

I soon found an ideal leafy position, certain that when Beau broke cover to approach the shed I'd see him soon enough and could quickly follow suit. Of course, remaining still, and becoming bored would be our initial enemies. Which got me thinking; Will might be a strapping, very fit looking specimen, but he's still only about nineteen years old. And yes, he has a military issue handgun: I pray his teachers at Duntroon taught him how to use it.

An hour later, Ho's converted furniture van came bumping along the dirt track which leads to his shed. I checked my watch; right, they get twenty minutes then we spring our trap.

Two dogs had suddenly started barking, or was it three? Regardless, these were undoubtedly guard dogs excited that their master had returned; proof positive they had not been aware of us ... but, they were off lead, which meant they would present a challenge to us when we struck, unless, unless, unless someone chained them up, no longer needed, now that Ho was back to exercise his control.

I'd no sooner embraced that possibility when two men emerged from the shed, and so help me God, they proceeded to clip chains onto the collars of *three* dogs, all three being rangy, ugly, and savage looking mongrel types.

Nonetheless, this flukish bit of good luck turned things squarely back to our advantage. I wondered if Aussie had seen them but easily convinced myself that he had. And though I couldn't see Beau in his hiding place I'm sure he was busily trying to keep Aussie's blood lust in check.

27

———————

Twenty minutes dragged by as if it had been an hour. Worse, mosquitoes had found me and doing their best to piss me off: how did they know I absolutely *hate* the little shits?

Movement in my peripheral vision caught my attention; it was Beau and Aussie moving together onto the open area which surrounded the shed. I moved quickly from my position to join them just seconds before Beth and Will caught up with us.

Beau then withdrew his gun and inserted a round into its firing chamber; we three immediately followed suit. As planned, he next gestured for us to approach the shed; Beau, Aussie and Will to take the front, Beth and I to each take one of the side doors.

Of course, our next moves also depended upon luck; that all three of the shed's doors were not locked, or that at least *one wasn't*! We had estimated it would take no more than twenty-five seconds to reach our appointed positions, whereafter Beau would fire a single shot, that being the signal for all of us to enter the shed in all haste.

At least my luck was in; my assigned door opened easily. I stepped inside and scanned the void, allowing a few seconds for my eyes to adjust to its low light level. And this is where I started to earn the fabulous salary I'd been receiving.

I looked towards the van just in time to see one of Ho's labourer's walking down the ramp with a sheep carcass draped across his right shoulder. He glanced over his left shoulder, no doubt to make sure he was not about to trip and go arse overhead ... but instead, saw me, or rather my gun, levelled directly at his head.

As I was about to say something like "arms up you're under arrest" when all Hell broke loose from the front of the shed. Two very different sounding gunshots were fired, almost simultaneously, and what sounded like the dog fight of all times had erupted.

'What's goin' on ya little prick?' my prisoner yelled, 'put that gun down or I'm gunna ...'

I fired my first shot which (somehow) luckily just missed the bloke's head. 'Gunna do what?'

The bloke correctly assessed my intentions and obediently started walking to where I was gesturing with my gun ... to the refrigerated storeroom no less.

'Hang on a second, you can't lock me in there, I'll freeze to death!'

'Better that than getting shot dead right where you're now standing. C'mon, move, or else!'

As soon as he entered the storeroom, I locked it but gave him one small concession; I left the interior light on. Ehhmm; one down and two to go.

I was about to venture to the front of the shed and lend my support, when Beth unexpectedly grabbed me by the arm and said, 'Top job darling, but the other blokes still in the van. I'll take care of him; you get up front and see what's going on.' Spoken like a seasoned livestock inspector; that's my Beth.

I hesitated. A bullet zipped past my left cheek. Second and third shots followed instantly, seeking the source of the original shot.

It was then silent; except for the dog fight which still raged outside. Right, that's two down, which leaves ... Ho!

Out of the gloom, Beau's voice echoed around the shed. 'I say, Ho, I think it's time you realised something. Your times up. You can surrender yourself peacefully like, or we'll happily collect the bounty on your head. It doesn't faze us whether that means dead, or alive. It's up to you.'

Before Beau got his answer, the dog fight abruptly ended. Aussie staggered into the shed's open front door, tongue hanging out, part of one of his ears missing and bleeding not only from his mouth and nose, but from several gashes on his flanks and on both of his front legs.

Another shot rang out. Aussie fell.

Two different sounding shots followed, almost instantaneously, then silence reigned.

Now furious, and quite stupidly, I was about to commit suicide by charging Ho's position, when young Will walked calmly from behind the van, his gun still smoking as he returned it to its holster. 'All clear, Beau, he was too slow,' he called, reassuringly. 'I think you'll find he's well and truly dead.'

Yes, I truly *was* relieved, but bloody Hell ... was this young man special, or what!

28

Shortly after, we met outside in front of the shed. Beau was on his knees beside Aussie, supporting his dear friend's head while talking quietly to him. 'Water, quick,' Beau pleaded.

I remembered seeing a water tank on the outside of the shed and bolted back to it hoping I'd find something in which to carry some water back for Aussie. My luck was in, an enamel handwash basin lay on the ground close to the tank's outlet tap.

'Is he still with us?' I asked, fearing the worst, and puffing heavily from my exertions. 'Please, tell me he's gunna be OK.'

'Get your shirt off darling, and start ripping it into pieces,' Beth ordered, 'I've got to clean his wounds and stop his blood loss quick smart, or he won't make it.

'See here,' said Beth as she pointed to a small hole in Aussie's shoulder. 'And here too, that's the exit wound. I think the shock of the bullet's impact floored him, but he's a tough bugger. Quick, give me some of that water and then, Beau, perhaps you could start cleaning his other wounds.'

'Don't spare the water, there's a full tank out the back.'

Will had been closely inspecting Aussie's wounds, while

muttering quietly to himself. 'There're four nasty ones; full pelt tears exposing his muscles and tendons. I've gotta operate.'

'Do you really know how too, Will?' I asked.

'Yep, all I need right now is for all exposed tissue to be washed as clean as possible. I always carry a few needles and silk thread for emergencies just like this. I can see that he's breathing by the rise and fall of his chest, but we also don't want Aussie going into shock. Beau, would you please drape your poncho over Aussie to keep him warm, but move it around as needed so that I can get to each injury site. Is he likely to bight me?'

'Not if I tell him not too,' Beau replied without a second thought.

What followed was incredible to watch; here was a nineteen-year-old Duntroon Academy graduate calmly and expertly sewing together seriously damaged sections of torn animal tissue, as if he'd been doing this sort of thing for years.

Beth and Beau nevertheless held Aussie firmly, just in case he moved. But he didn't, so, seeing there was little I could contribute, I stood and walked outside.

Well bugger me, you should have seen what I saw. There lay two huge dogs, dead; their throats ripped out and sporting a myriad of other nasty gashes though none as bad as that which had snuffed out their lives.

A third dog was alive, just. But not for long. I withdrew my gun and shot the poor beast in its head.

As I dragged the three corpses to one side of the track, I heard a vehicle, no, two vehicles, driving slowly towards the shed. A quick glance at my watch confirmed this backup team had arrived precisely on time: two divvy wagons, each with two uniformed officers, as scheduled.

'G'day lads, glad to see you. Mind you, you missed the real fun. Park anywhere but then please come with me.

'Backups arrived,' I yelled as we trooped past Aussie and his medical team. I paused just long enough for Beth to give me the "thumbs up", meaning *he's going to be OK*, rather than "get lost".

As we meandered down one side of the van, one of the backup officers asked nervously, 'do we need our guns, or not?'

'Please yourself son, but I don't reckon that little bastard sprawled on the floor over there will mind what you do … he's as dead as a dormouse.' At which point the officer threw up; not surprising really if you had seen the state of Ho's head and the pool of congealing blood which surrounded his shoulders.

'He gets to stay here until forensics finish their job, then he'll be removed by the ambos and driven to the Wagga morgue. Here, take this evidence bag and collect that idiot's gun, and don't touch it, it's vital evidence. And please, try not to step in that blood.

'Did you blokes know this mongrel has murdered eleven innocent sheep farmers in cold blood and caused enormous family sadness and upheavals? Even suicides!' The looks on the faces of all four lads said clearly, "you gotta be joking."

'I thought not, but come with me, I've got a couple of passengers for you. I just hope the stupid bastards haven't caught a real bad cold.'

'Right, all check that you have your handcuffs and gun at the ready, one up the spout, like. When I open this door here, you'll hopefully be greeted by two rather burly lads who will be enormously pleased to meet you. But, just in case their disposition is threatening in any way, you are authorised to shoot … preferably in their kneecaps.' Smiles all-round followed.

I hauled open the door to the refrigerated storeroom and there stood two very annoyed, half frozen souls. 'Your game's been well and truly nipped in the bud, boys. So, behave yourselves and you just might get some dinner tonight.

'By the way, your murderous friend, Mr. Hua, is no longer in the land of the living. So, please, arms stretched out in front, wrists together, and walk out slowly in single file. You come out first mate: honestly, you'll be glad I didn't shoot you because I *wasn't* bluffing.' Still, I hoped, he'd inevitably die wondering.

I don't think I've ever seen police officer's fit handcuffs as quickly as these lads did, nor since.

The four police officers then frog-marched the two remaining prisoners over to their divvy wagons and deposited one into each: next stop, the Wagga jail.

As previously agreed, one of those officers was to remain behind to assist the ambo medics to load Ho's body into their vehicle when it arrived, and to later help offload him at the Wagga morgue.

Ten minutes later we heard the now familiar whup, whup, whup of an approaching chopper; on schedule of course. By jeez that pilot was good, setting the chopper down gently without so much as a wobble, about twenty-five yards from where we stood.

Will immediately ran to the chopper and jumped aboard. He reappeared in about thirty seconds, carrying a small black bag, unmistakably a first aid kit ... for humans. He again ran back to our little gathering, dropped onto his knees next to Aussie and rumbled through the medical kit. He quickly located what he was looking for, ripped off its outer covering using his teeth and removed the cap from a large tube of ... well, something which looked like brown toothpaste.

As Will liberally covered the areas surrounding each of his beautifully performed surgery sites with that goop, Aussie only once raised a growl in protest. As soon as Will finished, he scooped him into his arms and headed back to the chopper, conveying an unspoken command for us to follow. 'Bring your poncho Andy,' he called over his shoulder, 'we still have to keep him warm.'

The chopper rose steadily, flying over the track leading from the shed. As we approached the intersection of the track with the main road, I noticed an ambulance turning onto the track. I nudged Beau and pointed; he nodded, smiled, then gave me a thumbs up while wiping his devilishly blue eyes; not tears for Ho, just the normal affliction which plagued him.

* * *

No sooner had we landed back at the Wagga Wagga Airport, than a small green panel-van with the words 'Wagga Veterinary Services" emblazoned on its sides, skidded to a halt close to the chopper.

Will was first to disembark. With Aussie in his arms, he jogged to the rear of the van where the vet had thrown open its rear door in readiness for his patient.

Beau was soon beside Will, intending I think, to accompany Aussie to the vet's surgery. However, Will put his hand on Beau's arm and gently manoeuvred him aside as the vet closed his van's door. There was no argument, but it was clear as the vet gunned his van's engine and then really stamped on the gas, that Beau was deeply saddened, his slumped shoulders being the giveaway of his emotions and fear of the unknown.

When Beth and I joined Beau and Will, Beth put her arm around Beau. But Will quickly interrupted our somber mood. 'He's in good hands folks and I'm sure Aussie'll survive this, but now's not the time to get too worried. After all, worrying is like sitting in a rocking chair; it gives you something to do, but you get nowhere. So, c'mon, we need to get over to the marquee and prepare for the debriefing.'

I know I smiled at Will's attempt to inject some levity, but it wasn't that so much, but rather, his innate authority which again impressed me for someone so young.

To my surprise as we approached the marquee, we were met by Kenneth (young Ken, as I came to think of him), the second of the two Duntroon helpers, and Gerry, the airport manager. 'Welcome back folks,' Ken cheerfully greeted us before Gerry had time to speak. 'All's in readiness for the debriefing, Beau, all personnel present, including the second strike-team. You'll be keen to know that the Wagga Police Station cells are now full ... nine prisoners in total. Well done, Beau.'

'It's been a fabulous team effort Ken,' I quickly added then stood aside and ushered Beth, Beau, young Will, and young Ken into the Marquee.

I was about to follow suit, but Gerry grabbed me by the elbow and indicated with a nod that he had something private on his mind. 'That young bloke, Ken ... he's been absolutely, bloody marvellous. Hasn't missed a beat all day, in fact he's essentially taken over the whole operation here. He arranged for delivery of portable toilets, monitored both outbound and inbound chopper flights, called off the second ambulance as soon as the second strike-team arrived back before you, arranged meals as needed and got immediate cooperation from the vet ... never pushy, like, just bloody-well gets things done.'

'Mate, I reckon I know exactly what you mean; both those lads are going places.'

* * *

As THE DEBRIEFING unfolded it was comforting that the second strike-team didn't endure what we did. No guard dogs or dog fight to contend with, three heavies who seemed indifferent to being caught red handed, and who didn't seem to know the difference between shit and clay, all their guns left in the driver's cabin of their furniture van ... and all doors unlocked.

However, that team also uncovered a stash of twelve hundred dollars, two .22 automatic rifles fitted with telescopic sights, ten boxes of ammunition, eleven unopened bottles of twelve-year-old Glenfiddich single malt whiskey and four balaclavas. For sure, it was going to take those mugs a fair bit of explaining. And, oh dear, that would more than *somewhat* have pissed Ho right off.

As the debriefing ended, Beau rose and graciously thanked everybody involved, suggesting that we had all taken a huge step forward in discouraging those who thought farm invasions and stock theft was an easy way to make a bob without the law interrupting their activities ... to stop and think again.

Loud applause and clapping followed, then we mingled and shook hands with everybody expressing our thanks for their timely and courageous contributions.

Beau and Beth and I looked for Will and Ken who had made themselves scarce, but it wasn't long before we spotted them in the process of packing the temporary accommodation tents into the back of the military trucks.

'Hey, you two, got a minute,' Beau called to them.

'For you Beau, any time,' Will replied.

'Yes sir, anytime,' Ken added. 'It's been a pleasure meeting all of you and good luck with your work in the future. We'd better get a move on though; we're expected back at Duntroon by nine o'clock. Anyway, if you need to contact us for any reason, our mutual friends in Canberra will pass any messages on to us.'

'We'll definitely keep in touch,' Beth said as she stepped forward to hug each of the boys in turn, then handed a slip of paper to Will. 'Here's our address and phone number if either or both of you are ever looking for work.'

'And again, thanks heaps, Will, for taking such good care of Aussie.'

'That's OK Beau; you've got nothing to worry about. Ken phoned the vet about ten minutes ago. Aussie's one tough hound and he's going to recover ... though he might be a bit lame for a while.'

* * *

We were about halfway back to the West Sale Airport when Beth broke our preoccupied silence. 'Is there anything nagging at either of you about today's events?'

Beau and I replied in the negative. "Nah", and "nope" sufficed.

'Well, doesn't it strike you as a bit odd that there was no sign of Lily at either property? And, during the debriefing, did you place any importance upon what the second strike-team spokesman reported ... remember what he found in those two attached outbuildings? It's my bet Ho and Lily have also been poaching native birds and reptiles from this region. And that's got to stop!'

'Agreed; as usual you're spot on Beth,' Beau added, 'but I've been wondering, as I'll bet you two have also ... is where do you think the money from Ho's thieving exploits ended up?

'It's my guess he's been in cahoots with some illegal gang operating in Vietnam; remember he was basically brought up by the Vietcong? His loss will be an inconvenience to them, but that won't stop them duffing livestock here, and besides, wildlife poaching is also a trade ... and will remain that way while Lily's still around.'

'Interestingly, I read an article recently,' I interrupted. It was about an escalating poaching pandemic in South Africa, Botswana and in Zimbabwe where some previously unrecorded and inventive poaching techniques are now being employed to trap and shoot elephants and rhinos, for their ivory of course, and then smuggling it to the highest bidders, particularly the Chinese. But what they're bloody well doing is decimating those endangered species. Sound a wee bit familiar? Perhaps it's *that* mob, not the remnants of the Vietcong who have been sponsoring Ho and Lily.

'Darling, your intuition puts you in the genius category, I mean it,' Beth responded, then articulated a statement which would once again profoundly impact our lives.

'We haven't seen the last of Lily, that's for sure. And you know what? I think now's the time to follow the money.'

29

As ordered by the News South Wales judiciary, all court proceedings involving those arrested in Wagga Wagga, and on both farm properties, were conducted behind closed doors.

The promised news blackout was rigorously implemented, but nevertheless, when the rulings and charges were released publicly about a month later, I was confident the impact of those outcomes would resonate for many months—if not for years—in most regional areas of Australia.

Young Will was not charged with murder (or manslaughter); after all, Ho was wanted either dead or alive Australia wide, and besides, we all testified that we had witnessed Ho level his gun first (though in reality, we hadn't!)

Beth was barred from directly representing either the defence, or prosecution team during Ho's court case due to the possibility of a there being a conflict of interest, but nevertheless, she spent many hours—out of hours—in quasi-legal consultation with the New South Wales elected Prosecuting Barrister.

There remains just one curiosity for me—though it's not a

compulsion to learn the answer, but—where the Hell *was* Ho buried? Forget it Andy, just move on.

* * *

THE END of year school holidays was looming, and life on our farm had returned to something resembling routine. Yet, Christmas was also constantly on our minds, and I have to say that Beth and I were ecstatic in anticipation of spending both events as a family.

Not being on the edge of one's wits 24/7 was a welcome change. However, dutifully, Beau phoned us either every three days or so, or just turned up out the blue for a cuppa and a yarn. It was clear he too was looking forward to catching up with Jack and Kelly, but also fishing for ideas for suitable Christmas presents.

Aussie's recovery was remarkably fast, and the scars around his mouth and on his body were almost invisible. However, his usual gait was a bit out of kilter; his back legs and body bearing slightly to Port. Nonetheless, he seemed totally unfazed by that affliction—plus the loss of half an ear—and somehow his *happy* smile remained unchanged.

Perhaps that had something to do with RB, who was expecting ... again!

However, Beau has promised RB that an appointment with a vet in Sale has been organised, in fact, I've seen a reminder note written in bold red characters on his kitchen calendar.

We've inherited a near exact copy of Aussie, in Betta, though he may not grow to be as large as his father. Hopefully he hasn't inherited Aussie's unsociable gene, but he has been blessed with amazing canine smarts. Beth reckons she's waiting for the day he actually starts talking with her. Regardless, Betta still bows to Aussie's alpha status and shares a doting friendship with Jack and Kelly.

Mind you, at that restful time of the evening after the flies have retired, and before the mozzies launch their blood-thirsty attacks, it's so nice to have Betta's company, particularly when he sits beside me leaning nonchalantly against my leg, just the two of us, together, watching the setting sun.

* * *

DURING THIS BREAK FROM WORK, we were essentially removed from the regular flow of statewide reports of minor farm equipment thefts and even the occasional livestock theft, however, two of those reports were not only laced with intent to steal, but ...?

In northwest Victoria, it came to our attention that an aggrieved farmer was the victim of a regular but unnoticed event and was seeking "reasonable retribution for interference"; whatever that meant.

It seemed that a nearby cattle breeder had been in the habit of transporting his latest receptive heifers to that unsuspecting neighbour's property, where, under the cover of darkness, he'd offload them into the paddock which held that farmer's best bull; one with a formidable servicing reputation.

Because of the size and remoteness of that farmer's property, it was easy for the bull to perform what comes naturally, without the farmer being any the wiser.

Up to a month later, that cunning cattle breeder would return in the depth of night, or when the farmer was away, and retrieve his now pregnant heifers.

Of course, all of that "toing-and-froing" transportation work was hard yakka for that bloke, and not without risk; but eventually the penny dropped.

Soon, a very different practise evolved and went unnoticed for up to three years until only recently, when the unsuspecting farmer returned home early from a visit to Horsham. It was more a case of bad luck rather than lack of planning which resulted in the shonky cattle breeder being caught red-handed while returning a borrowed champion bull.

We are still waiting to hear what charge, or charges, would, or could be applied, but in the meantime the quality of the rogue cattle breeder's herd will no doubt continue and remain the talk of the district.

* * *

THERE WAS another report which attracted our attention, about a drover who lived in South Australia, about one hundred miles north-west of Mildura.

Always on the lookout and desperate to make a quid, he decided to relieve a local grazier of a few hundred head of sheep, move them using his horse and dogs into a remote region, and thereafter stay with them until he could flog those sheep off at an upcoming bush auction.

But what this duffer didn't understand was that he had absolutely no sense of direction.

Three weeks later, he reached his ultimate destination but was bewildered and greatly embarrassed to be greeted by a team of newly recruited South Australian Livestock Theft Investigators who insisted he immediately return the stolen flock back into the exact same paddock from where he had nicked those now very tired sheep three weeks previously.

30

School for our kids concluded abruptly; the last year at boarding school for Kelly where she had been elected as the Girls School Captain.

No longer a child, her figure and good looks now challenged those of her mother. Kelly is also an absolute pleasure to be with around the farm, sharing her company and the maturity of her views on life, and willingness to do so many things without being asked.

Jack on the other hand is cricket mad and proving to be quite handy. Having just turned 15, he now opens the batting for Surrey Hills first eleven, in Melbourne's Eastern Suburban Cricket Competition. Perhaps Test cricket is on the cards for him? He's certainly a very focused young fella and deserves a bit of luck for all the time he spends practicing in the nets either at one of the grounds in Sale, or closer to home, at Briagolong. God only knows how many kilometres Beth and I spent driving him to and from matches and training sessions.

Jack also has a few other attributes, apart from his handsome face. For instance, he has a great sense of humour and delights in teasing his girlfriends but will not suffer fools gladly ... which has given him a bit of a reputation for ending fights rather than starting them.

By God, is that the most fabulous blend of genes, or what? Tonight, I'll have to share these observations with Beth.

* * *

NEIGHBOURS DROPPED by at all sorts of hours for either a hot bevvy or cold bubbles, and for a chat of course, to wish everyone compliments of the season and to congratulate our kids for their successes.

And, surprise, surprise I received a telegram from Zack, wishing everyone a merry Christmas and hinting at the possibility he might get the opportunity to pay us a visit, albeit vaguely "just some time in the new year". Yeah, right, but at least he was thinking about us.

The surprises continued.

First, Abbi Park and her brother Reggie from Bega arrived unannounced with a box of assorted cheeses from the famous Bega Cheese Factory and two large, insulated boxes filled with ice which covered about five kilos of oysters and at least the same weight of fresh prawns.

No more than an hour later, Beau arrived with Aussie and RB and two of her latest pups. They were all immediately swamped by our other guests, and introductions all round were made. 'So, where's the Christmas tree; where am I going to put this lot?' Beau asked while juggling an assortment of presents.

'Just plonk 'em on the back veranda for the mo,' I replied. 'Reggie, Jack and I are about to select one from that pine plantation on the way to Stockdale. Wanna come?'

'Yeah, why not; let's go,' Beau immediately replied. 'We'll take my Landy, it's got a half decent roof rack'.

And like I've said, the surprises weren't about to stop. No sooner had we arrived back at the farm, than our local copper, Alex, followed us down our driveway. And no sooner had he emerged from his police car, than he said to Beau, 'and where pray tell did you manage to get that beauty?'

'Ah, well, that's for me to know and for you to guess,' Beau replied without missing a beat.

'Well, how's about you show me where you got it,' Alex replied with a smile on his face, 'I've been so bloody busy I completely forgot to get ours.'

'No probs,' Beau replied jovially, 'but not until after we offload this one and have a beer, eh?' In fact, Alex was to have four beers and was obviously enjoying the company, particularly with Reggie, a fellow officer. This gave me and Abbi the chance to slip away: not only did we select a perfect tree, but we delivered it to the front door of Stratford Police Station.

As time for dinner approached, Jack and Abbi got our BarBQ going and it was no real surprise these two gravitated to each other; Jack teasing, Abbi pushing back and giggling at Jack's frustration, that he couldn't land a win over her. They'd make a good couple, pity about the tyranny of distance.

Not long after, it was great to unexpectedly hear Beth, Abbi and Kelly laughing on top note and then launching into their favourite Christmas carols, while all the time making cakes and putting the finishing touches to other Christmas delights.

And if that wasn't enough, they then set about decorating our Christmas tree, but not without first calling for volunteers. When that was finished, little of the tree was visible, but after all the gifts were positioned around it, a truly magnificent sight had been created. Many happy photos were taken; great memories recorded.

I was happily prodding the fire under the BarBQ and oblivious that the kitchen banter had paused when someone put their hand on my shoulder. I jumped and stood up far too quickly, and nearly over-balanced, but a strong set of arms grabbed me, stopping me from going arse-over-head.

It was Will, my valiant young friend from the Duntroon Military Academy.

G'day Andy, happy Christmas mate,' he spoke first, while grabbing my hand and shaking it firmly, probably because my gob was still open in surprise for, I was totally dumbstruck; we had *not* been expecting him.

'I'm assuming you nearly fell in excitement at seeing me, but you can't fool me, I can see you've wrestled the lids from a few VB's.' Cheeky bugger, but I smiled, nevertheless.

'Regardless, Andy, it's beaut to be able catch up; and you remember Ken too I hope? he lent us a hand on that Wagga project.'

'Yeah, of course, how the hell are you, Ken? Merry Christmas and please, make yourself at home. Here, let me relieve you of that tray, which, by the way, where'd you get it?'

'From the girls we met inside, they shoved it into my hands, and told us to deliver it to you; apparently, they're getting a bit hungry ... starving I think Beth said.'

You should have seen what was on that tray. It looked as if it was our intention to feed an army, the tray was resplendent with an assortment of huge steaks, rib eye fillet in fact, lamb cutlets galore, rissoles, and snags, thick and thin, of course.

'And I think Beth said something like ... "tell him to pull his finger out, or else".

Which we did in style, while chatting happily and putting further strain upon our dwindling supply of cold beer.

* * *

THE CHRISTMAS DINNER event which followed was *the best* I'd ever experienced. Beth and the girls had excelled themselves, with bowls of salads, even larger bowls of fruit salad and a couple of two-tier sponge cakes decorated in all-over white icing and red and green trimmings.

Beth also revealed a very well concealed surprise; that it was her and Kelly who had secretly invited and organised for our guests to "catch up" as their Christmas gift to me. And it sure was, for everyone. Presents exchanged hands, paper ripped from those gifts was scattered everywhere, and hugs and handshakes followed.

The seating arrangements at the dining room table didn't surprise me; well, not until I noticed Kelly sitting, or rather, rubbing shoulders with Will. Ehm!

And I chuckled to myself that Abbi was sitting next to Jack, happily tolerating his attentions.

As dinner concluded, Beth thanked everyone for attending our party and wished everyone a safe and happy festive season ... then sprung yet another surprise while she had everyone's attention. 'While I was rummaging through a few things the other day, I fell upon this,' she said happily while waving a large book above her head.

'Yep, it's our family photo album. Here, my darling, pass it down to Kelly would you.'

It wasn't long before Will and Kelly were in stitches with laughter, so much so that Will had to pass the album onto Abbi. A similar reaction followed which forced the album to do a lap of the table.

See what I mean; is Beth one very switched-on, caring lady, or what?

Anyway, you'd better face it Andy boy, your beautiful daughter and Will have fallen in love ... and at first sight, no less. More of Beth's doing, or just Cupid at his best?

And all the while, Aussie and Betta sat patiently together like a pair of (almost identical) sphinx, their eyes feasting on the food on the table and that which was disappearing into human mouths. Politely, they wagged their tails in anticipation of receiving their share, which they did, for Beau saw to that.

Eventually the house fell silent with the departure of our guests to their respective rooms. Rather than start clearing away the excesses of our dinner, I decided to go outside and sit on the veranda to unwind. But I never got there.

Instead, I was stopped dead when I nearly walked into Kelly and Will entwined and passionately kissing in the moonlight. I retreated, without any concern of being noticed.

When I climbed into bed, Beth asked quietly, 'Did you see those two on the veranda?'

'Yep.'

'So, what are you going to do?

'Absolutely nothing; though if it'd been anyone else, I'd have sent 'em packing.'

'Now, Andy, please hear me out, because, because, well, I've given them the OK to sleep together tonight. Besides, Kelly and I have had our "birds and bees" talk. So, please don't say anything in the morning.'

'Why would I, it was inevitable, eh? Not that different from our hard work on your desktop when we first met.'

'Except, there's no way Kelly's going to end up in the pudding club. Now get to sleep, or get over here, I need a hug.'

Like I said before, 'was this the greatest Christmas ever, or what?'

* * *

BOXING DAY EMERGED, though only four were up and in the land of the living before midday. Despite all the trappings of yesterday's magnificent feasting, Jack, Reggie, Ken, Aussie and Betta went for a run; about five kilometres the boys reckoned.

Ken claimed bragging rights for finishing first, though Jack counter-claimed that had Aussie and Betta stopped hazing him, he would have won easily.

When I eventually got out of bed, I made my way to the kitchen in need of a glass of Enos and perhaps an aspirin or two. I'd no sooner sat down than Kelly and Will, still entwined, walked into the kitchen.

Neither of them appeared self-conscience, nor guilty for that matter, and I wanted to keep it that way, so I said, 'About time you two; you're bloody lucky the sun hasn't blinded yah both.' At which point I slid the bottle of Enos across the table and continued, 'this, or would you two prefer a cuppa? Tea or coffee? I'll get it.'

Later, after I'd shaved, showered, and changed, Kelly grabbed me by the arm and escorted me outside, clearly intent on telling me something in private.

'Dad, you're the greatest, but nothing happened that shouldn't have.'

At which point we hugged. 'Been there, done that, just ask your mum,' I replied with an unexpected onset of tears.

'Yeah, I know, I've already done that, Dad.'

* * *

As that summer's afternoon advanced, shadows cast by the ancient red gums which grew randomly in our house paddock, unfailingly crept across the now very dry earth.

Re-energised by an afternoon nap, I caught up with Jack, Will, Ken and Reggie who were tinkering with my stubborn tractor which of late, refused to start.

'What's the go, boys?' I greeted them. 'Whatever the problem is, it's not the battery, I had it checked a fortnight ago.'

'Yep, the batteries got plenty of charge,' Reggie replied, 'It's not the alternator either. When did you last get her serviced, Andy? I reckon her timing's way out of whack.'

'Can't remember when she was last serviced,' I replied sheepishly. 'Can you get her started?'

'Oh yes, no problems,' Reggie reassured me. 'Just give me a few more minutes and we'll try again.'

'You might need this too,' Jack chimed in as he presented a spray can, of what, I had no idea it contained.

True to his words a few minutes later, Reggie said, 'That should do it. Hop up into the driver's seat Andy and give her a whirl when I raise my arm. He then scrambled onto the tractor's bonnet and held the spray can next to the engine's exhaust pipe.

Reggie raised his arm. I turned the on-off switch to "start", and Reggie started spraying "whatever" under the weather cowling on top of the exhaust pipe. 'Start yah bastard,' I heard him yell, just before the engine coughed and spluttered into life.

Smiling broadly, Reggie jumped to the ground, tinkered with the timing mechanism and without any fuss, set the engine throbbing evenly. He then tossed the mysterious can up to me; the label read ... Start You Bastard.

'Ehm, where did that come from Jack?'

'It was in the shed. Beau found it there a few weeks ago; reckons the previous owners of our place must have left it there.'

'Remind me to buy a few more cans of that stuff next time we're in town, eh.'

* * *

THERE WAS STILL plenty of daylight left and our guests were starting to rib each other and tell outrageous stories; mostly leg pulling but imbued with challenge.

Unexpectedly, Beau, carrying an armful of hessian bags and beaming broadly, returned to the back veranda. 'Right, you lot, so who's up for a bag race? Two per bag, fifty yards and first over the line wins a prize. 'What do yah reckon?'

'Yeah, come on, let's do it,' yelled Abbi as she grabbed Jack by his hand and hauled him off the veranda to select a bag.

'C'mon darling, we should be good at this,' Beth said, and quickly grabbed a bag from Beau for us.

It was no surprise Kelly was now dragging Will to our improvised starting line.

Beau and Ken then meticulously stepped out fifty yards, where they laid a rope across the ground to designate the finish line. They then raced back to the starting line where Beau called for each team to get into their chosen bag. Much easier to say than do, as we were all soon to discover.

'Right,' Beau called again. 'So, here's the rules, folks. It's OK to hold onto each other, but you've both got to be holding up the bag with at least one hand. No pushing or trying to trip your opponents. You'll find the easiest way to move forward is to jump in small jumps, like. If you go arse-over-head, it's OK to get back into you bag and have another go. You could still win.

'OK, are we all set? Looks like a good line ... soooo, GO!!

The track was slightly downhill which gave the impression this was going to be a doddle, but only two teams made it more than five jumps before crashing out. Which left Beth and me (leading, of course), but closely followed by Kelly and Will, who both also seemed to have got the hang of things. Much cheering was urging us on, but when we were within a yard or two of the finish rope, Beth deliberately pulled me sideways, sending us both tumbling earthward, landing with a thump.

My pride hurt, but only for as long as it took to follow Beth's nod and gaze to where Kelly and Will had just crashed over the winning line ahead of us.

Beth was beaming and now squeezing my hand; an accident on our part, be buggered! What I saw was Will holding Kelly to his chest, for perhaps ten seconds too long. 'Damn good catch that, I'd say, my love,' I happily whispered to Beth.

* * *

THAT VERY SPECIAL CHRISTMAS CAME, and unfortunately went, far too soon. I still occasionally wonder if everyone in their life gets to feel as lucky as Beth and me.

31

A few days into January, not long after our guests had all departed, Beau dropped by, carrying the usual milk, bread and a dozen eggs. However, Aussie and Betta had been tasked with sharing delivery of the local newspaper ... which soon landed at my feet.

As I picked up The Gippsland Times and thanked both dogs for their kind service, Beau quietly remarked, 'Turn to page seven, Andy, I've circled something which might interest both of yah.'

The article read: -

An Asian woman was recently questioned after being pulled over for having an over-wide trailer load. That load consisted of several cages, all containing common Australian birds. The lady in question presented a valid license to own those birds and no charges were laid.

However, the Victorian Police wishes to remind everyone that the capture and smuggling of any Australian bird, or birds, is illegal and anyone found guilty thereof, will receive either large fines, or imprisonment for not less than three years, or both.

All citizens are urged to report any suspicious dealings relating to this activity. Every report will be investigated and treated confidentially.

I passed the newspaper over to Beth and waited for her to finish reading the highlighted article.

'Heh! Seems Lily got lucky again,' Beth declared. 'And if I'm correct it means she's still up to no good somewhere in Victoria.'

'Or in South Australia, or in New south Wales,' I added, not unreasonably.

'I did some checking and asked the police whether they could provide a description of that particular lady,' said Beau, 'and based on what the highway copper said, there's no doubt in my mind it *was* her.

'But it gets even better, the license she provided was a dud; the number on the document correlated with nothing issued by The Victorian Wildlife Protection Authority. A forgery no less, but the name, Lily Nguyen, *was* on that document.'

'So now she's broken another Law,' Beth added somewhat cynically, 'which to my mind means she *is* still determined to operate illegally, probably not alone, and in cahoots with someone with a self-professed understanding of the law.'

'Have we been requested to follow this lead?' I asked.

'Well, yes,' said Beau, 'but it seems Canberra haven't yet got anything concrete regarding her actual whereabouts, but when they do, I believe they'll want us to relocate again.'

'That's Okay by us,' 'Beth replied while looking at me, assuming my unconditional approval, 'but what I can't get my mind around is why she's taking such risks. Yes, I understand that fauna smuggling is currently a relatively lucrative business, but is it worth copping a lengthy jail term?'

'If we only knew what, or who was driving her,' I suggested, somewhat needlessly, 'then maybe that'll lead us to the real money, and we can then put a stop to her.'

'True,' Beau replied, 'but this operation isn't strictly livestock theft, so we may get waved away.' *Wishful thinking old boy.*

* * *

Two weeks later, we got an update.

'You'd better pack a few bags,' Beau said calmly. 'It seems Canberra wants our help after all. You'll be pleased to learn that Zack, while in South Africa it seems, has uncovered something of "probable importance", and they want us to fly to Mildura and set up a nearby bush-setting headquarters to see what we can verify and uncover.

'Anyway, there's a bonus attached to this job; we'll be met by young Will.

'Did you know he grew up in Mildura before being accepted by Duntroon? He'll organise rental 4WD vehicles and whatever camping gear we'll need. And before you ask, yes, both Aussie and Betta will be joining us.'

* * *

Two days later, on the way to the West Sale Airport, we stopped at Stratford Police Station to let the local copper know of our common intentions to be off our respective farms for the next few weeks. Little did we know then how wrong that estimate would prove.

We eventually touched down at Mildura Airport, and true to form, Will was there waiting, smiling broadly but not alone as we were expecting. A strapping young Aboriginal man stood by his shoulder.

'Great that we all meet again, and so soon, eh,' said Will, 'but first I'd like you to meet my friend and teammate Clam Hunter. He's a local Barkindji man.'

'Actually, my name's Callum, but I grew up being the victim of Will's sense of humour, so Clam it is. I've never hunted clams in my life.' Ha, ha, good one, Clam ... I already like this bloke.

After introductions and some hugging (by Beth, not me), Aussie and Betta sidled up to Will and Clam.

'Hey Clam, this is Aussie who I've told you about,' said Will as he extended his hand and firmly shook Aussie's paw. 'He's been in the wars a bit, but he'll never take a backward step if a good fights in the offering.'

Will then stepped up to Betta and said fondly. 'And this is Betta, Aussie's number one son'. On cue, Betta repeated the handshake greeting, and added a few licks to Will's hand, for good luck, I guess.

Clam then stepped forward, but knelt in front of both dogs, leaving about a yard between them. A few seconds of hesitancy followed, but then Aussie, smiling, stepped forward and sat immediately in front of Clam, who by now had extended his right arm.

The usual welcoming handshake followed, but then Betta sidled up, not wanting to be left out and gently nudged Aussie to move over. Which, graciously he did, but not without first a low growl, and then a flickering of his top lip to expose his still very capable fangs.

As our group headed for the car rental desk, Will and I fell into step a few yards behind the others and then, when obviously out of earshot, Will said quietly, but with more than just a passing interest, 'So, Andy, how's Kelly?'

'Lonely, I suspect. Why not give her a call before we leave Mildura?'

* * *

After transferring our luggage into our almost new 4WD Nissan, Beth manoeuvred our plane into its assigned hangar.

Just minutes later we had crossed The Murray River, heading to a remote campsite about forty miles away on the bank of the meandering Darling River; roughly halfway between Mildura and Menindee.

Our three-vehicle convoy, all Nissan 4WD's, had Will, Beau, Aussie and Betta leading, with Beth, alone, next in line, followed last by Clam and me. This was a good arrangement; it gave me a chance to quiz Clam and learn more about Will ... our daughter's suitor. It also gave me the chance to study Clam.

There was nothing pretentious about this young man, his manner calm, polite, friendly ... his movements were smooth and well-coordinated, the hallmark of a natural athlete. His speech was perfect, yet Clam gave me the impression he probably suffered fools badly.

Clam, I must admit, was also a very capable driver, and would make an excellent guide, or perhaps an African safari leader. He obviously delighted in telling us about his homeland and pointed out features and critters we would otherwise have never seen.

'As Will correctly said,' Clam finally shifted conversation, 'this is Barkindji land, where Will and I have spent many days exploring and occasionally hunting. It's a magnificent part of Australia and blessed with many types of birds and reptiles as you've already seen.

'In the breeding season the budgies are so prevalent, they mass into flocks which can be in the hundreds of thousands. You can hear those flocks from half a mile away; all chatting on top note while making a loud whirring noise with their wings when the flock suddenly changes direction, or as they all attempt to land at the same time.

'Will and I grew up together in Mildura; our families were neighbours. Our mums had become great friends, as were our fathers, until my dad was bitten by an eastern brown snake. Will's dad did all he could to save my dad; but that's one deadly snake, the Eastern brown. My dad died in Will's father's arms, but somehow, but in vain, he managed to carry my dad for about three miles to a nearby farmhouse just in case help was available.

'We played Aussie Rules footy and cricket together, always in the same team, for years and years until, out of the blue, my application to attend The Duntroon Military Academy was accepted, unconditionally.

'Will joined the academy the following year, as did Ken, and we all became the best of mates. Unfortunately, Ken has elected to pursue a more military style career and he's now serving overseas, though I'm not permitted to say where.'

32

———————

The riverside camp site chosen by Will and Clam was perfect. They had slung two overlapping, large green tarpaulins overhead exploiting a combination of low hung branches and guys to hold the tarps in place, thus creating outdoorsy "open on three sides" breezy atmospherics, and of course, a large, shaded area beneath.

This site was about ten feet from the river's edge, with only four or five steps needed to either gather buckets of water as needed, or to take a running dive into the gently flowing, albeit slightly turbid water. You bewdy; no sharks, crocs, or nasty bitey, stingy, things to keep an eye out for.

The three Nissans and a dual axle horse float were parked side-by-side about five yards from this amazing haven, all protected by shade thrown by a stand of nearby red gum eucalyptus trees. The float I learnt later, held a few bales of lucerne hay, saddles, saddle blankets, bridles, and halters.

I looked around trying to locate the whereabouts of the two horses and eventually got a glimpse of them through the trees; hobbled I suspected, given their unnatural foraging gait. Both were light brown; walers I would later learn.

An empty flatbed trailer, no doubt that used for transporting all our tents and camping essentials up from Mildura, had been positioned beneath the tarps, furthermost from the river ... which left the balance of the shaded area as our communal space, a space already populated with five army style chairs and a fold-out table. Four canvas water bags were hanging in convenient to reach locations: it has never ceased to amaze me how cool the water in those bags could become, regardless of how hot the weather became. And, within arm's reach at different positions were five Tilley kerosene lamps.

For ease of access to items such as the two Coolgardie safes, bottled water, dry food storage bins, pannikins, and pots and pans, they were all placed on the flatbed trailer which conveniently served as a second table.

In the "forecourt" between our shade tarps and the riverbank was our fireplace; a ring of stones, roughly three feet in diameter. And, close by was a sizeable stack of dry branches, most broken into easy to manage lengths.

Behind the shaded area, four pale green army issue tents had been erected, each with about twelve yards of separation. One tent contained two wood and canvas stretcher beds (no doubt for Beth and me) while each of the other tents contained only one. A set of clean sheets were neatly folded on the end of each bed, and enamel wash basins were at the foot of each bed. But best of all, a generous drop of mosquito netting adorned the entrance of each tent.

Ah yes, the toilets. Long drops: one of the true delights of camping. There were two, one on either side of the shaded common area, but about forty yards distant. To ensure privacy, both facilities were surrounded by a canvas tarp with one side completely open, ensuring contentment with a complimentary view.

A spade, standing proudly atop a mound of freshly dug soil, was in readiness to commence the process of refilling the newly created long drops. But what if it rains ...? Surely not this time of year.

Overall ... not too shabby; well done lads. But bloody Hell it's getting hot.

* * *

As I arrived back at the communal tent for a drink, I was greeted by Aussie and Betta, both of whom were lying down, frantically licking their paws, and alternately using their front teeth to hopefully remove whatever was ailing them.

'Bindii,' Clam announced as he joined me. 'I should have remembered to put their boots on before they went exploring.

'I'll fix Aussie first, but Andy, you're going to have to hold him because this is going to hurt.

'Those bindii's can be real bastards in the country around here. No matter which way their seed pods land, one of their thorns will always be facing upwards, just waiting for some unsuspecting dingo, or roo or camel to step on it and then get a free ride for miles before falling off and regrowing after the next rains.

'I'll be back in a sec ... I'll bring sir back a few different sizes of boots. Colour won't really matter; I believe sir and his sidekick are both colour blind.' Yeah, right.

Clam worked fast, picking about five or six thorns from each of Aussie's paws without so much as a whimper. 'Here, Andy, dab some of this ointment onto each of his paws while I have a look at Betta's feet. That's a universal cleaning disinfectant and antiseptic. Don't let him lick it off, it'll make him crook in the guts.'

Betta did not fare quite so well. Probably because his juvenile paws were not yet as tough as Aussie's. Unfortunately, he had at least seven or eight thorns in each paw, but like his father, he too feigned curiosity over showing pain.

What followed was hilarious. After Clam had carefully fitted and laced up the boots for both dogs, he said, 'Now, Andy, release Aussie first; careful like.'

Initially, Aussie just stood there, looking at me as if wanting to say, 'So, now what?'

But the real fun started as I stood up and took a few steps to stretch my legs. Aussie, by habit, started to follow me, but took one step, stopped dead, and then frantically tried to shake the unaccustomed boot from his foot.

I continued to walk away, but Aussie, no doubt feeling compelled to follow, did so, but quickly realised he now had "something" very strange hanging from each foot.

Most people have heard the expression "like a cat on a hot tin roof", or perhaps, "carried on like a two-bob watch", but Aussie's performance was something else.

Apparently, as I started to walk away, Betta wriggled free from Clam, and not wanting to be left behind, he charged after Aussie. But when Betta took his second stride the penny dropped that his feet too, were in the grips of something very foreign and probably about to attack his feet.

Both dogs were soon throwing their legs about in all directions, jumping and spinning around, growling in frustration, yet gamely trying to walk and run normally, to catch up to me.

It was fun watching the pantomime of over-exaggerated leg lifting —in the right stepping order—but eventually they settled down and surprisingly soon got the hang of wearing their new "thorn proof boots".

So accustomed did both dogs become to wearing their boots, that each morning thereafter they refused to leave camp until we refitted them; not only because of the dreaded bindii's, but because the ground soon became very hot.

* * *

MID-AFTERNOON, Will and Clam, armed with five circular wire nets and two buckets, took us for a walk along the riverbank to a bend where the flow slowed as it ran into a gently swirling backwater.

After attaching somewhat rancid slivers of fatty lamb to the topside of our nets, we carefully cast them into the river, but no more than a yard from the bank. It wasn't long, no more than ten minutes, before Clam motioned for us to slowly retrieve our nets. You should have seen the yabbies! Collectively there were sixteen and the average size was about seven inches long. Beth had caught the most; me the least.

Will dashed about, helping us collect our rapidly retreating catch, and showed us how *not* to wear their powerful claws when picking them up.

Both dogs showed great courage, carefully stalking individuals from our catch and then springing back in mock alarm when their selected foe raised itself from the sand to wave and click their large claws in defiance. Great fun was had by all, though perhaps not so much for the yabbies.

This part of the river proved to be most bountiful, our buckets filling within half an hour, and yes, there's no prize for guessing what we had for dinner.

Appetites satisfied; we spent the next hour debating the merits of a plan which Will and Clam had hatched, a reconnaissance trip north, no less, lasting about four days. No dogs, just Will and Clam and their horses.

As the sun gradually set, Beth, Beau, Aussie, Betta, and me, for something to do, decided to go for a riverside walk. Will and Clam declined politely because they wanted to be fully kitted out, ready to set off on their trip at dawn.

We meandered about one hundred yards upstream to a sandy section of the riverbank where we sat side-by-side listening to the unique bush sounds and inhaling the fabulous, heady fragrances which enveloped us as the night threw its cloak over the day.

Sitting silently in the gently fading light we caught glimpses of birds, mostly cockatoos and parrots, a family of three kangaroos and two lizards (bluetongues?) go about quenching their thirst. Other cockatoos were screeching in muted tones as they flew through the surrounding eucalypts seeking a suitable roosting place. But best of all were the monotonous calls of boobook owls as they "talked" up and down the river.

A few bats arrived, fluttering, and darting about, trying to catch their dinner from the myriad of insects which hovered over the surface of the river.

Alas, it was time to retreat; the local mosquitoes were also now onto *our* scent.

Back at the communal shade tent we had just enough daylight remaining to allow us to light our five Tilley pressure lamps. Normally this would have been a disaster; we would have been inundated by ferocious swarms of blood sucking mozzies.

However, I hadn't previously spied the rolls of insect netting strategically attached overhead, but Beau and Beth certainly had, and knew exactly what to do for they were frantically engrossed in releasing the netting and overlapping each panel to create a floor to ceiling mosquito free zone. Neither Aussie nor Betta waited for an invitation to join us.

Will and Clam had again scored maximum points for their forethought.

* * *

I wasn't sure, exactly, what woke me the next morning. Most likely it was the sound of Will and Clam's horses as they headed away from the camp, though earlier I'm pretty sure it was Betta for he had become restless. I think he was trying to alert me to something unusual, and not too far away. 'Dingoes howling, young fella. Nothing to worry about, go back to sleep,' I grumbled. He did so, but at the foot of my stretcher. I couldn't help chuckling at the conniptions Beau was probably going through trying to refrain Aussie from checking out those dingoes.

Regardless, I couldn't get back to sleep. So, resigned to this, I got dressed as quietly as possible, hoping not to wake Beth. However, just as I was about to leave our tent, she asked, 'Where are you going, darling?'

'Nowhere in particular, do you want to come?

'Yep. Hang on a second, you can help me with my boots. Do you think Betta will want to tag along?

'What do you think? Look behind you.' Beth got our answer; Betta had commandeered the centre of my stretcher and pulled the top sheet over his body.

We set off upstream but first climbed the only nearby high ground. 'Best time of the day,' I said, after taking a deep breath of the fragrant, cool air.

'What about last night, that was lovely too?'

'Yes, it's a tossup alright.'

For the next few minutes we stood, wrapped in each other's arms, surveying the emerging, majestically beautiful colours of the surrounding countryside. The plains country was vast, yet infiltrated by a winding pathway of greenery which defined the course of the Darling River, for as far as the eye could see.

We walked on, back toward the little sandy beach where we had caught last night's dinner. There was a mist rolling from the higher ground, toward the river, where kookaburras were now launching into their strange rounds of laughter to welcome this day, and the first updrafts of warming air were gently rustling the canopies of the trees which bordered the river.

Our small, sandy riverside beach was as we had left it, however, something *was* different. Bird and reptile tracks, and those of both our dogs were still visible ... but now, so too were several naked footprints; not ours, for we had all been wearing our boots, as had both of our dogs.

'Friends of Clam's, I wonder?' Beth asked quietly.

33

Rather than sitting around our camp all day, Beth, Beau, and I decided to drive back to Mildura. We were going to need more toilet paper, food, particularly of the canned meat and veggie type, something similar for the dogs and a few loaves of bread ... and yes, something to read, newspapers and a few magazines.

Not to be overlooked, Aussie and Betta made a beeline for the front passenger seat of Beau's Nissan, making it clear that if anyone else wanted to ride in that vehicle, the backseat was for them.

However, the first thing we needed to do was fill both Nissans and buy more kerosene for the Tilley pressure lanterns, and while Beth and I took care of this, Beau strolled over the road to the Post Office.

Just as we were leaving the garage shop, I looked up to see Beau jogging back across the road to meet us.

'Quick, park the Nissans over there under those peppercorn trees,' he said excitedly, while puffing slightly and waving a sheet of yellow paper: no doubt a telegram. 'Have I got some news for you both or what!'

Once we were together, leaning comfortably against one of the

Nissans, Beau said, 'Things are about to heat up, I'd say. Let me read this to you … it's from our friends in Canberra.

'"High priority info rcd from Z. Interpol apparently on path to arresting renowned I'national forger.

If paths cross arrest immediately then escort under arms to nearest jail. Seize any/all his belongings: will need as evidence. Is linked to murders Germany and South Africa. Treat as dangerous.

German born; speaks German/English fluently. Is 80ish, thin build, wears thick glasses, stooped and totally bald.

Take great care."'

* * *

AFTER A PLEASANT PUB LUNCH, we drove back to our camp, but no sooner had we unpacked, than we were in for another surprise.

We could hear in the distance the sound of an engine approaching from downstream. And sure enough, about ten minutes later a small tinny fitted with a small outboard motor, with two blokes and a dog on board, drew level with our campsite … slowly towing a second tinny with five sheep on board. Ehmmm, this could be interesting, I thought.

Beau immediately waved, and "all friendly like", hailed them. 'G'day, fellas. You're just in time for a cuppa. Please, you're most welcome to join us.' They fell for it.

Beth and Beau soon had them comfortably seated, each with a mug of hot black tea in one hand, and a chocolate topped biscuit in the other. I dare say, both men, Bob Nunn and Alby Riddle, must have had some initial trepidation, however they gradually relaxed as we gently plied them with seemingly innocuous questions.

Bob's surname name suited him, for he had very little intellect and it was he who volunteered where he lived, even boasting at one stage that he hadn't paid any taxes for about thirty years. He came across as the bullying, smart arse type with very little compassion for anyone, even his mate, Alby.

Alby was at least one level lower in intelligence than Bob, in fact he was definitely not the full quid; perhaps as a result of an acquired brain injury. He had no idea about where he "actually lived", and happy it seemed to live an itinerate life. Nevertheless, I took a great dislike to Alby for the way he ogled Beth at every opportunity.

But at some stage they became uneasy with our questioning. No obvious signal passed between them but suddenly, in unison, both rose from their chair and hurried back toward their tinnies: no "thanks for the cuppa" and "no farewells".

Their attempt to escape was quickly discouraged by Aussie and Betta who had even more quickly placed themselves, snarling and bristling, into their retreating pathway. And, sensibly, their dog stayed in the lead tinny.

Both men were most upset having realised they'd been conned by a couple of plain clothed Livestock Theft and Investigation officers, one of them being a beautiful woman no less.

'Ahg, come on you lot,' Bob protested stupidly, 'all we wuz doin', wuz relievin' a poor bloody farmer of a few head which 'av been eatin' the farmer's paddocks bare, and sendin' 'im broke like.'

Bob then made an even greater fool of himself, by blatantly trying to bribe us. I sensibly took the almost brand new ten-dollar note he offered ... as evidence of course.

Beau officially charged them, preparatory to sending them on their way; minor felons maybe but we were duty bound to make our point that what they were doing was illegal.

Nevertheless, we allowed them to keep the sheep, on the proviso they make a representation to the Mildura police within the next ten days ... or else!

We almost laughed ourselves stupid after they disappeared around the next upstream bend in the river. The likelihood of our request being fulfilled was very low, but we also had our job to honour. So, unanimously we decided that on our way home to Sale, we'd meet with the Mildura Police and swap notes about these two blokes.

<h1 style="text-align:center">34</h1>

Four days after Will and Clam had gone on their reconnaissance ride, we were becoming just a wee bit anxious about their safety. However, we shouldn't have worried; at about three o'clock that afternoon they arrived back in camp, both looking tired and very dusty.

Beth supplied them with cool drinks and a small mountain of biscuits which disappeared from the serving plate in record time.

Meanwhile, Beau and I removed the saddles, saddle bags and swags which burdened the horses.

Soon after, both lads stood, then escorted their horses down the riverbank and into the water where they removed their bridles and set them free to do whatever grabbed them. Both horses waded to the opposite side of the river, where together they seemed to take great delight stamping their hooves hard into the shallow water, sending sizeable splashes in all directions.

Will and Clam had by now removed their boots and shirts and were dunking their heads into the water to remove any sweat and dust. After lying immersed in the water for a good ten minutes, they then retreated to their respective tents, only to emerge a few minutes later wearing clean sets of clothes.

I threw a few branches onto the fire while Beth presented a huge plate of fresh bread sandwiches, two equally fresh coffee scrolls and mugs of sweetened black tea all round. Like I've always said, Beth is *the* greatest host.

'Well lads, welcome back of course,' Beau said casually, 'In your own time, just go for it; please, tell all.'

* * *

WILL TOOK THE LEAD.

'Well, on the first morning we crossed the river and travelled north along the eastern bank. The only thing of note was that Clam sighted a small mob of aboriginals, so he spoke with them for a while. They didn't have much to pass on, only that they had seen a boat taking a few sheep upstream, which seemed a bit strange. Didn't mean much to us so we pressed on until we were about six miles from here, then crossed to the west bank.'

'What if I told you we intercepted those blokes?' Beau interrupted. 'Arrested 'em and got as much out of 'em as possible. Both no-bloody-hopers, and rude halfwits. Charged 'em with theft and bribery and gave them something to think about before we sent 'em packing.'

'Bribery, eh?', said Will, 'that's a bit unusual, folks around here don't normally have a lot of spare money to throw around.

'Anyway, we traveled north for another five miles or so on the west bank. Nothing much doing, only a few roos and a five-foot long eastern brown snake, so we called it a day.'

'Now it gets interesting, very interesting,' Clam continued.

'We were up and about early and hadn't gone more than half a mile before we spotted three things, all of which were most certainly out of place. Drawn up onto the riverbank were two tinnies, exactly what my brethren told us about. The second item looked like a hut of some sort, and third was a caravan which looked like it'd seen better days.

'We decided to wait out of sight behind a patch of scrub which extended up from the river, about eighty yards away from our most unexpected discovery. We had a clear line of sight, and so, when nobody surfaced in the next half an hour, we tied our horses to some saplings then crept along the riverbank until we came level with our find. A quick glance into the tinnies, revealed enough sheep droppings to confirm what my cousins had seen.

'Anyway, we pressed on, me to the left, Will to the right, but there was still no sound, other than that from some nearby birds. Within a minute we met up: there was definitely no dogs or people at this site, though there was plenty to indicate there had been, and recently.'

We paused when Beth brought our huge tea pot to the table for us to top up our mugs, then she disappeared, but not before promising to return with a snack ... which turned out to be a couple of dozen Anzac biscuits, all still warm. Delicioso! Bewdy, and bugger me, they were fabulous.

'Thanks Beth,' said Clam, 'But I'd better move on with the really good bits.

'Clearly, the hut we'd seen was a huge bird cage, an aviary I think it's called. Anyway, though it was serving a purpose, it's the worst bit of workmanship you'll ever see.'

'I do believe you mean *Heath Robinson*, or *Jerry-built*,' Beau said matter-of-factly. 'They're old-fashioned terms which basically mean something that's been built on the cheap and just whacked together without any thought for its effectiveness over time. But anyway, please go on boys.'

'All up,' Clam continued earnestly but with no indication of being fazed by Beau's interruption, 'we estimated there were at least eight to ten different bird species. Cockatoos and corellas, beautifully coloured lorikeets, budgies and several different finches. Some were already dead, or dying, and our initial urge was to immediately release the ones that were still living.'

Clam paused and sighed deeply, but after a few seconds he soldiered on. 'Anyway, we chose not to. We needed to first check out the caravan, and then follow the car tracks leading to and from the site. Besides, we could always release the birds before we rode back to our camp.'

'And, sadly,' Will interrupted, 'behind the aviary, nearest to the river, we counted thirty-two blue tongue lizards in a large wooden tray made with sides which were at least eighteen inches high. There was no way the poor buggers could escape, but at least a few boards had been placed randomly across the open top of the tray to provide *some* relief for them from the sun.

'The birds and lizards had water, but nowhere near enough and it was difficult to see how the remaining birds were getting enough shade given there was only one sheet of rusty old, corrugated iron on top of the cage ... and next to no shade from the few surrounding river red gums.'

'Yeah, but you should have seen what awaited us in that caravan, apart from the pong of mice and their pee,' Clam continued. 'Not only were there several bags of bird seed with their sides ripped open, and their contents scattered everywhere, but also an army of screw-top glass jars which contained thousands of different insects: mosquitoes, moths, katydids, flying ants—termites probably—the odd praying mantis, cockroaches, cicadas, and thousands of grasshoppers. God only knows how they collected that lot; it's not the sort of thing you can buy from your average pet shop.'

'Hey, Clam,' Will said excitedly, 'don't forget all those different sized cardboard cylinders, and that hoard of socks we found in that metal box. Is that evidence of smuggling, or what?'

'But best of all, we've taken photos of all this; not as many as we'd like, but our cameras are somewhat limited.'

35

───────

Clam continued. 'There was little sense in conducting any further investigations in the middle of the day; even had the sun not been Hell bent on having us die of thirst: to be seen in broad daylight was not part of our immediate game plan.

'Anyway, we strolled back to our horses and then walked them deeper into the riverbank scrub which threw some half decent shade. We ate a few of your biscuits Beth, then relaxed on our swags, where, I do believe, we somehow nodded off for a few hours.'

Will, now seeing an opening to continue their story chimed in. 'As the sun dipped toward the horizon, we walked back to the 'bird farm" as we now call it, and quickly followed the well-worn vehicle tracks which headed West.

'Having ascended the small ridge which separated the hinterland from the Darling, we soon came across a very old fence, holding up a closed and equally ancient gate, and uninterrupted tracks still heading due West.

'Regardless, the fence was good enough to keep the nearby flock of sheep from exploring. Clam soon discovered that not one of the now curious sheep had an ear tag, though *there was* plenty of painful looking evidence that they had.

'But that's not all,' Clam continued, 'we caught sight of a faint, single light, probably coming from a farmhouse about a mile away. Given it was now quite dark, for the moon had not yet risen, we set off to make a much closer inspection of that place.'

* * *

WILL AGAIN TOOK THE FLOOR. 'It took us about ten minutes to get within forty or so yards of an old farmhouse, which now had two lights on, one inside somewhere, and one on the verandah, adjacent to the front door. And in the far distance to the west, we could just see a car, and judging by the intermittent flashing of its red taillights, it was about to turn left, presumably South. It's my guess it was those two blokes from the tinnies, on their way to the nearest pub.

'However, there was another car, an old white ute ... a Ford as it turned out, parked under the carport right next to the front door. Don't worry, we've got its rego number; it's a New South Wales plate number.

'But we got lucky, given how foolishly close we'd approached the house. By that time, had there been a dog or more to contend with, our goose would have been well and truly cooked. But nothing, other than the muffled sound of two people inside talking.

'We froze—perhaps needlessly because we already had cover behind a mature lemon tree—when suddenly the front door creaked open, and the inside light was turned off.

'Two people came out of the house, an Asian woman we reckoned, and then an old codger bent over like a half open pocketknife. They made their way across the verandah and got into the ute; then the lady drove away; no hurry, like.'

'But we got even luckier, eh Will? It was so nice of them to leave their back door unlocked.'

Fidgeting with eagerness at what he was about to relate next, Clam nevertheless pressed on. 'We waited another ten minutes before entering the farmhouse and then immediately commenced a room-by-room search, turning lights on, and off, as needed. Only one

171

room, sort of an annex leading from the kitchen, had its door locked, but our training at the Academy soon had that sorted; Will was inside within thirty seconds, lights on.'

'At first I was a bit shocked,' Will continued with equal enthusiasm, 'but, in truth, I was confused. The beautiful paintings which adorned each wall seemed absurdly out of place amongst all the stuff which otherwise fills that room.

'There are two benches, one with many cans which at first inspection looked like paint, but when I sniffed a few of them, without doubt they contained ink ... because the smell is just like the whiff you get when you're the first to read the morning paper.

'There's also a sizeable collection of well used hand tools; small chisels, a selection of different sized mallets, bottles of methylated spirits and turpentine and a heap of dirty rags. At one end of that table there's a cleared space with a large overhead magnifying-glass mounted within an adjustable frame, and a globe to illuminate the space below it.'

'And on the other table,' Clam interrupted, while fidgeting excitedly, 'there's a modern looking manually operated printing press, two boxes of a high-quality white paper and stacks of very thin, clear plastic sheets ... and ten intricately engraved metal plates. How about that!? And, and ... there's also five stacks of our different denominations. Here, look, I nicked one of the ten-dollar notes.'

'Well, fancy that,' I chimed in, 'does mine look anything like that one?' The look on everyone's faces was priceless when I handed to Clam an exact copy of the ten-dollar note he was holding.

'Where on earth did you get that!?' Clam demanded out of genuine curiosity, rather than with any sense of jealousy.

'That's the note I relieved from that dropkick, Bob Nunn ... as evidence, like. Remember I told you about those two blokes who turned up in their tinnie towing some sheep? Strange bloke that, and only marginally smarter than his sidekick; well, that's what he thinks.

'Here, check this out,' I quickly added as I handed both notes to Beth. 'Compare their serial numbers; they're identical apart from their prefix characters.'

Beth nodded in agreement then passed the notes onto Beau who casually remarked, '*We* know they're definitely duds, but their quality could easily fool unsuspecting punters. Even the watermarks look real.'

'That's for sure, but just to finish off,' Will said as he took the notes back from Beau. 'We both took a few photos by the way, made sure the lights were turned off, then locked the door and took our leave. But we changed our minds and didn't release the birds and the bluetongues; far better that whoever returns to nail those two parasites get to arrest 'em red-handed first, and then release those critters. And well, that's about it.'

'Not quite,' I added, 'What about those paintings? It's my guess they're also counterfeits'.

'Or' Beth added, 'have they been stolen, and if so, who from?'

'The main thing is you've both made it back here unharmed,' said Beau, 'but regardless lads, you've done a fabulous job and you looked after the horses, so you may as well take it easy, or write up your report if you like; we'll keep out of your hair.

'Hang on a second lads,' Beau called as he retrieved a crumpled piece of yellow paper from his shirt pocket. Here Will, see what you make of this.'

From the day when I first met Will, until now, I'd never heard him swear, not once ... a trait which had put him in good stead as a potential son-in-law.

'Christ all mighty Beau!' Will roared, 'We could have arrested both of those bastards on the spot if we'd bloody well known this!' No harm done, in my opinion, Will is still number one for our beautiful daughter's hand.

* * *

THAT NIGHT, as Beth and I lay listening to the sounds of the outback night, I quietly commented to her, 'I say, my gorgeous clever girl. I bet you weren't expecting this outcome when you suggested we needed to follow the money.'

Beth just yawned, rolled over and sleepily whispered, 'Maybe there's more to do yet, my handsome man; now please, get to sleep.'

36

Immediately after breakfast the following morning, a decision was taken. Without any doubt in our collective minds, and because of the detailed descriptions of our suspects, we knew exactly where to find and capture, Lily, an unabashed devotee of sheep and cattle theft in Australia, and a foreign bloke, his name not yet known to us, who was wanted by Interpol for grand scale currency counterfeiting.

It was high time to return to our respective homes, report our findings to Canberra and await further instructions, if any. After all, we were not being paid to be front-line Federal Police ... just livestock theft and investigation officers. Yeah, right.

By midday, our wonderful campsite was bare; shade tarps and tents removed and all other trappings that had made our stay here so relaxing and comfortable were now securely packed onto the tandem trailer. Neither horse had shown any reluctance to walk up, and into their float. Walers, forever proud and cooperative.

After handshakes all round, Beth first gave Clam a hug, then walked up to Will and repeated her embrace, albeit one which lingered a smidgen longer, but only noticeable by someone who had a vested interest in both.

'Hey Will, before we hit the road,' I interrupted, 'please, don't forget to get your photos to your mates in Canberra. And for heaven's sake give Kelly a call, asap.'

37

Our return flight to Sale was uneventful; Beth piloting with Aussie and Betta being her copilots. Beau and I played "hostess", handing drinks and sandwiches to those upfront.

* * *

THREE DAYS LATER, Will phoned with some unexpected, but not altogether surprising news. He called, not on the pretext of wanting to talk with Kelly—or so he said—but to let Beth and I know he'd been given the task of leading a team of Federal Police in their quest to arrest Lily and the counterfeiter ... tomorrow, at high noon! Which ruled Beau, Beth and me out of that action.

The real surprise was that Clam had been assigned to a special investigations squad, to be stationed in Europe; their remit being to uncover the legitimate owners of the paintings which adorned our suspect's workshop and, hopefully, to track down an international team of counterfeiters, and put them away.

Clam, apparently, was already in transit. Yep, a First Nation

Aboriginal man to represent Australia ... which also ruled out any more of our team from any first-hand involvement in that little caper.

I couldn't help thinking ... *he's a damn good lad, our Clam; definitely got his head screwed on proper, like.*

Will now seemed to have run out of anything else to say, and I bet his mouth was dry in anticipation of what needed to be said next. So, graciously I said, 'Congratulations Will; but hang on a second, I'll get Kelly for you. Cheers, son.'

Fifty minutes later, after my initial three minutes talking with Will, Kelly returned the phone to its cradle. She then gracefully waltzed by me wearing a dreamy smile and said as she disappeared back into her room. 'Thanks Dad, you're the best.' That was nice, but I already know that.

* * *

Four days flew by, and true to form, the phone rang as soon as Beth and I sat down on our veranda chairs to enjoy a few fly and mozzie free minutes and to watch the sunset while finishing our last cuppa for the day.

Beth raced inside but quickly returned, mouthing, "it's Will", before placing the phone on our table and selecting the loudspeaker button.

'Go ahead mate, we're on loudspeaker,' I said quickly, 'it's just me and Beth here at the mo,'

'OK, well, I've got some news that'll no doubt be of interest. We arrested Lily and that German bloke. I'm only allowed to refer to him as Fritz, not his real name though.

'Anyway, we nailed 'em at 2:00am. There were five of us, all armed, and by the jeeze was Lily upset; threw a tantrum, more to do with distracting those of us inside, to give Fritz a chance to clear out via a back door, but he was in for a surprise. Walked straight into the barrel of J-boy's handgun. Can't tell you who J-boy is; security and all that.'

'And where are they now, pray tell,' I asked.

'Can only say that they're in remand either in Sydney, or Melbourne. They've both been charged with a string of offences, so they won't be going anywhere in the short term, though I'm aware that paperwork for Fritz's extradition has already been filed by Interpol.'

'Well done, Will,' Beth said eagerly, 'but what became of the birds and the blue tongues?'

'Ah, yes.' Well, we took Lily down to the bird cage and questioned her at length. She admitted to paying Bob and Alby to "acquire" sheep on her behalf, but refused to say where she was selling her sheep or getting them processed. Definitely not at her last operation near Wagga Wagga that's for sure. And she was unmoving regarding telling us who were collecting the birds and lizards for her.

'We took plenty of photos, then threw open the door to the bird cage. It took a few minutes for the birds to realise their freedom was being offered, but eventually they all got the right idea and scarpered. Regrettably, there were at least sixty or seventy dead on the floor. What a waste of such beautiful creatures.

'As far as the lizards are concerned, well, we simply upended their crate and they took off, most headed towards the river.

'Oh yeah, before we took off, the lads tied a rope around the bird cage, then tied the other end to the bull-bar of one our 4 x 4 ute's. As the ute backed up, it didn't take long before the aviary became a heap of wire and kindling.'

'And the caravan?' Beth asked.

'Took heaps for photos as evidence, then we torched it.'

'Any news from Clam per chance?' I asked.

'Not yet, too early to know how he's getting on. I'll let you know as soon as I hear anything.'

'And what about the fake notes?'

'No free samples, but more than a million dollars of evidence.'

'Good God, but what about all the other paraphernalia?' Beth enquired, then added, just for completeness' sake. 'The paintings, the fake plates and that printing press, what's to become of that lot?'

'I can assure you it's in very safe hands and won't see the light of day again until the court case gets under way. Though, Beth, I heard Interpol will be given first call on all that stuff.

'There's just one more thing you need to know. There has been and will continue to be a media blackout on this episode. As you probably already know, everything will proceed behind closed doors, and nothing will be issued to the media for at least three months. It's hoped that when a media release eventually surfaces, it'll scare the bejeezus out of anyone thinking to test their luck at stealing sheep and cattle anywhere in Australia.'

We said our farewells but didn't ring off. As Beth and I headed back inside, Kelly conveniently danced from the kitchen and picked up the phone, making sure she first switched it back to normal mode before speaking.

'I say, my darling man and father of two,' said Beth, the one who never misses anything, 'did you notice how our daughter's face lit up when she picked up the phone?' Of course, I had.

38

Five relatively quiet months passed. In fact, no farm invasions or stock thefts were brought to our attention during that period. However, Gippsland is only one small area of our great land, and it makes you wonder how many illegal rural activities continued unnoticed, elsewhere.

However, toward the end of that period, we received an update from Clam.

Apparently, Interpol, the Belgian Police and Insurance company detectives identified the rightful owners of nine of the paintings which we seized from Lily's remote farm. They were all returned to those lucky folk, however, the legal owners of two of those paintings remain unidentified. Clam's theory is that perhaps in two- or three-years' time, a wealthy art collector will step forward and reclaim them, for a price of course and guaranteed assurance of anonymity.

As for Fritz, he was deported, not to Germany as we had speculated, but to the USA, together with the failed hardware he'd created to defraud Australian enterprises and citizens.

What the Americans wanted, was waterproof evidence which, up until now, had eluded their war crimes investigators, due to the disappearance of their number one suspect. The charges pending, simply put, were that Fritz had played a significant role in creating counterfeit US dollars during WW2; more specifically, that he helped make the plates used to produce different denomination fake US currency notes, and in such quantity that significantly undermined the Ally's war ending efforts.

Good luck getting out of that now Fritzie boy, I thought.

* * *

A MONTH LATER, Will phoned.

He had not given up on his investigations with Lily, and had applied for, and obtained permission to visit her in a high security Melbourne based women's prison, and yes, we accepted his invitation to join him; after all he'd be driving down from Canberra and could collect us on the way. And yes, there was an ulterior motive for volunteering his service ... Kelly! The smile on Beth's face clearly conveyed, 'that's fine by us.'

It's never nice to enter a prison precinct, whether as a visitor or, as I imagined, as a long-term guest. After we were ushered to an interview room, Lily, handcuffed, was led in. This was not the perfect environment in which to interview a felon, but at least it was just the four of us in that room and unlikely to be disturbed.

Will took the lead. 'So, Lily, we trust you're being treated properly and that you're comfortable enough to honestly answer a few questions? I think you know who we are, and what we need to finalise.

'So, please, tell us in your own words, what drove you to your criminal behaviour?'

'Ho ... an maybe get plenty rich,' Lily replied openly and, I think, frankly.

'But did you expect the consequences from Ho's methods? You do know that he murdered at least twelve innocent Australian people, and that you are now considered an accomplice to all those murders?

'That no fair, Ho kill those people because he sick in his head.'

'So why did you stay with him?'

'Our daughter, she need him as much me do.'

'Your daughter is in good hands, Lily. She's in State care and being treated with love and understanding.'

'OK, that velly good to know, but what you really wahn from me?'

'Lily, listen to me,' Beth interjected, 'I'm a Barrister, do you know what that is?' Lily nodded.

'Good. Under our laws in Australia, you are likely to spend the rest of your life in jail for breaking those laws, for fraud, theft, and complicity in murder. Unfortunately, after you are convicted, you will hardly ever get to see your daughter, only occasionally perhaps.

'But if you can help us, we might be able to reduce your sentence. Your daughter ... she is growing into a lovely young woman and will need you to hold her hand and guide her through the challenges she is already experiencing. Do you understand what I'm saying Lily?'

Ten or so seconds of silence reigned before Lily said in a measured manner, 'Oh yes, I unnerstand, you try blackmail me.'

I couldn't believe she would come to that conclusion, so I dived in. 'Lily you're being irresponsible and a damn fool; we here, are your last and probably only chance you'll get, to *not* spend the rest of your life in a place like this. C'mon woman, wake up to yourself.' Well done Andy, you've just made the woman cry.

At this development, Beth moved to sit beside Lily and draped an arm around her shoulders. Her crying soon abated, then stopped just as Will handed her his neatly folded handkerchief.

'What we'd like to know Lily,' Will continued, 'is what became of the profits you made from stealing sheep, for example.

'I invent things, to make our work much easy for Ho, but needed much cash money to build and pay workers. You know, like them mobile butcher systems and transport vans.'

'Lily,' Beth said in her most reassuring voice, 'did you buy the materials and pay your workers with counterfeit, you know, with fake money?

'Yes.'

'But Lily,' Beth continued, 'you didn't make the fake money, did you?'

'No.'

'So, how did you meet Fritz, I mean that old German man who was staying with you?'

'Ho, he knew him from when he lived in Vietnam; they like father son. Their gang very big, have much money from poaching much elephant ivory and rhino horn, in Sou Afric, Botswana an' Zimbab which all then go back to gang in Vietnam before being sized an' deliver to China. Much good arrangement, big money flow back to Vietnam gang.

'Anyway, Ho decides go here and work on own; make *heaps* he always believe. That old man followed later but they keep in touch ... agreed to use that old farm as safe shelter if things ever get too big gamble.'

'But, Lily,' I pleaded carefully, 'we still don't know how Ho thought he could make his fortune?'

'He always setting up many different teams from Sale to Wagga Wagga, Eden and Mildura and pay them real good with fake dollars, but takes all profits in real dollars ... for all his hard work and cunning he always say.'

'Thank you, Lily, I chipped in, 'what can you tell us about the bird and reptile trafficking you were involved with?'

'That just one of his idees. He get team of young men up from Adlaide to do all dirty work an he pay 'em with fake dollars. But it no work out too good; local black fellas got all upset and start throwing their boomrangs at Ho's boys. Some get hurt too, did you know? So they go back Adlaide.'

'Times up, I think Lily,' said Will as he moved to finish our inter-rogations, 'but is there anything else you can tell us before we have to leave you?'

'Yes, you may as well know of other Ho's idees; he had me working on new ways of changin' stock brands, using chemicals and not just hot irons. Much quick an' easy.'

After thanking Lily for her admissions, we retreated courteously, but not before I heard Beth saying covertly to Lily, 'I'll visit your daughter while I'm here in Melbourne and pass on your love ... and I'll see if I can get the OK for her to write to you.'

Beth made good her promise.

39

When we arrived home that night, well after eleven o'clock as I recall, it was quite a surprise to find Beau waiting patiently for us. He'd nodded off in front of the lounge room fire he must have set for himself, but Aussie, RB and Betta had soon put an end to his dreams once they heard the unfamiliar noise of Will's hire car rolling down our driveway.

After quick greetings, Beau busied himself filling the kettle for mandatory "arrival home cuppa's"... which gave the rest of us the opportunity to disappear for a few minutes to freshen up.

As we wandered back into the kitchen Beau had not only filled our mugs with steaming hot tea but had already placed a dozen or so of our favourite strawberry-filled biscuits onto a plate which he'd placed in the middle of the kitchen table.

'You're an angel Beau,' said Beth, 'I've been thinking about this for the last fifty k's; thanks heaps.'

'No problem, you're always doing the same for me. So, how'd things turn out?

'We got multiple confessions from Lily, which was most unexpected,' Will was quick to reply, 'but we're now sort of morally obliged to see she receives some leniency in sentencing and that her daughter receives visiting rights. None of which would have been possible without Beth's compassion and Andy's forthright advice.'

'Well done, you lot,' Kelly's unanticipated voice came from the open hallway door where no doubt she'd been standing unnoticed for some time, 'but can't this wait until the morning?'

'Oh, hello luv,' Beth said, as she rose from the table and hugged Kelly, 'is everything OK?'

'Yes Mum, and it's got a lot better now,' she said cheekily as she sashayed over to Will and plonked herself into his lap. If you think Will might have looked embarrassed, well you'd be wrong; he just wrapped his arms around her and kissed her flush on her lips.

'Anyway, Beau, I think we can guess why you've dropped by,' I chimed in, 'you've been talking with Canberra, yes?'

'Correct; we've been invited to investigate some very recent thefts that have been reported around a place called Rainbow, that's a small town at the southern edge of the Victorian Mallee. And they would very much appreciate it if we could start an investigation, tomorrow like.'

'Which means we'll need to fly out from West Sale early tomorrow, if, and that's a big if, a plane is available at short notice.'

'There's no problem with that, it's all been arranged. I've been guaranteed the Beechcraft will be refuelled, fully checked allover and ready for take-off, any time after 5:00am.'

'Well, c'mon, what's stopping us, let's finish packing and get on the move,' I jested with exaggerated and false enthusiasm.

'Seriously though, can you join us Will?'

'No can do, bugger it, I need formal written approval and there's no way that can be done before five o'clock tomorrow, besides I've got to return the hire car by mid-morning.'

'And Beau, I take it you've got your kit with you'll be ready to move by 4:30am?'

'Yep, as will Aussie and Betta; you can count on it.'

'Of course, so Beau, you take one of the side bedrooms ... and you two lovebirds had best take the front guest room.' Good God, the words were barely out of my mouth before Kelly was dragging a bemused but very compliant Will along the hallway.

* * *

AS WE APPROACHED RAINBOW, it was clear there would not be an airport landing. What concerned me, just a bit, was where the hell we *would* land, and who would have decided whether that site was suitable. But right now, I could not see anything that might indicate where I should land.

I glanced at Beth, my copilot on this trip ... much to the chagrin of Aussie. She met my gaze, raised her eyebrows, and shrugged her shoulders.

I nodded and decided to do another circuit of the small town, albeit a kilometre or so, further away. I'd no sooner levelled out when Beth, excitedly yelled, and pointed. 'There! Three hundred yards to starboard.'

'That's our man, what's he trying to indicate do you reckon?'

'That paddock's been mown recently I'd say, to look like an airfield. The strip looks clear to me; no scrub, ditches, or stock anywhere; should be a doddle, put her down, darling.'

The surface of the airstrip was as smooth as one laid with bitumen, well almost, but nevertheless the Beechcraft behaved perfectly and slowed to walking pace by the time we reached the end of the mown section. I then turned our plane around and taxied back to where the only person in sight waved a greeting and gave us the thumbs up. To stop I gathered: next, apply brakes, feather both engines, stop fuel flow, turn off both engines ... and everybody, out please.

Beth already had her seat belt off, but even though she moved aside, I swear that Aussie and Betta deliberately hip and shouldered her out of the way and by so doing, sent her sprawling onto my lap. Now, I can understand their needs were greater than mine at that moment, but it did fleetingly cross my mind that had nobody else been around, I may have taken full advantage of Beth's predicament.

Once we were all on the ground, the first thing I noticed was Aussie and Betta poised motionlessly close to adjacent trees, near-side legs raised and both wearing that now familiar smile on their faces in that moment of greatest relief. Ehm; good idea actually.

After much surgical scratching of the ground with their hind legs, they turned in unison, sprinted back to our gathering and sat shoulder to shoulder beside Beau, albeit now gazing intently at our welcoming committee of one.

'By Christ, I hope you've fed those two,' muttered our host, not fully convinced he was just being jovial.

'You're OK mate, they like you, and they're on their best behaviour, so relax, eh,' Beau replied. 'You must be Mr. Morgan; pleased to meet you,' was all Beau could say before he was brusquely cut off. Standing abruptly to his full height of at least six feet, he then said, '*Captain* Gareth Morgan, I'll have you know, First RAAF Bomber Command, now retired. And that landing sir, was exemplary.'

'None of my doing Gareth; congratulate this bloke, his name's Andy, Livestock Investigator Andy Stevens, actually. And this lovely lady here is Beth, Andy's wife. She's not only a top bush pilot, but also a very capable Livestock theft Investigator. And my name's Beau, Beau Dickinson, and well, I'm sort of in charge of this investigation.'

'And these two boys, their names are ...?'

'The bigger one is Aussie, and the other one's Betta.'

'Need I ask why you call them by those names?'

'Of course, you can, but not right now, we'll tell all later. But in the meantime, by all means shake hands with them and introduce yourself.'

The good captain, judging by the perplexed expression on his face, seemed most impressed when in turn he accepted the right paw of each dog as it was offered up to him.

'Beautiful lads, eh Beau, but I'm not sure how you'll utilize their talents.'

'It'll depend upon the circumstances Gareth,' I interrupted, intending to give Beau a breather and wishing to change the subject. 'So, what's the go, how many head have you lost?'

'Now, that's a really good question,' Gareth replied thoughtfully before replying. 'To date I'd say, ehmm, I dunno exactly ... probably two hundred and fifty thousand, give or take.'

'WHHAAAT!?', we *all educated and knowing* Livestock Theft Investigators chorused in disbelief.

'Didn't your boss tell you I'm a bee farmer,' Gareth smirked, 'and that some bastard has been nicking my hives?'

Beau, Beth and I looked at each other and then cracked up laughing. However, Beth somehow placated Gareth, assuring him we meant no disrespect, simply that this was our first ever project to help an apiarist!

'No offence taken folks,' Gareth replied good naturedly, 'but it *is* my only source of income, which according to the Ag Department, bees have equal status along with sheep, cattle, pigs, goats, chooks, and even horses.

'Anyway, grab your gear; this'll be my wife coming over to collect us.'

* * *

AFTER DROPPING Gareth's wife back at her General Store in downtown Rainbow (as we euphemistically referred to it with much hilarity on our return flight), Gareth drove us out of town, northward in the direction to where he had first noticed a reduction in the number of his beehives.

'My operation's not huge,' Gareth confided, 'but I own ninety functional and thriving hives which I placed in equal numbers at three different locations. When you do that, the bees take advantage of what's growing nearby and that eventually means I get three very different types of honey; you know, different colours, aromas and taste of course.

'And given there's been good water flowing from Lake Albacutya at this time of the year for a change, this should be a great season, except that some no-hopers keep taking off with my best hives. I've reported those thefts, twice, to the district copper and to be fair, he has somehow got into the right ear because, here you all are.'

'Strangely though, I'd visited all three hive sites before it dawned on me that their numbers appeared reduced, but it wasn't really obvious until my second routine check when it became overwhelmingly obvious something was amiss.'

We'd driven no more than ten kilometres before Gareth slowed his 4 x 4, then turned off the road and stopped at a gate. I did the honours, opening, and after Gareth drove through, closed it, and then looped a very meagre chain around a section of the gates vertical frame and hitched the chains tabbed end onto the fence post spigot.

The track we then followed was years old in its making but showed signs of quite recent vehicular use. Having bounced and lurched along for at least another two kilometres through stands of scribbly gum and manuka scrub, we were glad when a clearing came into view ... except that when we got out, there was a horrendous pong hanging about, and, where we had not seen it before entering the clearing, was a Holden station wagon hooked up to a garden trailer loaded with five hives ... and just four or five yards further away were four neat rows of hives.

'Hang on folks. Quickly, get back inside. Before we can go anywhere, we all have to suit up, you can't go anywhere near those hives on that trailer, there's some very upset bees over there.'

Without any argument from us, Gareth swiftly reversed along the track, back to about fifty yards from the clearing. 'Now, quick, everyone out, I'll show you how to don my special suits. Don't worry, all my suits will fit anybody. Just grab one and put it on asap!'

It was Beau who first noticed Aussie's and Betta's agitation from being harassed by an increasing number of upset bees, but before his dogs could retreat out of harm's way, Beau threw open the tail gate of Gareth's 4 x 4. Neither dog hesitated and immediately after they were both inside, Beau slammed the tailgate shut.

Though suited up, we sat in Gareth's 4 x 4 for fifteen or so minutes, windows wound up fully, hoping our winged friends would piss off and leave us alone.

It was Gareth's call to leave the safety of his vehicle, though he left it for another ten minutes before suggesting we could then commence our investigations.

We tentatively exited the 4 x 4 and Gareth immediately lit his three handheld smoke generators, because smoke, he assured us, is the only time proven method for subduing swarming bees; apparently, they become passive and disinterested in attacking. Ehm, well, fingers crossed.

Having left Aussie and Betta behind in the 4 x 4 we slowly approached the station wagon. Regrettably, it didn't take long before what I witnessed made me wish we hadn't come on this journey.

I tried to shield Beth from seeing the two sprawled bodies, about ten yards apart, but her curiosity trumped my best intentions.

'Oh, my God, Andy,' she gasped and grabbed my arm. 'That's appalling; what a terrible way to go.' There was no mistaking that for a fact; their heads, particularly their faces, and all their exposed arms and hands were hideously swollen, which would make their immediate identification impossible, no doubt the result of what looked like thousands of bee stings.

I was suddenly conscious that Beau and Gareth were now standing beside us, both rigid in shock.

However, Gareth was the first to regain his composure. 'Oh, Christ Almighty, they had no protection whatsoever ... what in God's name did they think they were doing!? It wasn't suicide they had in mind, the bloody idiots! Complete novices, or desperate for money, or both, I'd say.'

It was Beau who now took control of this situation. 'If it's OK by you Gareth, we need to move these bodies, so I suggest we first get as many photographs as possible, then remove those hives from that trailer. I've seen you've got a tarp in your 4 x 4, so let's use it to collect the bodies and to move them into the trailer. I'll drive the station wagon, but I'll follow the rest of you in Gareth's 4 X 4, back to Rainbow. OK?'

'Sounds like a plan Beau, but before we can do anything mate, we have to give both bodies, those hives, and inside the station wagon, a really thorough smoking treatment.'

While Beth immediately busied herself taking photos to capture forensic images for evidence, we three men manned the smokers and got busy. Yes, this had to be done, but our efforts produced the most disgusting and nauseating smell of putrefying flesh and burning gum leaves that you could never imagine. (So bad was that stench, that even today, thirty years on, I still occasionally reckon I can smell it.)

We waited about ten minutes for the air to clear before Beau and I walked to the body furthermost from the trailer. With some effort and feeling disgusted, we clumsily manipulated it onto one half of the tarp, which we then folded over the corpse. Gareth helped drag the tarp over to the second body where we repeated that gruesome task.

'OK, this might be the worst bit, but it has to be done,' said Beau. 'C'mon, one of us on each corner, we all lift on the count of three, then lift and slide them as best you can onto the trailer.'

It wasn't as bad or difficult as I first thought, no doubt made easier by Beth's gallant effort. What a woman!

However, as I moved around the trailer tucking the tarp under and around the bodies, a noticed a wallet; old, but well padded. I pocketed it and then ran to the 4 x 4 to join Beth, and Gareth, who wasted no time in getting its engine started. It was nice to be welcomed aboard by Aussie and Betta who both clambered all over me, vying for the opportunity to indulge me with their warm wet tongues.

40

The drive back to the road gate was no less uncomfortable, but it gave me time to rummage through the wallet I'd collected. However, once both vehicles were through the gate, I asked Gareth to stop and come with me back to the still open gate.

'So, what gives Andy?' a now puzzled Gareth asked. 'Surely you don't need my help to close the gate?'

'No mate, I don't need your help, just watch this,' I said, as Beau and Beth joined us, wondering what the holdup could possibly be.'

I proceeded to swing the gate closed, and then walked to about the middle of its span. Next, I firmly gripped the top of the gate's frame and lifted, jiggled the whole gate, and lifted again with just enough brute force to pop the gates hinge pins from the fence post pivot rings ... then dropped the gate onto the side of the track.

'Pretty easy, eh? How long did that take me, Gareth? What, sixty seconds, tops?'

'I'd say that's spot on, but so what young fella?'

'Well, how long would it have taken me if you'd installed a gate with built in anti-theft hinges?'

'Dunno, I didn't know you could buy such a gate.'

'Yeah, they're readily available, and they don't really cost that much extra. Your local Stock and Station Agent should have advised you of that option.

'By the way, his name wouldn't happen to be Mr. Frederick Inches by any chance?'

'Well, well, yes, it is as a matter of fact,' Gareth replied awkwardly. Why?'

I passed the wallet to Gareth, and I think he damn near feinted with shock as the realisation settled upon him.

'I sincerely hope not, but perhaps, just perhaps, could the other body be that of his son?'

* * *

BACK AT RAINBOW, Gareth detailed to his wife what we had discovered. Stoically, she volunteered to explain matters to her friend, Mrs. Inches, however, Beau quickly explained that that was the job of the local regional police officer.

Gareth next phoned the hospital at Horsham, who advised him they would immediately send a suitable vehicle to collect both bodies. Judging from the brevity of that conversation, not too many questions were asked by the despatcher.

That might have sounded like good luck, for us, to immediately head back to Sale, but as I was about to ask Gareth for a lift back to the airstrip, a police car most unexpectedly drove up the main street and parked almost directly in front of our small gathering outside of the General Store.

'G'day Sergeant Philips,' Gareth called to him as he stepped from his patrol car, 'how'd you get here so quickly?'

'I'm well, thanks for asking, Gareth, but what do you mean?' replied the officer as he walked up to Gareth and shook his hand.

'There's been two deaths on my property, Ron. We think it's Mr. Inches and his son.'

'Oh yeah, what makes you say that? Is it, or isn't it? And where are the bodies?'

'Actually officer,' I said quickly, 'it's rather difficult to make positive IDs because of their present condition, but that's them both in the trailer next to where you're standing.

'However, if I were you, I'd not be too keen to remove that tarpaulin, for any reason, particularly if your curiosity is compelling you to get a full blast of that smell.'

'That bad, eh?'

'Yes, it is! Here, I found this wallet on one of the gentlemen.'

'Right, thank you, but who are you, and what brings you all to Rainbow?'

At this point, the officer withdrew his notepad, then Beau stepped forward to explain that an ambulance was on the way, and to make obligatory introductions.

'How about we all move down the street a bit to get away from the pong,' said sergeant Philips. 'I need to ask you all several questions and you must remain with me until that ambulance arrives, which might take an hour or two. OK?'

And with that word of finality came any chance that our assumed luck of an early departure would materialise. The situation could have been worse I suppose, but midday was, after all, still a few hours away.

* * *

The ambulance arrived at about ten past noon and, God love both medico's, they departed ten minutes later.

Sergeant Philips thanked us for our co-operation, and we shook hands all round as he departed, however, as he walked to his car he stopped and looked appraisingly at Aussie and Betta. 'Nice dogs, Beau,' he said. 'I don't suppose you'd consider selling the younger one?'

'Not likely mate, he's still earning his stripes. However, Ron, I've got three back home on my farm who are going to be just like him. Call me in two months' time and I'll see what I can arrange if you're still interested.'

'Sounds like a plan, I'll do that. But just a friendly word of advice; both of your dogs should be wearing collars.'

'Oh yes, I know that, but when they're on a job I give 'em permission not to wear them, just in case they get snagged on something, like.'

Here it comes, Beau had just set Ron up. 'Perhaps you'd like to put their collars on while we put our kits into Gareth's 4 x 4?'

Naively, or just in the spirit of co-operation, Ron replied, 'Yeah, OK, can do, but where are their collars?'

'I'd like to see you do that Ron,' I quickly chimed in, strictly in the spirit of supporting our men in blue, of course, 'but you're guaranteed to lose an arm or two if you were to try.'

'You're a bugger Beau, I didn't see that coming. Anyway, I'll be in touch.'

'I'm already looking forward to that Ron. And mate, don't forget to include reference to Beth's photos in your report. Cheers.'

* * *

MINUTES LATER, we piled into Gareth's 4 x 4 and headed back to the improvised airstrip.

As Beth commenced the engine startup routine, I noticed Gareth, frantically displaying the old RAAF's "cut engine" signal, while simultaneously jogging over to the Beechcraft and obviously doing his best not to drop the medium sized cardboard box he was carrying.

I nudged Beth to stop her pre-flight routine, then threw open the door on my side of the fuselage. 'What's the problem Gareth?'

'No problem. Here, take this, I almost forgot. Hope you like honey. Cheers!'

* * *

THE FLIGHT HOME WAS PERFECT; what else could you expect? Beth was piloting and Aussie was in his element teaching Betta the finer points of navigation ... yeah, well, you know what I mean.

Mind you, there were a few things about this last project which we pondered on our return flight, which made it different from those which proceeded it.

First, our investigation team was on standby, available, and ready to move immediately without being inhibited by the tyranny of distance. Second, our team is now operating with several years of firsthand experience under our belts. Third, we were getting positive, meaningful, and measurable results. The perpetrators, bee thieves in this case, had effectively killed themselves in the act, and fifth, unlike most other stock thefts, there was no supply or distribution chains to contend with. And, as Beth reminded us, this project did not have Ho Hua's fingerprints all over it for a change.

But, most importantly, we all felt that Canberra was listening.

41

———

The day after our return to Sale, we received another call for assistance from Canberra.

From a farmer managing a small sheep flock about fifty kilometers southwest of Echuca, we learnt that his sheep had been targeted, not for their meat, but for their wool. Obviously, he was most surprised and angry to find several hundred of his sheep had been shorn ... yet he hadn't planned on doing that for at least another fortnight.

And of course, there was no sign of the stolen fleeces.

* * *

By mid-afternoon we were met by Will at the Echuca airport. In another hired Nissan 4 x 4, we were soon on our way to that farmer's property where, upon arrival and after enthusiastic greetings, we were then plied with scones with jam and cream, and mugs of steaming hot tea: the best of typical Australian hospitality.

Our discussions went well into the afternoon; the basics being addressed, with typical question and answer progression as follows.

Q1. What do you believe we are up against?

A1. My gut feeling is that there's a gang of men cruising Central Victoria who borrow a mob of sheep for a few hours and lift as many fleeces as possible from them before returning the entire mob back to where they came from.

Q2. Has this ever happened to you before?

A2. No.

Q3. How long ago did the theft occur?

A3. Not exactly sure; probably no more than five or six days ago.

Q4. Did you see or hear anything which might have made you want to investigate?

A4. No.

Q5. Have you noticed if any of your roadside gates have been tampered with?

A5. No.

Q6. Have you come across any blokes you've never seen before?

A6. At last, hesitation ... Yes, as a matter of fact there were three blokes at the Commercial last Wednesday night who I've never seen before ... but not everyone drinks at the Commercial, so perhaps they're regulars from another pub.

Frustrating, but something to work on.

* * *

THAT NIGHT, we hatched a plan: it was time for Will to shine, and that he did.

There were three pubs in Echuca, the venues where the "players" were most likely to toast their illegally gotten gains. And no matter how well a drinker reckons he can hold his liquor, that's a fallacy. Eventually, with the right amount of persuasion and ego flattery, they become "flappy mouthed" and reveal all, believing they are invincible and beyond suspicion. Bloody idiots and slow learners, or both, I'd say, and easy pray for a properly tuned-in undercover investigator.

We had also learnt over time that thieves have a predisposition to immediately start spending their newfound wealth; usually highly priced material objects such as a brand new 4 x 4, a flashy Holden ute, a lengthy European river cruise, or expensive jewellery for either their long-suffering wife, or secret lover.

Our first move was to visit the Senior Sergeant at the Horsham Police Station, to introduce our team and to lay out our plan, well, Will's really.

At first, the Senior, Mr. Anton Blackler, understandably took offence at our intrusion into his town, but to his credit also quickly saw the merit and wisdom in co-operating fully when Beau produced Canberra's letter which effectively directed immediate local police support when we requested it.

Anton personally volunteered to immediately start investigating the last eight months of sales records of the local businesses we recommended. He also called in his only detective, briefed him, and sent him on his way to see what he could uncover with respect to any unusual peaks in local wool clip sales.

Part of our strategy was for Beth and me to call on the local jeweller and feign interest in a specific highly priced piece and try to gauge the owner's trustworthiness when Beth eventually hinted at wanting to see other, more flamboyant pieces and perhaps negotiate a mutually beneficial deal.

It was bloody marvellous to see the dramatic change on the owner's face when Beth, in her sexiest voice, then unexpectedly challenged him to show us his sales records for the past eight months. From shock I suspect, the poor bugger farted much louder than he obviously intended, and I think he pissed his pants in harmony ... but despite his embarrassment, he moved surprisingly quickly to hand over the records we needed to see. Regardless, this bloke was definitely on our short list of suspects.

Will, however, had his work cut out, that's for sure. His plan was to consecutively roam into all three of Horsham's pubs and engage in friendly country style banter with every patron on the premises. At first that sounded barely possible, but it was Wednesday, usually the least busy trading day of the week.

Mind you, he did look the part; two or three days of beard growth, slightly soiled pale green button-down shirt, far more soiled dark green trousers, well-worn R.M. Williams boots and of course a broad brimmed hat which had definitely seen better days.

During six hours, virtually non-stop, Will chattered with every barfly, no-hoper, drunk and shifty looking character and shouted every one of them a beer before moving on. How the hell he stayed sober during this time was a bit of a mystery, but all was revealed when he wobbled into the police station at about 4:30 pm.

As you know, there is a lot I really like about Will, but I was always surprised how one so youthful could pull off exploits like this. But then again, he had, already, in my company, shot dead a ruthless murderer with precision and unfathomable poise.

The "trick" to his drinking marathon, he explained, was four-fold. Every beer he drank was a shandy, he always left dregs in his glass, whenever he frequented the toilet he drank copious amounts of water, and when he felt himself getting "a bit under the weather", resorted to a technique learnt while at the Duntroon Military Academy; that is, he would shove his index finger down his throat to induce immediate spasms of vomiting.

Those toilet visits served another purpose, they gave Will the chance to secretly record the name of every character he met, and in most cases where they lived and what they did for a crust.

Beau, on the other hand, had a lovely time. He went from place to place around the town and sat with Aussie and Betta in front of the supermarket, different butcher shops, a Newsagency, a dentist surgery, the stock feed outlet and both banks. Beau, being Beau, easily struck up friendly conversations with passersby who stopped to admire Aussie and Betta who sat faithfully at his side.

Beau too collected a considerable list of names, but surprisingly it was when outside the dentist surgery that Beau got the first hint of a rumour from an old lady, that a shadowy bunch of disgruntled shearers had got their heads together and formed a team of travelling shearing contractors.

At 6:00pm, as agreed, we convened a meeting back at the police station and started wading through every bit of information which looked even remotely co-incidental.

Will, however, was undoubtedly very weary, his eyelids fluttering and periodically jerking his head up just as sleep threatened to fully embrace him.

Though his head did eventually touch the desktop, when Anton mentioned the name, Counsellor Brian Martin, Will suddenly sat bolt upright, now wide awake. 'Anton, say that name again, I think we've got one of them!

'Does that Counsellor have a brother?' Will asked.

'Let me think,' said Anton.

But Anton's sole detective, "Tiger" Blake, a nondescript, yet alert bloke, answered for his boss. 'Why, yes, he does, Les, Les Martin. Not only that, but I've asked some very discrete questions of my second cousin who happens to work for Elders down in Hamilton, and he's scratching his head and wondering how the hell could Les Martin possibly afford the new Toyota 4 x 4 he's just ordered.

'It's my bet Will that we're about to nail not one, but two greedy felons.'

'Which probably means,' said Beth in a considered tone, 'that this rogue gang of shearers are in cahoots with someone working for Elders, who is illegally "receiving" and then brokering the sale of the stolen wool clip ... and later sharing the proceeds with that gang.'

'And Tiger, there may be more felons to be unearthed,' I chimed in. 'Beth and I think you should have an in-depth conversation with your local jeweller.'

'Right, Tiger, I want you to take two constables of your choice with you,' Anton ordered brusquely, 'and go find and arrest Counsellor Martin and his brother, asap like. Get them back here and slot them into separate cells, away from each other. I'll apprehend the jeweller bloke and give him a bed here for the night; I know where he lives if he's closed his shop for the day.'

As for Will, judging by his contented snoring, I don't think he had heard a single word during the past ten minutes.

* * *

Our team remained in Echuca for the next three days while Anton and Tiger finalised charge sheets, not for three, but for eight men and a woman suspected of theft of a farmer's assets, receiving stolen goods, to deception and selling stolen goods ... and other lesser charges I've forgotten about.

The most satisfying outcome from our perspective was that the entire supply and distribution chain of several stolen wool clips had been fatally dealt with before it could flourish any further. Well done Senior Sergeant Anton Blackler, and detective Tiger Blake ... both good men.

Whilst there was no evidence that our old adversaries, Ho Hua and Lily Nguen, had any input in the formation of that Echuca gang, there was also no guarantee others in the future would not risk emulating this gang's tactics.

All eight of those offenders were convicted; eight served prison terms ranging from two to six years. The jeweller committed suicide.

42

A month after we returned from Echuca, Aussie died.

According to Beau, he seemed to be in his usual good health the day before his passing, the only indication that something was wrong was when he politely sniffed his dinner, then turned and walked away ... and that's nature's way of letting us know something is not right, and not just for dogs.

About an hour later, Beau found Aussie lying on the driveway covered in bloody vomit and his faeces, urine, and twigs and grit. He was silent, though shaking, twitching and occasionally, hideously, arching his back in physical torment.

Beth and I were devastated with grief when we heard this, not just for the sudden loss of our wonderful protector, but for Beau too, when, with tears running down his cheeks and sobbing, he described how Aussie had passed while in his arms.

What sent Beau into moments of intense grief was when he bravely described Aussie's final passing: with one mighty effort, Aussie had forced his right near side paw into his hand and delivered one final lick of affection onto the back of his hand.

We didn't see Beau for another week. He'd gone bush, taking

Aussie with him, to no doubt bury his great friend near to his favourite place beside the upper reaches of Valencia Creek.

But we three weren't the only ones to mourn; Betta underwent an amazing change. It wasn't just his endless hours of howling throughout the night, but that he would run up to the front gate as if expecting Aussie would surely return in every vehicle which drove past our farm.

But time cures all and time creates goodness. However, I'm not sure whether RB ever overcame the sudden disappearance of her soul mate.

Beth and I discussed this awful event with our local vet. He listened politely, but when we pleaded to learn what killed Aussie, he said with genuine empathy and more than just a hint of anger. 'Well, the symptoms of snake bite and certain types of poisoning present in much the same manner, but I'm afraid that from your description of Aussie's last moments, it's my professional opinion he was poisoned, probably deliberately. I'm so sorry folks, but I'll wager it was 1080.

'It's a damn shame because I'm positive Aussie would have won hands down, the new "best presented working dog category" in this year's show. In fact, from a conformity point of view, Aussie was the best I've ever seen.'

Beth and I did not speak until I stopped our car in our backyard. 'You do know, my darling,' said Beth through a bout of tears and much sniffling, 'that we must find the bastard who did this, before Beau does.'

43

I've been told that retribution comes in many forms.

As a courtesy, I called Will in Canberra to explain, as best I could, what had happened. He was shocked and saddened, I could tell, but he responded as you might expect.

The next morning, just as I sat down to finish my breakfast on the back verandah with Beth, a Nissan 4 x 4 drove down our driveway. Yes, it was Will. And no sooner had he stepped from his vehicle, than our back door flew open, and Kelly raced across the verandah and launched herself into his arms.

There was absolutely no misunderstanding where this relationship was headed, and I was mighty proud.

Betta also made his presence known, welcoming Will with a couple of muted "coughs", a smile, fierce tail wagging and then the customary handshake once Will had unhanded my daughter.

After Beth had almost squeezed the breath from Will, she dashed off toward the kitchen, but stopped abruptly and called, 'Have you had breakfast, or do you just want a cuppa, darling?' That endearment was so natural, but it didn't go unnoticed by yours truly.

'I'm a bit peckish, I must say ... and a coffee for a change would go down nicely, thanks Beth.'

While Beth and Kelly dashed off to the kitchen, Will and I shook hands, then I carried his kit bag onto the verandah. 'Bloody hell, Will, what took you so long to get here,' I jested.

'I could have got here earlier had the owner of the car hire company not been marooned at the local pub.

'So, do we have anything to work on; anything at all?'

'Nah, not a thing other than the vet's diagnosis; that bloody 1080, he reckons.'

Unexpectedly, Kelly, who had just rejoined us carrying a huge pot of coffee and a jug of milk, suddenly chimed in. 'Maybe it's got something to do with the Sale Show, though I doubt it ... surely everyone loves dogs, their own in particular, of course.'

Silence reigned, but only for a few seconds before her implication dawned on us.

* * *

'Hey Beth,' I yelled from the passenger side window of Will's 4 x 4 as it crept up our driveway. 'Will and I have to go and see a bloke about a horse; be back in few hours, OK?'

It was a bit rude I suppose, not asking the girls to come with us, but Beth knew all about that "horse euphemism" and knew full well sometimes boys just needed to be boys ... and that things could possibly get ugly. We drew no protests, so Will put his foot down.

Under the pretext of wanting to make a last-minute enrolment into one of the canine events, The Sale Information Centre gave us the contact details for the President of the Sale Show Organising Committee.

Not fifteen minutes later, we had all we needed; the names of all entrants in the new category of "best presented working dog", and there was Aussie's name; his breed recorded as Australian red kelpie. At that stage, only one other entrant was recorded as such; with the owner's name, address and contact phone number listed below.

That address took us to a small, nearby settlement called Newry.

Will parked the Nissan inside the driveway to prevent any easy retreat for one, Mr. Dennis Pritchard. He soon appeared, swearing on top note and needlessly threw a piece of firewood at a yapping dog which was only doing what guard dogs are meant to do. A handsome red kelpie, no less.

Will was first out of the 4 x 4 and said to Mr. Pritchard in very plain English, 'No need to do that, yah cruel bastard, he's only trying to protect you, yah dopey mug.'

'So, what's it to you how I manage my own business? For all I care you can both piss off, right now, or I'll call the cops.'

'That won't help you one iota, Dennis,' I took great pleasure in saying, 'because we *are* the cops, and you're coming for a ride with us.'

'Be buggered if I will, just try it and see what happens'.

'OK', Will replied matter-of-factly, and immediately strode toward Dennis, 'have it your own way then'.

Dennis obviously thought the better of his reckless challenge and turned to run, but Will grabbed him by the neck of his boiler suit and threw him quite harshly I thought, flat onto his back.

'Now get up, and get in the Nissan, or I'll deal with you right here and now.'

'Yeah, yeah, all right but what the bloody Hell's going on? You can't do this, it's kidnapping; that's against the bloody law.'

'Not in your case, Dennis,' I chimed in, just stick both hands behind your back; I'm gonna cuff you and you'll have to like it or lump it. Now, just get in the car and we'll all go and have a nice little chat, somewhere quiet like.' I glanced at Will and received a quick wink.

Twenty minutes or so later, Will turned off the made road and drove onto a pine plantation maintenance track. After a few turns we bounced into a small clearing where I'm pretty sure none of us really knew where we were.

Will was first out of the ute then hauled Dennis from his seat. As I exited, Will nonchalantly, though loud enough for Dennis to hear, said to me, 'grab that shovel in the back, mate, and lets' go for that walk we promised him.'

By the look on Will's face and his general demeanour, he certainly appeared as if he meant business, particularly when he retrieved a double-barrelled shotgun from behind the 4 x 4 driver's seat and shouted, 'Right, get moving Dennis, straight ahead!'

I caught on quickly; for effect, getting behind Dennis and giving him a decent shove.

We walked another forty or so yards amongst the rows of pine trees before Will stopped. 'OK, Dennis, turn around so that I can uncuff you. And while I'm at it, how about you tell us what you reckoned you'd achieve by poisoning our dog?

'I say, Andrew, give him something to do while he decides what he's going to tell us ... give him that shovel, he can start digging his grave, or so help me God, I'll give him both barrels. What's up, Dennis, cat got your tongue?'

At this stage, even I was getting a bit worried that Will might be overdoing things just a bit, but strangely I forced myself to relax; surely this was all a pantomime.

'OK, OK,' Dennis was now pleading, our gruesome intentions having fully registered with him. 'Look, I wanted the trophy was all; that's all I wanted ... and the two hundred bucks that goes with it. Honest, that's all.'

'And the only way you could possibly win that trophy and the money was if you could eliminate our dog, Aussie. Isn't that correct? Keep digging you bastard.'

Will hadn't finished. To my surprise he produced a small package from a pocket, unwrapped what looked like an innocent piece of dark chocolate and offered it to Dennis. 'It'll make you think more clearly about things, Dennis. Go on, eat it! If you don't, I'll bloody well stuff it so far down your throat, you'll go cross-eyed.'

Dennis tentatively took the offering and chewed. Will never took his eyes off Dennis, but as soon as he'd finished swallowing, Will asked in a voice veiled with disgust, 'Did you know, Dennis, that 1080 is colourless, odourless ... *and tasteless?*

'So, now Dennis, how do you feel? And ... do you think your grave is deep enough yet?'

In response, Dennis screamed and pleaded and begged until his voice was reduced to a desperate whisper ... then slumped onto his knees into his almost completed grave.

'Or rather, would you prefer I give you both barrels? Either way you're going to suffer as poor bloody Aussie did.'

Dennis, at this stage, was a sobbing wreck and to tell the truth, I was now hoping Will might relent ... but like I said, he hadn't finished.

I was on the verge of interfering, but Will shoved the poor bugger onto his back, then lowered the shotgun so that both barrels rested on Dennis's belly.

'Listen carefully you heap of shit, I'm only gunna tell you this once and only once. You're going to leave Victoria, forever, and within a week, and if I, or any of my colleagues ever see you here again, you *will* be dead meat, guaranteed. Got it?'

Dennis was trying to say something, but Will ignored him. Then, before I could stop him, he pulled both triggers; nothing followed, but for the double "clunk" of both hammers. Correct, the gun wasn't loaded. 'And not a word to anyone about our little chat to anyone, OK?'

With that done, Will nodded his head indicating to me it was time for us to retreat to the Nissan. 'Leave him, the bastard can find his own way home.'

* * *

As soon as we commenced the drive back to the farm, Will burst into laughter and thumped the steering wheel in ecstasy. 'I've still got it, what a performance, eh Andy? Best damn effort since I passed the Academy's acting course. But where did *you* learn to act like that?'

'I've always been a quick learner son, but *I* was pretty convincing too, eh?'

'We should walk the boards together some time; we'd make a great double act.'

'Listen, let's get serious for a few minutes, we need to decide just how much we reveal to the girls.'

'You mean, like, convincing, and honest but very little detail? I reckon we can do that. However, as you can appreciate Andy, my official report to Canberra must include chapter and verse for our impunity to remain intact.'

* * *

AND SUCCEED WE DID, though we separately gave Beau the full account when he returned home two days later. It was hard not to notice the look on his face, I suspect it conveyed his appreciation, relief ... and our arguably warped sense of humour.

* * *

BUT THIS ENTIRE event had one more twist to its tail. Unbeknown to all of us, my gorgeous daughter, having earlier learnt about the upcoming Ag show, felt it was a bit unfair not to enter RB and Betta, after all, they too were magnificent working dogs; well, a dog and a bitch of course.

Naturally, there was no sign of Dennis or his kelpie at the judging ... and the first prize had to be shared.

RB and Betta didn't seem all that fussed having to wear white ribbons around their necks on the drive home.

And like I said earlier, retribution comes in many forms.

44

———————

Normality returned to our farming routines which allowed Beth and I to indulge our penchant for travel. We flew to Sydney, climbed the Harbour Bridge for a second time, and attended the Sydney Opera house and listened to The Sydney Symphony Orchestra perform a magnificent rendition of Beethoven's 9th symphony.

We also flew to Heron Island and unintentionally overstayed, so good was the service, food, weather and having so many beautiful places to swim, including the impressive pool at our motel, that we actually forgot our departure date.

But all good things must come to an end.

While refuelling in Sydney, I rang Beau to ask if he'd heard anything from Canberra, hoping against hope he hadn't, and that we could therefore extend our holiday.

No such luck, Canberra had received reports from two adjacent cattle graziers in north-central New South Wales and wanted to know if there was any reason, we could not be available to assist with an immediate investigation.

'How could we possibly refuse,' Beth taunted, 'perhaps it'll stop us from spending so much time lazing around doing nothing.'

We were expected to fly to Wilcannia, posthaste, where we would be met two days later by Beau, Will, Kelly (yes, Kelly) and Betta.

'So, what sort of a place is Wilcannia?' I asked.

'It's a small town located within the Central Darling Shire, in northwestern New South Wales,' Beth read from the tourist journal she'd collected years ago.

'It's way north of where we went looking for Lily that time, but it's on the Darling River. Way back in time it was the third largest inland port in Australia during the river boat era of the mid-19th century. And according to this journal, Wilcannia has a population of about five hundred people.'

* * *

OUR MOTEL ROOMS had seen better days, but were adequate for our purpose; comfortable, clean, and fitted with an air conditioner which only made desperate calls for help when it was shutting down.

* * *

IMMEDIATELY AFTER OUR team had freshened up from their flight (compliments of our man in Canberra), Beau called a meeting, primarily to bring Beth and me up to date.

'Stick close to Will, Kel, even if he's outnumbered ten to one.'

'Yes, dad. I'm sure I'll manage that.' Cheeky little bugger.

'OK, here's the basics,' Beau commenced. 'It seems two farmers have stumbled onto something, though it's already cost each of them about forty head. It might also interest you Canberra think that somehow the tactics of these thieves may have Ho's grubby little fingers all over this.

'Has anyone else here heard of chemical branding? Remember when Lily brought it up when we last interviewed her? I'm aware of that technique, but never used it.'

'Yes, to both questions,' I interrupted. 'I've read somewhere recently that talked about chemical branding. But it's not new, it's been around for a few years, basically to minimise the pain and stress caused to the animal after being hit by a traditional branding iron. The chemical brand is temporary, but a convenient and legal way to ensure much faster stock transition through the yards.

'And, regarding Lily, it's never been certain that what she says, is true, or just another ploy to change the subject.'

'Anyway,' said Beau, 'this chemical branding is quite simple. Much easier and quicker to perform and there's no contest needed to wrestle the beast to the ground. The cattle are simply driven into a crush and worked on while they're still standing.

'It's essentially a technique of overlaying the thief's template cutout of their selected brand pattern, and then freezing a combination of chemicals over the voids in the template. The chemicals deprive the hair follicles of their normal environment and within a few hours the associated hairs drop off, leaving an easily visible brand.

'And, I'll bet, the branding and the processing of cattle through the yards, and their despatch through the abattoirs is all over before anyone is the wiser ... leaving no recourse for the unlucky farmer to recover any money.

'And even if some of the stolen cattle are passed in, they can be transported quickly to any destination, where, after just a few weeks, or maybe a month, the thieves can at their leisure, rebrand those animals with a legally registered brand configuration, using their own home-made branding iron. All "out of sight, out of mind" operations stuff.'

'What about stock which already have permanent brands made by applying a branding iron?' Will interjected.

'Much the same way as I've just described, but with a subtle difference. The thieves do what the master cattle rustlers did up here, one hundred years ago.'

'Meaning, what?' asked Will.

'I can tell you that,' Kelly piped up, 'they modify the owner's brand configuration using a sneaky shaped branding iron which basically produces a different brand shape.' Good girl, Kel.

'You're on the money, Kelly, well almost,' Beau added. 'Today, the thieves use a well-designed template which overlays the owner's original brand, then they apply the chemicals which in turn creates the altered configuration they want.'

'I've been thinking,' said Beth, while Beau took a breather, 'it's Australian folk lore that our early drovers moved huge mobs of cattle from Central Queensland to Adelaide, and Wilcannia was an important stayover. But those drovers took great pride in not losing any of those cattle, other than the one's which died along the way. They also had to contend with opportunistic rustler's no doubt, but still managed to keep losses to an absolute minimum.'

'Why bring that up, mum?' Kelly asked innocently.

'Isn't it reasonable that some modern-day graziers should take the blame for their reported losses? They have means at their disposal to deter and keep stock thieves at bay, but it seems to me those olden day drovers took greater care of other people's property, than did the owner, just like today.

'I'm not advocating the actions of those we're dealing with here are acceptable, they're not, but they are taking advantage of other people's complacency. It's an attitudinal matter which I believe our government is responsible to eliminate, but as yet, we've seen bugger all in terms of providing funding and resources to address this problem.'

Silence reigned as we all considered the truth in what Beth had to say.

'So, what do you suggest, Beau?' Will asked politely.

'I think we'd be wasting our time trying to locate these blokes, the country around here is massive, there's only six of us and we are without the use of a plane.

'So, we wait for them to come to us?' I asked, which seemed logical, but realising how open-ended our wait might be.

'Yep, that's exactly what I have in mind.'

Beth had something else to add. 'It's only a gut feeling, but I don't think our friend Mr. Ho has been involved in this. First, it's a very long way from where he traditionally operated, and second, Lily didn't invent the chemical branding technique so there was no kudos in it to tickle his ego, so to speak.'

* * *

THAT AFTERNOON WE BECAME TOURISTS, separately wandering around the town, immersing ourselves in local gossip and checking out the small historical museum.

Kelly, ever inquisitive, dragged Will into the stock and station agent's building and was quick to find a chalk board notice which confirmed the next livestock auction in Wilcannia was scheduled to take place in just two days' time and cover a yarding of twelve hundred cattle. There were five of the larger New South Wales buyers registered to attend, but of course we had no idea how many locals might roll up.

By now the heat was getting the better of us, including Betta, so we spent a few hours in the motel's pool before retiring to our rooms for a snooze.

We later enquired where the town's Police Station was located and looked forward to meeting the only policeman in town. We were in luck (I think?) and caught up with him just as he was arriving to his home from a patrol.

We were fresh and relaxed, and I dare say, Constable Taylor was tired and looking forward to a cold beer, but definitely not looking forward to meeting us to discuss "local matters" or interested in hearing about our proposed involvement in monitoring what goes on at a typical Wilcannia cattle auction.

In fact, I've never met a police officer less helpful, or standoffish or downright rude as this bloke, even after Beau thrust a copy of Canberra's letter into his hand.

Beth and Kelly were also somewhat taken aback, later letting the rest us know it was their women's intuition that this cop could not be trusted. He certainly wouldn't be left out of Will's next report to our man in Canberra.

45

Auction day began early for us. As each livestock transport truck arrived, they were allocated off-loading ramps. Most drivers were quick to unlock and slide open the tailgate to allow unloading to commence.

As Beau was by far the most experienced in performing that task, he took up the best possible position from which to inspect each beast as the first consignment made its way down the ramp leading into the holding pens.

'Nothing out of order with that lot,' said Beau quietly, 'quite good condition actually. But let's get across to the next truck to be unloaded.'

Each of the truck drivers were amiable enough and easily fell under Beau's "yarding nouse" and appreciated his helpful tips … until the fourth truck tried to reverse into place.

This driver, impatient and obviously nowhere as experienced in reversing such a large vehicle as were the previous drivers, had, as Beau put it, "a real bad case of shit on the liver."

After a couple of unsuccessful attempts to align his truck up with the off-loading ramp, Beau trotted over and offered some well-intended advise. But all we heard from that driver was, 'Piss off yah silly old bastard, what would you know? Go on, piss off and mind yah own business.'

What an ungrateful piece of work he was, but I think we all tumbled to the fact that he was worked up over something not related to his lack of driving skills for he seemed needlessly anxious.

We took up similar positions as the earlier unloading's had proceeded ... and waited. Eventually, after his fifth attempt, he manoeuvred into the correct position, but not without crunching the tailgate of his truck into the off-loading ramps' framework.

And here was where things now got interesting. As soon as this load of cattle were in their holding pens, Beau quickly met with us and said, 'two things, folks. Co-incidentally, there just happens to be eighty head in that pen, and second, they all have chemical brands, I'd swear my last dollar on it.'

'So, what now Beau?' Will asked,' do we collar him now?'

'Nah, let's just continue our inspection of the fifth and last truck, and then see what the sale throws up.'

* * *

AN HOUR AND A HALF LATER, the last bids were accepted, and then each seller and buyer retired to the main office to settle their transactions. Some of the trader's headed to the on-site kiosk for a cuppa and a yarn before hitting the road, but not our very agitated friend who made a beeline for his truck.

We had made his day even more annoying when he discovered his truck was as dead as a dodo, compliments of Will's handywork in removing its fuel line. And, unfortunately, I missed how Will went about handcuffing him. He could tell me later.

Nevertheless, Beau, Beth and I, and Betta, waited out of sight until the accountant had finished recording his final transaction record, then we swooped.

To our surprise, that obnoxious copper, who we'd met just a few days previously but not seen earlier, was in the process of signing those documents, that he, Constable Taylor, had born witness that the auction's legal obligations had been conducted legally and above board. (Or words to that effect.)

And it didn't escape our attention that there was not only a three-quarter empty bottle of Johny Walker whisky and two almost empty glass tumblers on the table ... plus, a stack of bank notes in front of our now obviously, untrustworthy keeper of the peace.

'Get out of this office, all of you, you've got no right to be here,' Constable Taylor roared.

'Or what?' Will's voice boomed back, thank God, for we were not expecting him back in time to witness this bust, and I had reservations if the five of us could physically take control of this situation. As I said, these two crooks (alleged crooks!) were big bastards.

Nevertheless, it was Will's turn to swoop. In just a few quick steps he was face to face with Constable Taylor and pushed him hard in the chest, sending him tumbling arse over-head, backwards. So well executed was Will's attack that he somehow, mid fall, relieved Taylor of his service revolver.

The accountant, bewildered I guess, thought it better to make a run for it, but quickly changed his mind when Betta, hackles raised, snarling most disturbingly, and showing his now very large fangs, loomed in front of him. That was most interesting; I'd witnessed Aussie do this on more than one occasion, but as I later learned, none of us had trained Betta to react this way.

While Will was in the process of handcuffing Constable Taylor, he threw another pair of cuffs to Kelly and called over to her, 'there you are, my darling, learn how to cuff a crook.'

46

___

Having collected the very incriminating documents and the money, we waited while Beth and Kelly finished taking the last of their many photos then frogmarched both foul-mouthed gentleman (another euphemism) to our hire car and nudged them into its rear seat, to join their suspected accomplice. Their common demeanour, at best, would be described as a mix of shock, loathing, and realisation that their days of illegal trading and easy pickings were well and truly over.

All three were driven by Will and me to Wilcannia's small Police Station and we then deposited them into its even smaller, and only cell.

Meanwhile, Beau, Beth and Kelly had remained at the saleyards to drape blue and white crime scene tape to the accountant's office door, and around the driver's transport truck.

At the first opportunity after returning to our motel, Beau phoned the Senior Sergeant at the Wagga Wagga Police Station to explain the events of the past few days and requested his help.

Will then did much the same to update Canberra, but out of our collective earshot, of course.

'Well, that's us sorted,' Beau advised happily enough, 'there's a five-seater on its way here to collect our slippery friends. Whoever's in charge will sign for our evidence, and they'll leave their forensic tech here until he's finished giving the once over to the truck and the office. It'll be up to the Senior in Wagga to formally arrest and charge those blokes.'

The boys from Wagga were the opposite of Constable Taylor, one of their own, but soon to find himself disgraced, dismissed from the New South Wales Police Force, and cooling his heels in a cell for the next five or six years.

* * *

However, to our great surprise, during yet another trial behind closed doors, we soon realised we'd made a mistake in thinking our nemesis, Ho Hua, had no influence in this fraud.

It was revealed that Ho had prayed on Constable Taylor's weakness; his inability to repay considerable gambling debts. And Taylor had jumped all over Ho's offer that he would pay off those debts, in return for a favour, or two.

However, the outcome, after Taylor had ensconced Ho into the trust of the previously mentioned cattle rustlers, was that Taylor was remunerated in cash ... albeit, in counterfeit dollars!

I can see now why the good police officer would be in such a permanent state of distrust, and SOL ... shit on the liver. But that in no way excluded him from being excused from being convicted for his role in a chemical branding rort.

We all had a good laugh at how things can play out.

Other bonuses from our team's perspective, were that the unhappy cattle graziers were reacquainted with their stolen cattle, while those who had physically perpetrated the altered branding were located and arrested.

47

––––––––––

ot all our callouts involved hundreds, and sometimes thousands of kilometres of travelling.

After our visit to Wilcannia, all had been quiet in our region, until one afternoon our telephone rang. It was Alex, the local officer in charge at Stratford Police Station. 'I say, Andy, have you got time to pay me a visit? I've got two blokes here who I'm not sure should be arrested or sent to an asylum in Melbourne. And if you would, see if can get Beau to come in with you, and bring Beth too, as witnesses, like.'

Curiosity and respect got to all of us and an hour later we arrived at Alex's cop shop.

Before we were to meet his guests, Alex sat us down and launched into his story, or rather, his dilemma.

Both blokes, Stephen, and Ron Herbert, were known to the South Australian Police, but had recently moved to Gippsland for a change of scenery.

They had hatched a plan which, in their minds "would be a cinch", and went something like this.

It had occurred to them they were both getting a bit long in the tooth to continue using their "normal sheep rustling techniques".

Why continue busting their guts when all they had to do ... was wait for their prize to come to them?

So, during the previous week and immediately after the livestock sales, they followed their "target", a stockman with a tandem transporter carrying three hundred sheep, destined for a property near Yarram about seventy kilometres south of Sale.

With some degree of recklessness, they forced the driver off the road and with considerable daring on Stephen's behalf, pulled his ute to a stop directly in front of the truck.

The enraged driver was no contest for the brothers who manhandled him into the scribbly gum scrub next to the road and proceeded to tie the exasperated stockman to an old waratah tree ... and then blindfolded him with a large hand towel. I shook my head at this revelation, wondering if the brothers really believed the hand towel would demonstrate any sensible purpose, in later questioning.

Anyway, Alex cleared his throat and pressed on.

The brothers then "hid" their ute on the opposite side of the road, for whatever lame reason, because anyone driving back to Sale would easily spot it.

Unbeknown to Alex at this stage, the brothers had recently purchased a sixty-acre property just south of the small settlement of Woodside.

Anyway, having driven the truck onto their property and off loaded the sheep, the brothers then positioned it up against the boundary fence where a meagre stand of gum trees and some scrub was intended to conceal the truck from everyone heading south seeing it ... or so they thought.

Two days later, the brothers presented themselves to Alex, wanting to make an official complaint that some rotten bastards had stolen their sheep. Yes, really; truck and all.

By this stage Alex had received word from the Sale Police to keep a look out for the Herbert brothers. Apparently, they'd both been seen by a plain clothed detective while at the auction, who believed they seemed to be taking an unnatural interest in a trader's purchases.

So, Alex listened to their story, but somehow cajoled the brothers to relax in one of the cells while he "made further enquires on their behalf".

But by now, we had arrived at the 'Stratty" cop shop and were about to meet these hapless chaps. What followed was incredible.

Ron, the older brother demanded to know what had become of *their* sheep.'

'But Ron,' Beth countered, 'you haven't got any proof that they're legally yours. You know, like a receipt. And remember, those sheep weren't lost, or given to you.'

'Ah, that's all bullshit,' yelled Stephen, 'the sheep were in our paddock so they're ours ... possession is ninety percent of the law. That's the law, you lot should know that.'

With that said, we adjourned our meeting with the brothers and concluded they didn't know what day it was let alone be capable of managing themselves through the judicial system.

* * *

A week later I received a phone call from Alex. 'Mate, you're not going to believe this, but those Herbert boys are in for a surprise.

'Apparently, the legal owner of those sheep, and two of his mates, went looking for his transporter having decided to take things into his own hands, agreeing, for no other reason, that he had to start looking somewhere, and opted to take a run down the Sale-to-Yarram road.

'As it transpired, more from good luck than anything else, they recognised the owner's transporter tucked behind a not so dense stand of roadside scrub and gum trees.

'The interesting thing was that the brother's had taken themselves fishing down at Port Albert, so the owner and his mates and their dogs, totally uninterrupted, rounded up the sheep, reloaded them onto the transporter and then drove back to the owner's property.

'And the absurd thing is that those idiot brothers had conveniently left the transporter's keys in the ignition switch.

48

———

'Hey, Dad,' Jack yelled from his idling motor bike, 'how well do you know that new bloke who moved into the Barton's place out at Perry Bridge?'

'Met him briefly about four months ago. Quiet sort of bloke, but he's OK, I guess. Chook farmer as I recall. Why's that?'

'It's just that I was riding past his place about an hour ago, minding my own business, and he told me to piss off; that I was disturbing his animals. But there was no stock to be seen anywhere, or any chooks for that matter. Is that a bit odd, or what?'

'Good job, son. His name's Bert something; ah yes, Bert Meiers, I'm pretty sure. I'll give Beau a call and make a few enquiries. But keep this under your hat, we don't want him getting suspicious if too many people get nosey, like.'

'No probs, I'll be back in about an hour; my shout tonight, eh?' A good lad, our son Jack. Of course, after all, I've taught him well.

Beau had never met Mr. Meiers but took the time to speak to our man in Canberra to see what could be unearthed.

True to form, the following day we received a faxed copy of Bert's profile. Nothing major recorded, nor a threatening type, but does have a tendency which had twice put him in front of a magistrate on the suspicion of stealing kid's pets, usually lambs ... which of course raised our antenna's, and demanded an immediate chat with Bert.

* * *

OVER THE FOLLOWING FORTNIGHT, Beau, Beth, and I took turns to cruise by Bert's property, where the house and its surrounding outbuildings were set back from the road by at least sixty yards. Our objective: to look for anything unusual which might invite us to pay him a visit.

'No family, apparently,' Beth said, 'just the one car, an old Toyota ute in the carport; no bikes, or toys, or any sign of pets.'

'There's five original outbuildings,' I added, 'of various vintage, and they've all been reboarded and given a lick of paint. All the sort of practical conversions you'd make if you were going to breed chooks.'

Beau then chimed in. 'But did you notice the five-strand wire fencing that runs along the back of the largest shed and then heads off towards the scrub at the back of the house block? It looks like a fence better suited to keeping in sheep, than chooks.

'And the positioning of that fence would be bloody hard to see from the road, or to see whether there was anything in that paddock, which makes me just a wee bit suspicious about what our friend is up to. You know, like, out of sight, out of mind.'

Silence reigned while we considered a course of action.

Beth was first to speak. 'I studied the basics of the criminal mind when at Uni. I haven't remembered everything, but I do know all criminals have common traits.

'You're right Beau. On top of their agenda is believing that out of sight, out of mind, is their number one ally.

'A close second is an aversion to paying tax, and its bedfellow of believing they shouldn't have to pay for anything.'

'And what else, Sherlock Holmes?' I couldn't resist saying, 'this is really interesting.'

'Well, we've already experienced their absolute self-interest, and lack of compassion or concern as to how their actions can wreck other people's lives.

'And risk is always seen by criminals as minimal, and inevitably overestimate their skills, believing no one else could ever outsmart them.

'Another couple of things worth remembering is that most criminals are an impatient lot, unable to refrain from spending their ill-gotten gains. And some convince themselves that big is not always best.

'There's another type of criminal who relies on certain people to keep them at arm's length from the police, while making a quick quid for themselves.

'The moral to their style of operation is, to never employ a person before they produce a Police Check clearing them from any previous unsociable activities, particularly where livestock is involved. And, it goes without saying, farmers should never discuss their plans regarding stock numbers or their likely relocations. You never know when one of your workers is also paid to spy on your plans.

'However, such is the criminal mind that they inevitably succumb to either complacency, or an ever-greater need for other people's hard-earned wealth.'

'So, Beth, what you're really saying,' Beau asked, 'is that we should pay Bert a visit?'

'Yes, but I want our Jack to tag along.'

God Almighty, how did I ever deserve to meet and marry this amazing woman?

* * *

A WEEK LATER, Alex, Beau, Beth, Jack, me, and Betta met at Stratford Police Station at 7:30 a.m.

Thirty minutes later we had surreptitiously surrounded Bert's house, and two minutes later, Beau, Alex and I were hammering on the front door of Bert's house.

'Open up Bert,' Alex called loudly. 'I need to talk with you about your chooks.'

Reluctantly, Bert opened his door. 'I don't have any chooks; what's the big idea waking me up at this goddamn hour?'

'No chooks? Then, I need to talk to you about your sheep.'

'What sheep? I don't have any sheep. What's got into you Constable?'

'Then, to prove your statements to me, and to my witnesses, you'd best let us inspect your sheds; all of them. OK?'

'No, that's not OK. You can't just come charging onto my property without a search warrant.'

'We thought you'd say that, so here, clap your eyes on this Bert,' Alex replied while handing him the two sheets of paper which constituted our official search warrant. 'So, let's get started, shall we?'

Bert's bristling demeanour changed immediately, as did his entire body language; his shoulders slumped, and his gaze suddenly focused upon a small area on the ground in front of him ... giving the appearance of a broken soul.

The largest shed revealed, as best that I could describe it, a sheep nursery. The shed had been divided along its length, into twenty small enclosures, each comfortably holding four lambs.

There was no sign of either any mistreatment, or undernourishment of the lambs, quite the opposite. All were plump, about thirteen to fourteen weeks old and seemed indifferent to the observations of our team. And none had been ear-tagged, tail docked or castrated.

'Now Bert', answer me this,' Beau asked politely enough, 'how and when do these little blokes get outside for some fresh air?'

'Every morning until about eight thirty this time of the year, and again late in the arvo until it's almost dark.'

'And you reckon they get enough grass to eat during those times?'

'Yeah, of course, look at them. Do they look starved to you?'

'That's not the main point, Mr. Meiers,' Beth interrupted, 'are you bottle feeding them with the right ingredients?'

'Yes, of course.'

'Then tell us,' Bert, 'how do you go about getting your hands on this many lambs, and where are you getting them?'

'Easy, really. I wait for the lambing season to get into full swing, then I jump fences and grab a few at a time. The farmers aren't going to miss two or three newborns, here and there. If they do notice, they usually reckon feral foxes are to blame, given the number that those bloody foxes kill, unchecked like.'

'Right, Bert,' Alex asked bluntly. 'How do you go about offloading these lambs? You must be making money somehow, so, I want every name and contact number for every person or company that you trade with.'

'And if I don't, what'll happen?'

'Bert, listen carefully,' Beth continued. 'I'm a barrister and I can tell you that for withholding information, you'll get at least another two years detention ... and that's on top of the mandatory five years you're going to receive, regardless.'

'OK young fella,' I said to Jack, 'see how you go fitting these cuffs to Mr. Meiers.'

'Yeah, yeah, alright,' the luckless Mr. Meiers stuttered, 'but how did you lot get onto me?'

'Bert, that's for us to know, and for you to forever wonder about.

* * *

BERT RECEIVED five years of prison time. His customers, fourteen in all and ranging in age from six to seventy years, were given either a "stern Police warning", or copped substantial fines for receiving goods known to have been stolen.

Inspection of Bert's other sheds revealed the beginning of another enterprise, a plethora of bird traps and empty bird cages.

Though only a relatively minor felony in monetary terms, it was a good feeling to have shut down Bert's operations knowing vigilance, well planned investigations and a prompt arrest all contributed to that success and, hopefully, acted as an ongoing warning.

49

So quiet was the ensuing five months that Beth and I had almost completed arrangements for a five-week holiday to South Africa when out of the blue, Beau received a phone call from our man in Canberra.

In his customary way, Beau arrived unannounced with bread and half a dozen of his own homemade cinnamon doughnuts. Betta and RB, as usual, handed me the morning paper, for which Beth gave each of them their favourite reward, a pig's ear.

'You're a bit stingy with the doughnuts mate,' I gently chided Beau, 'I suppose you've already gutsed the first dozen?'

'Yeah, something like that, though these two have taken a liking to 'em too.'

'So, what gives mate?' I asked. 'Here, take a gander at this pamphlet we picked up from the Travel Agent last week. Can't wait to see those big cats, and rhinos; it's only eight days now before we take off. Which, by the way, should give you plenty of time to join us, if you want to change your mind. Like I said, it'll be our shout, and our pleasure to have your company.'

'Oh No!' Beth gasped, her hand partially covering her mouth, 'Take that look off your face Mr. Beau Dickenson; I can tell you've been asked to second us for another project. It'd better be bloody good to trump our holiday!' Beth was angry; for as you know she very seldom resorts to swearing; my bad influence probably.

'Yes, I'm afraid so, Beth, but please, hear me out.

'I tell you what, if you agree to helping me on this one, I'll definitely go on that trip to Africa with you. And we all know Jill is always talking about one day getting to see elephants up close, and the massive herds of migrating wildebeest and zebras, so we shouldn't have any trouble convincing her to tag along with us.'

'Yeah, that's all well and good,' I chimed in, 'but we'll have to cancel our tickets and accommodation and so forth, and that'll cost an arm and a leg ... unless, unless we can shift our departure date without charge, using Jill and me as a sweetener for the Travel Agent.'

'Does that mean you're both in?'

Silence reigned, but not for long. I looked from Beau to Beth, who gave me the slightest of nods, followed by the smallest of self-satisfied smiles. 'I'll go and have a chat with the Travel Agent this arvo,' Beth said with unexpected enthusiasm, 'you know, just to see they're on the job and that they get cracking.'

'Good on you Beth,' Beau replied with obvious delight. 'As soon as you let me know what dates they can accommodate us, I'll let Canberra know; but bear in mind we need to get moving on our assignment, by Tuesday ... that's just three days from now.'

* * *

TRUE TO THEIR PROMISE, and by midday the following day, the Travel Agent phoned Beth to advise her they had called on a few favours and that all our ticketing arrangements, for four adults, flying First Class with Qantas Airways, from Tullamarine to Johannesburg, had been rebooked and confirmed. This meant we now had another ten days up our collective sleeve to put our latest mission to bed before winging our way to South Africa.

* * *

WHEN BEAU REJOINED us the next morning, he had the news we needed to get our plans under way.

'Well, folks, it seems a farmer who lives on a property about forty k's northwest of Violet Town has been in touch to report a problem with his herd of forty-two Angus cattle. Apparently, almost overnight, they all somehow seem to have lost their previous condition.

'But hang on, before you ask, this may still turn out to be something for a veterinarian to investigate, but Canberra reckons there's a whiff of no good going on ... that's why their need for us to investigate first.

'Violet Town is a small rail-line community, just off the Hume Highway. There's a serviceable airport there, and only two hangars, but not much else.'

'That's OK, mate,' I reassured Beau. 'Beth and I will arrange everything with the boys at the West Sale Airport regarding refuelling arrangements, and they'll also organise local accommodation and a hire car, and for someplace to secure our plane. With luck, one of those hangars will be available.'

* * *

WE EASILY LOCATED the property in question and, as instructed, landed the Beechcraft on the dirt road leading up to the homestead, not an unusual procedure in the outback.

Having tumbled from the plane, Betta first of course, we three walked up to the couple waiting for us at the bottom of their home's front steps. Greetings all-round were performed, including Betta's ever so polite, now customary paw offerings.

Mr. and Mrs. Welch were retiring types, almost shy at first, but after we'd all had a cuppa and a slice of chocolate sponge cake, both were nevertheless keen to find out what was going on with their cattle.

'So, Mr. Welch,' Beau asked calmly, 'how old were your cattle at the time you paid for them?'

'The purchase document says twenty months, though to look at them, you'd have to say they're more like two-year-olds, and all of them were in really good nick. Just look at the feed I've got here.'

'So, what happened, and when?'

'I was going into town four days ago, to do the shopping like,' Mrs. Welch interrupted. 'It almost took my breath away when I saw those that were up near the house were all looking so poorly.'

'Was there anything that looked suspicious?' I asked. 'Anything at all? No matter how small.'

'No, nothing,' our equally bewildered hosts replied in unison.

'No roadside gate tampering, car or truck tracks, or anything like that,' Beth suggested.

'Nope, nothing like that.'

'Two or three more questions,' Beau pushed once more.

'Were all forty-two of your cattle ear-tagged?'

'Well, no, not this lot, Mr. Welch replied openly, 'we're still waiting to receive the new one's we ordered a few weeks back.'

'And they were all males?'

'Yes, all steers. All one purchase from the one breeder, parentage verified on the receipt of purchase. Here's the receipt, they were all delivered the same day of purchase.'

'So, this puts their arrival here, what, a month before you first noticed how emaciated they suddenly looked.

'Yes, that's correct.'

'And all had been branded?'

'Well, yes, but only temporary chemical branding; I intended to brand them properly with my registered brand at the same time I fit their ear tags.'

'Ehhmm. So, we're back to, *when* they became ill ... or?' Beau reiterated.

'It's really hard to say,' Mr. Welch replied, 'though it must have been while we were in Albury on holiday over the Queen's Birthday long weekend.'

'Now, please, don't be offended by my very last question for today, but look, we need to know all those people with who you discussed your then upcoming holidays ... particularly anyone who showed an unexpected interest. You know, with questions like, how long will you be away, can we feed your dogs, or even, can we collect your mail, or even all those sorts of questions.'

Deeply concerned looks passed between the elderly couple, but Mr. Welch responded, 'those people are our friends and neighbours who we've known for years. It's unimaginable any of them might, you know, ever do the wrong thing by us.'

Once again, thank God for Beth who reassuringly took Mrs. Welch's hand and said, while looking at her squarely, eye to eye. 'We are not implying your friends are untrustworthy, it's just that their observations during the time you were on holidays, just might give us a lead or two.

'So, please folks, put your heads together. We really do need to talk with as many locals as possible. We're all staying at the motel in Violet Town, so when you feel up to it, please call us with your recollections.

'Just one last thing. Please, *don't* talk to any of those people about this while we conduct our investigations ... promise?'

Frustrated, we bid farewell to the Welch's, but not before assuring them we would update them as soon as we possibly could.

'You can leave that dog of yours here with us, if you wish,' Mr. Welch offered in surprisingly good humour.

'No bloody way,' Beau replied with equal affability. 'He can't stay, he's gotta keep his flying hours up.'

50

'**G**od damn it, it looks like they've broken just about every commonsense rule of thumb,' I said as soon as we were airborne. 'My bet's there's a very clever bloke operating in the vicinity, or a smartarse team, who think the law's an ass. But whoever's involved are about to come a gutzer.'

* * *

Following a typical pub dinner, and an ice-cold pot of Carlton Draught, we gravitated to the outdoor beer garden to weigh up what we'd gathered so far.

Casually, Beau asked, 'I say, Andy, what makes you so confident it's the work of locals?'

'I didn't say that exactly, it's just that there's something going on here we haven't seen before. And the Welch's made no mention of their neighbours experiencing the same sort of thing. I'm sure if they weren't the only ones, they'd have said something to us.

'I haven't got the experience you have Beau, but I'd wager the Welch's cattle are much older than just two years; stock in condition prime don't just lose half their body weight in a few weeks. Those cattle they showed us today are badly undernourished. They're not sick, they're old and have been doing it tough.

'They will, I dare say, recover somewhat on the feed where they are now, but I don't reckon they're the cattle the Welch's paid for.'

'So, darling,' Beth chimed in, 'I think what you're saying is there's been an unlawful exchange of stock. But, nevertheless, we'll need to prove our suspicions, which means notifying the local vet, asap, to get blood samples.'

'Well done you two,' Beau quickly added, 'that's exactly what's been nagging at the back of my mind, but first and foremost we have to locate the whereabouts of the Welch's correct and lawful cattle, so the vet can also take blood samples from them for primary herd contrast checks.'

* * *

WE THEN GOT LUCKY.

While contemplating our options, I took a call from our daughter, Kelly. She was "just checking" to see that Beth and I were OK and listened politely while I explained what we were up against.

Having unburdened my frustration, Kelly, innocently replied, 'So, if it's stock substitution, it had to occur between the day the Welch's offloaded their cattle and the day the Welch's returned to their farm after their long weekend holiday.

'Sooo, if it were me, I'd start by checking the auction sales records at all the nearby sale yards for anybody who bought any quantity of ageing angus cattle, between those dates. Why don't you call Will and see if there's any way, he can fast-track that sort of info? Luv yah Dad, but can I talk to Mum now?'

Smart girl, our Kelly.

* * *

WHEN BETH and Kelly had finished their chat, I immediately phoned Will and bounced Kelly's suggestion off him. 'It's worth a try Andy,' he agreed enthusiastically, 'I'll clear it with your man in Canberra, and get back to you asap.'

In fact, I didn't have long to wait. My feet had barely hit the floor the following morning when the hotel manager put a phone call through to our room; not surprisingly, it was Will. 'Time you lot got cracking Andy; I think I've got what you're looking for. Got a pen and paper handy?'

'Cheeky bugger, and good morning to you, my boy. Go for it, what've you got?'

'We checked the records of the closest three sale yards to the Welch's property, only one had an auction-yard sale during the period you advised: just three purchases. One was by a New South Wales grazier not far from Albury. He's been checked out, salt of the earth type; you can safely rule him out. He purchased three pens: a mix of types totalling 87 head.

'Another sale, 42 Angus steers, went to a Mr. Welch.

'And lucky last, 42 ageing angus steers, all choppers and not long destined for this world ... usually going into dog food. Apparently, they were almost given away to one Mr. Gregory Arnold on the same day. And, furthermore, it turns out Mr. Arnold happens to live just six kilometre's from the Welch's property.

'So, if you're ready, you'd better start writing down how to get the Arnold place.'

'Great work Will, we're on it. And thanks heaps.'

Over breakfast I briefed Beth and Beau, but just as I was about to have a second cuppa, the motel manager said there was a call awaiting me in our room.

'Hello, it's Andy Stevens speaking, can I help you?'

It was Mrs. Welch calling to advise she had a list of all those who she and her husband considered to be friends and neighbours they could trust, and asked if we could call in to collect their list.

Of course, we would, but not until we had paid a visit to Mr. Arnold ... whose name incredulously appeared first on Mrs. Welch's list!

That call could have lasted an hour, but I had to take the risk of not offending her by calling off our chat, for, as Will put it, we'd better get cracking.

* * *

AN HOUR LATER, we arrived at the Arnold farm.

Two men greeted us, Gregory, and his younger brother Laurie. After introducing our team, and showing them our official credentials, their initial openness fell away, and a surliness punctuated their demeanour.

'Why do you want to inspect *our* cattle? There's nothing at all wrong with them,' Gregory protested.

'I'm sure there's not,' I replied in a matter-of-fact manner, 'but Mr. Arnold, that's not for you to decide.'

I figured then, that if they were both not pissed-off by Beau's simple request, then what we'd next be asking them, most certainly would.

Reluctantly, the brothers walked with us to inspect their herd. There was no mistake that the cattle before us were anything but two-year-olds, and all in prime condition.

'So, boys, I suppose you a have receipt for the purchase of these animals?' Beth asked in her most unnerving tone of voice.

By the looks on the brothers' faces and the glances which passed between them, I got the feeling they might soon leg it. But rather than release Betta, I moved my jacket just enough to reveal the handle of my holstered handgun.

'If you can't answer that question either, boys,' Beth continued, 'can you tell us exactly what day these cattle found their way onto your property?'

Having received no replies, Beau then changed tack. 'You do realise, due to your failure to produce evidence of ownership and your lack of cooperation, that I'm now going to arrest both of you for cattle theft; and not only will that be very costly, but you'll both be spending a mandatory jail term of five years.'

'Unless you both come clean,' Beth casually, enticingly, added. 'If you cooperate, I may be able to reduce your fines and jail terms, but it's now entirely up to you.'

For further impact, of course, I added, 'For what it's worth, I think both of you blokes should be ashamed of yourselves. You've done the dirty on a couple of your neighbours; really nice folk, who both trusted you and who considered you both as friends ... just to make a few lousy bucks.'

* * *

WE SPENT the rest of the afternoon in the Arnold brothers' kitchen, clarifying the background and reasons for their actions.

'Right, so Gregory and Laurie,' Beau said, 'tell us why you embarked on this swap plan of yours? Just the truth please, and no embellishments.'

'Yeah, well, I'm embarrassed to say,' Gregory started our conversation going, 'but, what we did was a last resort sort of thing. You see, I've got Jack the Dancer, and all the treatments I've been getting have just about sent both of us broke.'

'But it was my idea really,' a crest fallen Laurie said, 'You see, I was at the same auction and witnessed Mr. Welch's successful bid for those beautiful Angus. Something just got to me; I saw an opportunity and just went with it, on the spur of the moment, like. I risked everything but succeeded with my bid for those older cattle, yes, all forty-two of them.'

'And why, exactly did you make that call?' I interrupted.

'Well, I knew the Welch's had purchased forty-two head, so a swap of forty-two new, for forty-two old, would give us time to do a direct swap, and potentially not be noticed too soon, giving us time to off-load the Welch's steers before anyone became the wiser ... and provide us with a motzer so we could pay for Greg's next lot of cancer treatment.

'Anyway,' Laurie continued, 'real early on the Saturday of the Queen's Birthday long weekend, it was pretty easy to walk Welch's animals along the long paddock, and then put 'em into a separate paddock at our place.

'We then walked our old boys back the opposite way and pushed them into the Welch's property. Job done before midday, and I'll be damned if I can remember seeing a single vehicle. No witnesses, like. A minimal risk earner, or so I thought.'

'None of which makes what you've done acceptable,' Beth replied, 'but your apparent honesty and medical battle just might win you a few days of acquittal.

* * *

MEANINGFUL APOLOGIES WERE MADE by the Arnold brothers to the Welch's. And that, along with sincere regret for their stupid actions, not only clearly influenced the judge's-imposed fines, but significantly reduced the prison terms he had initially imposed from five to just two and a half years.

But there was another interesting twist to this story.

The Welch's made a heartwarming and pragmatic approach to the judge, which saw both brothers being released into the care of the Welch's for a period of two years, on the proviso they work off their fines ... already paid on their behalf by the Welch's.

But what the public never learnt was that all the cancer treatment, transfusions, and subsequent home care costs, were paid for by Mr. and Mrs. Welch, until Gergory's death about three years later.

Which, in a most unforeseeable way, probably came about by Kelly's offhanded, innocent deduction intended only to help me.

By God, am I a lucky father, or what?

51

Our man in Canberra acknowledged our need for a break and happily endorsed the need—at our age, no less—for a decent break.

Oh yes, I was telling you about our plans to travel overseas. Well, we made it back from Violet Town with plenty of time to spare to get to Melbourne before our scheduled flight.

Kelly and Jack were more than capable of taking care of things on the farm, but if any help was needed, at any time, then Will was a phone call and only three hours away. Mind you, Kelly put up a damn good case for Will to stay over "just in case".

Beth was sympathetic to Kelly's pleas: my only concern was that Jack might feel left out in his own home. I shouldn't have worried, he told me up front, 'Don't be stupid Dad. Will's a great guy; besides, they'll be getting married next year, I reckon.'

Yeah, right, thanks for letting me know.

Anyway, Kelly won out, and Will was transferred to Sale the day before Beau, Jill, Beth, and I flew First Class to Johannesburg, via Sydney and Singapore.

* * *

IT WASN'T until we discovered the delights of Qantas's First-Class Customer Lounge in Sydney, that Beau found his feet, so to speak. We had a ninety-minute void to fill before boarding our connecting flight to Singapore, and it wasn't long before Beau and Jill were happily chatting with four travellers: two sisters and their husbands, South African, and all about Beau's and Jill's age ... all cattle farmers yet separated by nearly half the world.

After Beth and I were introduced, we soon discovered our itineraries were in lock step. Not only were we all destined for a six-day side trip (via Johannesburg), but we would be on the exact same flights to and return from Madagascar.

During that initial meeting, we soon got to learn that stock theft, particularly of cattle, was not confined to Australia, and that "on the spot retribution" in South Africa and neighbouring Botswana was often the norm, and that without a body or any witnesses, judicial systems and police often received some workload relief.

And of course, it wasn't long before Beau had our newfound friends dwelling on his every word as he related one of his priceless classics.

* * *

I RELATE BEAU'S STORY, which follows, without wanting to glorify theft in any way, but I want everyone to know that humour lurks everywhere, even in the realms of the most vengeful, manipulative, inventive and ruthless of felons.

* * *

THERE WAS ONCE a livestock trader of dubious character who lived in Sale. I'll call him Fred, though that's not his real name.

Though in general, Fred was not well-liked, nevertheless at just about every sale yard auction he attended, he did very little to ever change his ways.

On the other hand, it was agreed by most that he was a very smart operator and dealer ... but one who cared nothing about who he let know how good he was. Nobody, just nobody had the smarts to pull the wool over his eyes he'd tell anyone who wanted to listen.

Fred's reputation had even spread to those who "unofficially managed" the central hub of Victoria's stock exchange facilities at Newmarket, a few kilometre's from Melbourne's CBD.

Unaware that one of those Newmarket "bosses" (I'll call him, Syd) had taken umbrage at the challenge which Fred represented, decided to pay him a visit (along with a couple of his mates), at Sale's upcoming heifer auction sale.

Syd soon identified Fred, big noting himself in the saleyard kiosk. Syd then sidled up to his quarry and, as cattlemen do, easily engaged in conversation with Fred ... and soon learnt that he had seven magnificent Angus heifers which he boasted would bring him a nice little earner.

What Fred neither expected, nor didn't care less about, was that Syd purchased those seven heifers. And, from what Fred had learnt from that friendly bloke, he could make another killing at the Newmarket heifer sale the next day.

Syd quickly loaded his purchase, drove back to Newmarket and then penned his heifers overnight in one of his "self-managed pens".

Fred rose at 4:00am the next morning anticipating the rush of excitement as he always did when he visited Newmarket. *'Once again Freddy boy, there's an easy bob or two to be made from these city centric cowboys.'*

Syd and his men soon recognised Fred. 'G'day mate,' Syd jovially greeted Fred. 'You'll not regret coming here today, there's some lovely cattle here, none better than the pen I've picked out for yah. Come with me; you've gotta see them for yourself. And Fred, you know I'll look after you; buy 'em from me and you won't go wrong. Know what I mean?'

Fred liked what he saw. The pen held fifteen almost identical Angus heifers and immediately agreed to Syd's asking price, even though they were more expensive than he really wanted to pay ...

which was more than what he got for those he had sold the day before.

Syd provided the necessary paperwork, signatures were applied, and Fred handed over his money, in cash.

After Syd had helped Fred load his fifteen heifers, and after one last handshake, Fred hit the M1, proud of himself for securing such an easy deal.

Of course, what Fred didn't know was that Syd and his mates were at the Newmarket pub laughing their heads off.

As for Fred, I wonder how he felt after he got home and offloaded his lovelies ... when seven of them ran off to their mothers!

THE LAUGHTER which followed was such that the pilot of our plane came to investigate, but rather than chastise us for our raucousness, insisted Beau retell his story ... via the plane's intercom.

Yet, there persists a pseudo acceptance that stories like this are OK; humorous yes, nobody got hurt, Fred was embarrassed, and those who masterminded the clear message to Fred that his days as a credible trader were over, all do nothing to address blatant fraud.

52

———————

By mutual consent our holiday was extended by another month at the behest of our man in Canberra, not that we really needed it, but because Clam was in hospital in Bruges, in Belgium, compliments of a bullet which had passed through his left side.

It was also suggested we could spend some time with him, perhaps even help with his rehabilitation.

As we approached the steps leading up to the hospital's entrance doors, there was Clam in a full-length dressing gown, slightly stooped, hair sticking up like a birch broom, but nothing could hide his happy, brilliant smile. Oh yes, he was supported by a very attractive nurse in full white uniform.

My first reaction was, 'who the hell told him he'd be receiving visitors?' But for the time being, not knowing that could wait.

In just a few paces, Beth had her arms around him in an embrace his own mother would have been proud. When they parted, both unashamedly had tears in their eyes.

'It's so great to see you, and thanks so much for dropping by,' Clam said, having quickly recovered his emotions. 'Nice to meet you, Jill. I sort of feel that I already know you; Beau has often talked about

you. But, anyway, how's Will, and Kelly and Jack of course, and Aussie
...?'

Silence reigned but Clam suddenly showed signs of awkwardness. 'Have I said something I shouldn't have? No, it's worse, isn't it?
Please tell me what's happened ... is there something I should know?'

'Relax son,' Beau said, choking back a tear. 'We've lost Aussie;
some bastard poisoned him.'

Discreetly, the nurse intervened and said in near perfect English.
'Please, monsieur's and madame's, come this way. Monsieur *Call-hum*
must not be overtaxed, and I see you need privacy. Please, follow me.'

I too had to choke back a few tears as Beau and Beth, arms
around Clam's shoulders, supported and guided him into a waiting
room with a table laden with iced sponge cakes, fancy biscuits, a bowl
of fruit, a platter of cheeses, a carafe of red wine and pots of hot
brewed coffee.

Stuffed, and feeling mellow from the effects a few glasses of excellent Belgian wine, Beau turned his full attention upon Clam. 'So,
Clam, what on earth led to you getting shot?'

'Our team had been tracking an American bloke suspected of
stealing two paintings by German master Albrecht Durer, best known
for his engravings and prints. All up, worth more than five to six
million US dollars at a private auction.

'I can't go into all the ins-and-outs going on behind the scenes,
but we had set up a sting which involved conducting a bogus auction:
bogus to us, but not to any would be art thief wishing to add to his
collection.

'Anyway, all was going well. We had lured our suspect to attend
our sale and he seemed genuinely interested in another of Durer's
works. His accomplice, an older lady, who was earlier introduced to
us as his mother, suddenly started abusing one of our team who was
masquerading nearby as a drink waiter, for being a clumsy lout,
which in fact *was* his role to "appear to accidentally, yet on purpose"
knock over one of the galleries potted display plants so that it fell
across her shoulders, neck, and her head.

'We were in luck, her hair, which we suspected to be a wig,

became tangled in the plant's foliage and when she stood up, it slid from her head and landed on the floor.

'She then became extremely agitated, swearing and carrying on, but seemed more concerned about concealing her face; her real face … that of a much younger woman, who, more than one of us immediately recognised her as another suspect to the original Durer thefts.

'But in a flash, she reached into her handbag and produced a small handgun, but before she targeted a specific person, I attacked and dislodged her piece, but I hadn't counted on our main suspect, who by now had his own gun levelled directly at me and fired.

'I was too slow, and that was that. His bullet went into my lower back, near my hip, and exited just below and to the right of my belly button. However, with the loving care of nurse Gerdie, I'll live.'

'And what happened to that couple?' Jill asked, 'If they lived, it'll be interesting to see who makes claim to them.'

'You're right there. Both surrendered quick smart when they realised they'd fallen for our con. Right now, they're in a high security jail in Brussels. However, there's legal debate going on as to whether they should be charged under Belgian, French or USA Law. They're innocent under Belgian and French law until they can prove otherwise, or the Americans will insist they be extradited and tried under USA law which says they're guilty and must prove their innocence.'

'Either way,' Jill replied, 'I'm bloody glad I'm not in their shoes. And if I recall what Beau has told me over the years, none of this would have been revealed if your team hadn't put a stop to that sheep thieving bastard, Ho Hua.' Jill was right come to think about it.

At that moment, nurse Gerdie returned to the waiting room, no longer dressed in her uniform, but now wearing denim jeans, a lilac long sleeved shirt and tan sandals. An oversized carry bag draped casually over her shoulder and sunglasses were perched on the top of her blonde hair which was now pulled back into a ponytail. At a guess, a few years older than Clam … but drop dead gorgeous.

'By the way, Gerde is also my boss,' Clam said cheerfully, with just a hint of mischief at what was about to be revealed. 'But not for long, we're getting married in August, just two months from today.' Bloody hell, young folk move quick these days, but then again, Beth was my undoing at about the same age.

And a fabulous couple they were, now side by side, arms enfolding each other; Clam, as handsome an Australian Aboriginal man you'll ever see, and Gerde, an absolute classical Belgian beauty.

'Please, keep a lid on this,' said Clam, 'I haven't told Will yet, though your man in Canberra has given us his blessings.'

'And do not worry,' Gerde added, '*Call-hum*, he'll live, his surgeon did an excellent job. Lovely to meet you all, but I must see a man about a horse; hoo-roo for now.' A quick kiss applied passionately to Clam's lips, then a big smile, a cheerful wave to us all and she was gone, skipping down the hospital front steps. What a girl; a fast learner too, eh?

* * *

BETH ROTATED her time between playing the tourist with Beau, Jill, and I, and working at the hospital to oversee Clam's rehabilitation. This gave Gerde time to pursue a gang hell bent on threatening and then stealing artisan cheeses from innocent, hardworking farmer's ... not just a few kilograms of cheese, but truck loads! Sound familiar?

But that aside, there was a highlight not to be missed by Beau and Jill; the Global Equestrian Championships held in the Flemish Region of Belgium. There were representatives from around the world competing for professional skill recognition and the most prestigious and lucrative equine prizes. Ireland won, South Africa were runners up and Australia came a very creditable fourth. An amazing event to witness: if only I could ride like any of those competitors.

Alas, all good things come to an end. Besides, to be honest, we were all becoming a bit homesick.

53

It's not every day you get an ultimatum when flying at thirty-five thousand feet.

Mine came from Beth while we were snuggled comfortably together; her head resting on my shoulder. I thought she was sleeping, so I was a bit supprised when she asked, softly, but just loud enough for me to catch what she had to say over the background rumble of the jet's engines. 'Darling, as much as I love you, I can't keep doing what our man in Canberra expects of us. I just can't. I'd much rather spend more time with you and our family; it's time we retired.'

I pondered her demand for about thirty seconds then whispered, 'OK, let's do it.' I expected a verbal reply, but no, all I got was a firm squeeze of my right hand in acceptance of my pledge.

Beth's breathing then became a gentle rhythm and she didn't wake up until our plane started its descent into Singapore's Changi airport.

* * *

Beth and I were bushed when we arrived at our farm, but that didn't stop Kelly, Jack, Will, Betta and RB making a welcoming fuss over us. Over several cups of tea, we happily swapped stories, but the need for sleep was rapidly overtaking us.

The next morning Will announced he was about to start his drive back to Canberra: apparently, they couldn't do without him. Yeah, right. Kelly was morose, but accepting, Jack had already gone to work at a nearby dairy, Betta kept dropping a ball at my feet, and RB had cajoled her way onto Beth's lap.

As Will got into his car, he wound down his window and said to me,' Andy, get Kelly to tell you about our one and only investigation while you were away. And, oh, by the way, can I have your permission to marry Kelly?'

'Yah silly bugger, of course you can; what took you so long? I replied proudly and, I must say, feeling greatly honoured as we firmly shook hands through his car's window. 'I'll let Beth know straight away. Drive safely, son.'

'No need to Andy, Beth already knows. She said to tell you that if you decline, it's OK for me to gut you on the spot!'

* * *

That evening after dinner, we sat around the lounge room fire sharing a few more stories about our holiday experiences, though under Beth's threat of getting myself gutted yet again, I did not raise our meeting with Clam, other than that he seemed to be fitting into life in Europe rather well.

Of course, the news of Will and Kelly getting married held centre court, which left Beth and Kelly in tears, and me and Jack pondering why it is that women find it so easy to show their emotions.

After a short pause, Jack changed the subject. 'It's been really quiet on the stock theft scene, according to Will. That's a good thing, isn't it? Perhaps those idiots are getting the message. However, we did bring a couple of local women to heel, but, go on Kel, you should tell this one for Mum and Dad.'

'OK. You'd been on holiday for about a month when Will received some intel about a couple of sisters who live over at Newry.

'Jack and I knew these girls from our primary school days. We never got on with them, they were pests, always nicking things from the school tuck-shop, smoking, and swearing, and showing off.

'Over time, we learned about a few things they'd got up to with their boyfriends, which involved the police; anyway, they had, and still have poor reputations. Tarts the both, and some of their not so nice boyfriends have spent time in prison.

'Mr. Verbunt, that Old Dutch dairy farmer at Newry, apparently felt sorry for them and employed them to help him with milking and feeding out his small herd of twenty or so store cattle.

'However, the girls did the wrong thing by him, not turning up for work because they were too badly hungover.

'But unbeknown to him, on those days, they weren't sick at all, they were taking further advantage of him by lifting one or two of his steers, stripping their ear tags and replacing them with their own and then putting them through the sale yards at Traralgon.

'They were successful for a while before the old bloke woke up to what was going on: he reported it and that's when Will and Jack and I got involved.

'Will quickly discovered that each theft occurred during the week prior to each Traralgon cattle sale market, and realising the next sale was only ten days away, organised for Mr. Verbunt to carry on as usual, and behave as if he was totally ignorant of the inevitable theft to soon follow.

'On sale day, the sisters arrived, but only after Mr. Verbunt's two steers had been penned, that Will struck. The girls could not provide any evidence of ownership and were humiliated when Mr. Verbunt turned up to identify and reclaim his animals.

'The sisters, having been caught red handed, not only lost their jobs but copped heavy fines for livestock theft. For elder abuse, they each received a prison term of one year.' Things at last were getting the attention they deserved.

'Well done you three,' I said proudly, 'but I've also got some other news.'

'Go on darling, tell them!' Beth burst out.

'Well, kids, your mum and I have attended our last LTI job; I've spoken with Beau, and he's passed on our intentions to retire; effective immediately. Not only that, but Beau has followed suit.'

Kelly screamed and rushed to hug Beth and me. Jack simply punched the air and yelled ... 'YYYESS, at long bloody last!'

* * *

BUT A NATIONAL TRAGEDY WAS UNFOLDING: an election.

As a result of the change to Australia's Government which followed, a badly misinformed decision was taken soon after ... to dramatically cut most funds and resources previously guaranteed to stamp out farm invasions and livestock theft!!

Thanks for nothing.

54

The date, time and place for Kelly's and Will's wedding was locked in but approaching quickly.

The reception would be held at our farm, invitations had been posted and catering details were all well in hand. A professional cameraman had been teed up, so too were the bride's gown and bridesmaid's ensembles and groomsmen outfits; the lucky ones being Abbi from Eden, and Jack, but who on earth was going to be the best man?

We found out, just two days before the wedding when Clam and Gerde arrived unannounced ... it was Clam, of course. All had been arranged with the compliments of the Duntroon Military Academy, and of course, our man in Canberra. If time and protocol permit, I'd like to one day meet that bloke.

What really surprised Beth and I was that Beau offered to perform the MC duties, and being a teetotaler, also volunteered to man the bar.

Yet, that gesture was trumped by Alex, the local Stratford cop. His brother, the singer with a Melbourne based, five-piece band also turned up unannounced to set up their sound system on the day before the wedding. All gratis, despite my protestations, they should receive payment.

* * *

THE WEDDING SERVICE was held in the All-Staints' Anglican Church in Briagolong, a small town where Kelly and Jack had attended their primary school years.

"Our church" was full to overflowing, festooned inside with multiple bunches of brightly coloured flowers and huge bunches of gum tree cuttings which provided a beautiful visual and fragrant work of art.

The Minister applied himself with patience, good humour and a respectful calling to defend all religious commitments ... then issued one last Amen to conclude his service.

The milling crowd of guests and onlookers cheered and clapped enthusiastically as Kelly and Will walked arm-in-arm from the church; whereafter the photographer fired off his first hundred shots, capturing that moment.

What followed wasn't exactly chaos, let's just say that judging by the clouds of confetti and rice which rained over Kelly and Will, it was going to take days to clean up. The principal mess makers were me, Beth, Jack, Beau, Clam and Gerde.

As Kelly and Will climbed into the back of my 4 x 4, I turned to Beth, caught her ecstatic smile, and quickly realised I wasn't the only one with tears of joy rolling down their face for our little girl, now a beautiful wife, and for Will, now our second son.

* * *

WHEN GUESTS STARTED ARRIVING at our farm for the reception party, a huge fire was lit in the home paddock, about sixty yards from the back of the house. The area surrounding the fire had been mown super-low to minimise any threat of causing a grassfire. The weather forecast was for a clear night with no wind, and perhaps frost close to dawn tomorrow. A huge stack of firewood was close by, surely enough to sustain our fire throughout the night if required.

Four portable toilets had been positioned closer to the back of the house where lighting was provided from the verandah. A generator had been hired to provide power for a system of coloured lights festooned across the back yard and reasonably close to the fire. I must find out who arranged this, it looked fantastic.

Beau threw himself into getting a tent erected, ready to receive his fridge from home, his huge icebox, and bags of ice, soon to arrive from the Briagolong pub.

Kelly and Will received every guest who showered them with gifts, hugs and engaging words of kindness and wisdom.

And oh yes, the only hiccup was that the trestle tables and chairs were nowhere to be seen. It transpired that the delivery driver had got lost, but returned to Stratford Police Station for directions, just as Alex and his wife were leaving to attend our party.

As it transpired, the caterers followed Alex and the "trestle truck" down our driveway and it wasn't long after that the first of many refreshments were served by Beau, amid an increasing level of happy chatter and laughter.

If Betta and RB were confused, well they didn't show it. By the time our meals were ready to be shuttled out to our guests, both mother and son had shaken hands with everyone, at least twice.

Speeches followed, mine included, immediately after the main course. The highlight though, occurred as Clam finished his best man's speech and presented Will with a large white envelope.

Will was making a show of wrestling with the envelope to open it, when suddenly some documents and two airplane tickets fell onto the trestle in front of him. The penny dropped when Will passed the tickets to Kelly. 'Oh, my God, thank you so much Clam, you sneaky bugger,' she called to him.

By this time Clam, Kelly, Will and Gerde were on their feet, hugging and laughing, particularly Kelly who seemed almost over-whelmed. As they returned to their chairs, Clam gathered up one of the documents left on their trestle and called for everyone's attention.

'Well folks, I know I promised no more speeches, but I think you're all busting to know what you've just witnessed. You see, Kelly and Will have just received an invitation to attend my marriage to Gerde, in Belgium in five weeks' time ... compliments of the Duntroon Military Academy: all expenses paid! How about that?!'

Spontaneous cheers and much clapping followed, during which my eyes first met Beth's and then Kelly's; another magical, loving, and proud moment shared by nobody else but us three.

As dessert, hot tea and coffee arrived, the band struck up ... wow, were they good. A perfect mood of contentment descended upon our festivities; the moon had risen, the fire crackled merrily, everyone was now sated and feeling the release of their inhibitions, when Will and Kelly stepped onto our makeshift dance floor.

Beth and I had the honour of following, and the four of us were soon waltzing and rotating our ways around the dance floor. Gerde and Clam followed, then Jack and Abbi ... then everyone else who'd caught the spirit of this time.

During a refreshment break for the band, Beth and I, and Kelly and Will sat together, getting our breaths back, when I remembered something. 'By the way, you two,' I said as I withdrew an envelope from my trousers' back pocket, 'Our wedding gift for you both. It's no good visiting Europe for just a few days, you'll need this to have a good look around for four months', at least.'

A single sheet of paper read something like ... *the bearer of this document is entitled to receive ten thousand USA dollars upon presentation of suitable proof of identity.*

'You won't receive cash by the way', Beth said quickly, 'just traveler's checks. For God's sake don't lose them. And please, keep this a secret until you return home. We don't want people thinking we were too lazy to buy you a special gift.'

'Oh Mum, this is unbelievable! I'm sure we'll love Europe, but I've always wanted to see Africa, so Will, my darling husband in arms, would you care to join me for a quick honeymoon safari in South Africa on the way home? What do you say?'

'Thought you'd never ask; perhaps we might catch up with those folks Mum and Dad met.'

Mum and Dad! Indeed ... thanks Will, I'm truly honoured.

'Which, by the way,' I added, 'have you two had any thoughts about where you'd like to live?'

* * *

AS THE NIGHT MELTED AWAY, Beth whispered into my ear while we were dancing slowly around the dance floor, 'Darling, everything has been so lovely tonight. I'm not sure whether Kelly is enjoying this more than I am. And I really do love you to bits Andy, but do you think we need to worry about Jack; he and Abbi seem to have become very lovey-dovey.'

'And Beth, you're the best that's ever happened to me,' I whispered back. 'Can't say I've ever seen him quite like this, I'd say he's ... ahem, ahem ...'

I quickly looked Beth square in the eyes, but before I could say what I needed to say, something clicked between us, and we both mouthed ... 'besotted!'

'Fear not, I'll have a word with him tomorrow. Maybe you should have a quiet word with Abbi.'

Though the fire was now on the retreat, the band played on. Those still on the dance floor were becoming increasingly wobblier, except for Jack and Abbi who were just standing there gazing into each other's eyes.

Finally, the band finished playing and our guests started heading for their homes, but not without first saying a quick goodnight and thanking Beth and me for turning on such a terrific night.

Bugger cleaning up, that could wait until tomorrow, or more correctly, until sometime later today because it was 3:00am!

Jack and Abbi never protested when we suggested it was time for bed; not the best choice of my words I agree, however, they both said good night to Beth and I and wandered apart, both a bit dazed I think ... Abbi to her tent, Jack to his inside bedroom.

Those who were staying over, fearing they'd never find their way home, gratefully retired to their tents.

Beau was our last guest to leave, but not without putting out the fire, just in case.

I was about to turn off the outdoor lights when Beth took my hand and turned me back to the veranda's handrail. 'Can you feel it, Andy? A part of our life is leaving this place, but we shouldn't be sad.'

'No, we shouldn't. But yes, I *can* feel it, my beautiful bride, we've surely been blessed, eh?'

I then took Beth into my arms. We hugged, sharing sobs of joy, and so help my God, I could somehow feel Beth's love surging through me; so intense, and something which I never thought was possible.

55

Three years on, and despite now supposedly retired, Beth and I encouraged, even pleaded on occasions with Federal politicians, to review their responsibility to better support farmers and farming communities.

Our best, though most distressing statistical evidence for the urgent need to provide adequate funds to do so, came in the form of escalating numbers of farm invasions and stock thefts since they came to power. And just as those figures rose around Australia, so did the number rural business bankruptcy's ... and suicides.

However, two positive things emerged, the first being that Will and Clam both received promotions. Will was given an Australia wide role to liaise with State and Federal Ministers to help them understand the re-emergence and seriousness of the growing problems facing rural enterprise ... a task fundamentally impossible when it became more and more evident that accountants, not law makers, were just not interested in opening the nations purse strings.

Clam on the other hand, became the force behind the force in Belgium to usher in powerful new laws designed to not only frustrate would-be rural thieves, but to see that unprecedented, and significant, prison terms would become the norm.

Jack on the other hand, surprised us somewhat. As much as he loved playing cricket, and despite his ascension to First Class cricket, he followed his heart and moved to Eden to live with Abbi, now his fiancé. However, an even bigger surprise followed when he let it slip, he was on a short list to be inducted into the Duntroon Military Academy. We knew Jack had physical ability and an unusually high IQ, something he seldom bragged about: he'd be a perfect fit.

He eventually confessed that Will and Clam, but more importantly, Beau, had twisted his arm to give the academy a go. Nevertheless, our son would possibly be exposed to life and death situations just as Will had been, when in self defence, he shot dead Ho Hua. This did not sit well with Beth and me, but Jack was his own man: he wouldn't want our approval, yet we'd be the first to know if he ever changed his mind.

So much for our hope of spending more time with our kids. Kelly and Will now live in Canberra, and surprise, surprise, Beth, and I were about to become grandparents.

* * *

WE STILL TRAVELLED EXPANSIVELY around Australia, including multiple trips to Canberra and Bega, but due to a most unexpected affliction which caused my legs to jump uncontrollably without notice, I cancelled my pilot's license.

Beth followed suit shortly after when on a flight back from Melbourne she somehow dislodged her prescription sunglasses and panicked slightly when she couldn't find them. Had Betta not been with us, and not found and then cleverly placed her glasses onto Beth's lap, I don't want to think about what *could* have happened.

Anyway, our Duchess was sold off and went to heaven via a wrecker's yard, and with it went many memories. We donated her proceeds to The Wagga Wagga Airport Management.

'Penny for your thoughts, my beautiful bride,' I whispered into Beth's ear while she sat in her bikini on her favourite deckchair, sipping a Pims and lemonade, and reading a flashy looking real estate magazine.

'Do you ever miss our old house in Bondi?'

'Yes, often; particularly early in the morning or as the sun sets ... or when it's humid and there's a storm building out to sea. Why pray tell?'

'Well, our old place is up for sale; see, there, middle of page three.'

* * *

THE FOLLOWING WEEK, out of interest, but not entirely overwhelmed with nostalgia, we returned to Bondi. However, I think we both knew within ten minutes that we wanted to reclaim our patch of paradise. The previous owners had made a few interesting modifications and had kept the place in excellent condition: an offer was made and accepted. Two months later we again became Bondi residents.

Though it upset us that Betta would remain behind, we agreed with Beau that the best outcome was not to permanently expose him to an environment so unfamiliar as metropolitan Sydney. Besides, Beau admitted he needed the company, and we could never provide Betta with the care and attention they both needed.

56

It was easy settling in; more like returning home from a holiday, than moving into a new house.

We both rejoined the only remaining gym in Bondi and swam nearly every day. I dared not drive anymore given the chronic unpredictability of my legs, however, Beth had no objection to becoming my chauffeur when we decided to revisit our favourite walking tracks, or to drop into a country pub for coffee or lunch.

* * *

Six months flew by, and during that time a pleasant routine evolved. A quick swim in the late afternoon followed by an hour or so of sunbaking on the grassed area above the beach; just the two of us, content, sitting shoulder to shoulder on our beach chairs soaking in the view, talking, or saying nothing, just lost in our thoughts.

On an unusually humid and warm midweek day, we staggered from the waves and, hand in hand, walked up the beach to where our chairs were awaiting us. Halfway up the beach, I paused to let Beth get her breath, then we looked ahead, took two steps ... and we both stopped dead.

'Well, I'll be buggered,' I said, still puffing. 'It's Kelly and Will and our number one granddaughter, young Jacqui, I do believe.'

'Yes, it is ... what a surprise, eh?' Beth replied excitedly as we shuffled up the last of the beach to meet them.

Hugs and kisses and handshakes followed. 'How'd you know we'd be here, and how come on a Wednesday?' I enquired, genuinely intrigued.

Kelly was the first to respond. 'Will and I have a surprise for you ... but hang on, no, I'm not pregnant! Go on Will, you tell them.'

'OK, but first let's all take a seat and relax. Jacqui, go and sit with Nan please.

'Right, do you recognise that bloke walking this way along the beach?'

Silence reigned. I gasped, nearly choked actually. 'Good God Almighty, it's Zack!'

'No Andy, it's your brother, Levy.'

Beth handed Jacqui to Will then ran down to the beach and threw her arms around Levy. She quickly grabbed his hand and returned with him in tow to our gathering.

'Well, I'll be buggered,' I almost shouted, 'look what the cat just dragged in. How long has it been, what, seven or eight years?'

'Ten, actually.' Regardless, we shook hands and embraced. I felt no awkwardness, lingering bitterness, or regret at good times lost, but rather, an intense relief that we had found one another again.

Kelly quickly suggested we head back to our house and continue our get together, besides it was getting hotter and even more humid, and Jacqui needed to sleep.

With Jacqui soon in the land of nod, we positioned ourselves around our verandah table to witness the offshore build-up of dark clouds, erratic lightning, and the rumble of distant thunder.

'So, Levy,' I initiated a start to our chat, 'who pray tell organissed this fabulous surprise?'

'Guilty as charged,' Will replied. 'I thought it would be a fantastic opportunity to learn more about the role Levy has been playing over the past couple of decades. Even though I was living and working within Canberra, I never ran into him until a few weeks ago when he walked unannounced into my office, primarily to announce his retirement and to fill me in. I'll let Levy explain; over to you, sir.'

* * *

'FIRST, you should all know I've already met with Beau and explained to him all which I'm about to tell you. I can't, even though I've officially retired, relate everything because I'm duty bound by a non-disclosure agreement which doesn't lapse for another seven years.

'What I can tell you is all those conversations which Beau had with "your man in Canberra", were in fact with me, via a voice scrambling system. It was an essential security protocol, and Beau has confirmed he was never the wiser that it was me pulling the strings during all that time. Even in the beginning when I went out of my way, pretending to upset him. It was also me who recruited Will and Clam, and of late, your son, Jack. He'll do well.

'You all played such an amazing, courageous, and reliable role for which I am extremely grateful. I really believed we were starting to make a real difference in the service and protection of our farming communities, until of course those Goddam politicians focused more upon shutting us down than embracing the potential of securing millions of dollars in tax revenue. Blind Freddy could see their policies were city-centric, unjust, and would damage our economy.'

'So, is anyone driving a livestock theft initiative?' I chimed in, 'or what?'

'Yes, as a matter of fact, there is,' Levy replied and pointed to Will, 'you're looking at him. Clam by the way, has been absorbed into the Belgian police force and will continue to do them proud.'

'OK, time for a break,' Kelly said, 'anyone for pizza and a cold beer?'

* * *

WHILE WE DEVOURED OUR PIZZAS, we watched in awe nature's fireworks exploding out to sea.

And with that gathering storm a warm breeze wafted over our verandah, the perfect complement to our collective mood.

While my story could end here, you might be wondering about the inheritance left to me; no, to me *and* Levy.

Well, no matter how hard I tried to convince Levy he was entitled to half of that inheritance, he flatly refused it.

Finally, Beth, with her usual wisdom, intervened. 'Stop arguing you two. Why don't you set up a recurring scholarship to be administered by The Duntroon Military Academy? You could call it something like, "The A and L Stevens Memorial Scholarship."'

'You know what, that's not a bad idea,' Levy replied enthusiastically.

'So, you reckon that'll bring about some relief for our farmers?' I asked.

'Not on its own, no,' Levy said thoughtfully, 'but it just might create some impetus to end what's still happening. But God only knows when.'

THE END.

TREVOR TUCKER

Inspired by the joy and intense satisfaction of writing my first four books, *"Ned Kelly's Son"*, *"The Stolen maps... Australia's greatest maritime secret?"*, *"Aussie Anecdotes" and "A sense of Justice"* ... plus the success of their sales, I embarked upon my fifth authorial adventure.

God Only Knows When was written in response to the ongoing, shameful culture which has existed in Australia, essentially unchecked, since the earliest days of Colonization, i.e., that of farm invasion and livestock theft.

For those who have suffered from this blight, I truly hope this novel provides some comfort that farm invasions, and livestock theft will neither be tolerated, nor remain underfunded in the future.

Livestock theft (in particular) is an outrageous criminal act and some unusually brave men, and women, are putting their lives on the line every day, somewhere in Australia (or overseas), to capture these audacious, and occasionally, homicidal criminals. However, for good reason, you are unlikely to ever hear in the public domain the voices of those good folk ... or to learn of their successes.

To help eliminate those who think it's OK to prey upon innocent, hardworking farmers, six words of advice are becoming more important than ever: -

1. Join Farm Watch.
2. Get to know your local Livestock Investigator.
3. Invest in current security technologies.

4. Never tell strangers about your daily routines, or when you intend to be away from your farm.
5. Treat with suspicion any person who flaunts newfound wealth.
6. Fit anti-theft gates to all roadside gates.

Writing is a most satisfying outlet for creativity … both challenging, and relaxing. However, writing is not just escapism, but rather the compulsion of a glorious illness which I call, **The Dreamer's Disease**, i.e., that the more you give, the more you receive.

Having retired from the oil and gas industry, my other interests include when possible, spending time with my kids, and grandkids, fishing, reading, bike riding, watching Test cricket and AFL football (in both men's and women's formats), and listening to classical music … but most of all, enjoying the life-changing experiences of travelling the world.

AUTHOR'S COMMENT

Having delved into the realities of the dark side of stock theft, it must be understood that the "act of theft" is not the sole issue, but just one obnoxious and selfish link in a chain of organised illegal intent.

Those participants who allow "the trade" to function and prosper, not only impact the bottom line of honest farmers directly, but far too frequently, indirectly, contribute to their suicide. Logically, the actions of **all involved participants** make them equally implicit in those farmer's deaths ... and are all therefore equally responsible for the sorrow and depression they inflict upon so many families.

Historically, several well-intentioned plans to stamp out the livestock trade have failed due to the vastness of Australia, haphazard recruitment and non-professional training of farm theft investigators, ineffective perpetrator punishment ... and the complacency of politicians.

What is not properly understood is that under the current policing regime, any success in prosecuting an offender (or offenders) usually involves just one identified point in the livestock theft supply chain. Not only is their eventual punishment trivial at best, but therefore of little or NO impediment to others who are all too willing to restore an interrupted supply chain link.

Enforceable laws which make it pointless for any person to participate in, and/or support in any way, any livestock theft supply chain operating in Australia, are long overdue. In other words, "render the trade unprofitable and useless".

Punishment should include, *for every guilty supply chain perpetrator*: -

- Mandatory imprisonment of at least ten years.
- Huge fines.
- Being banned from working in their previous place of business for at least another five years after their release from prison.

Yet, none of these measures will become cornerstone deterrents unless there is an allocation of appropriate, ongoing funds for personnel recruitment, training, accommodation, transport, and salaries "to empower simultaneous, whole of supply chain interventions."

Furthermore, most urgent of all, retrospective compensation must be provided for all those traumatised and disadvantaged by livestock theft, and ongoing medical and mental counselling must also be provided free of charge to those affected.

While I cannot use names, in order to protect the anonymity of those who bravely put themselves on the line to protect our farmers, I was encouraged to continue my research for this book by members of the following: Australian Federal Police; Interpol; Victorian Police; Victorian Livestock Theft Investigation; responsible livestock traders; and Farm Watch participants.

www.ingramcontent.com/pod-product-compliance
Lightning Source LLC
Chambersburg PA
CBHW051258210726
48287CB00002B/554